Praise for

SUSAN DODD

"*The Mourners' Bench* finds its considerable power in Dodd's patient excavation of the complex aftereffects of tragedy on the lives of the people who emerge—alive if not whole—on the other side. . . . [It] does a splendid job of showing two people engaged in a last-minute effort, fueled by both love and guilt, to understand the present and the past." —*New York Times Book Review*

"Exuberant and sharp-witted." —*The New Yorker* (on *Mamaw*)

"A powerful love story. . . . [A] tour de force." —*Denver Rocky Mountain News* (on *The Mourners' Bench*)

"Dodd . . . proves she has an undeniable gift for creating alluring characters. . . . The beauty of Dodd's writing lies in contradictions, the wonderful incongruities in her characters and the eagerness with which they still approach the casual cruelties of love." —*Greensboro News & Record*

"*The Mourners' Bench* is a great love ballad, an old-timey hymn, a song that both grieves and rejoices. In this exquisitely crafted novel, Susan Dodd has taken grief and despair and magically sung them into hope." —Jill McCorkle

"*Mamaw* transcends its time. . . . There are sentences on every page that turn on every light in the house. *Mamaw* is fresh, strong, and plainly beautiful." —Pete Dexter, author of *Paris Trout*

"In Dodd's hands, a quiet Raymond Carveresque world turns unexpectedly operatic." —*Booklist* (on *O Careless Love*)

"A dazzling range of characters and settings, a compassionate understanding for connection, a zest for negotiating the contemporary sexual battlefield, a keen ear for snappy, tart dialogue, and a felicitous use of language distinguish Dodd's new collection. . . . A standout." —*Publishers Weekly* (on *O Careless Love*)

Trudy Austin

About the Author

SUSAN DODD is the author of six previous books, including *The Silent Woman*, *The Mourners' Bench*, and *Mamaw*. Her work has been honored by the Friends of American Writers, the National Endowment for the Arts, and the Faulkner Society, among others. She lives in Ocracoke, North Carolina.

O Careless Love

STORIES *and a* NOVELLA

Susan Dodd

Perennial

An Imprint of HarperCollinsPublishers

Some of these stories were originally published in the following books and periodicals: "So Far You Can't Imagine" in Writers Harvest 2 (San Diego: Harcourt Brace, 1996); "The Lost Art of Sleep" in The American Voice, no. 27; "Lady Chatterley's Root Canal" in The Iowa Review 25, no. 3; "Lokey Man" in The Ohio Review, no. 55; "In France They Turn to Stone When They Die" in Ploughshares 21, no. 1. "Ethiopia" received the 1995 Medal for the Novella from the Pirate's Alley Faulkner Society and was published in The Double Dealer Redux (New Orleans, 1996).

A hardcover edition of this book was published in 1999 by William Morrow.

HarperCollins books may be purchased for educational, business, or sales promotional use. For information please write: Special Markets Department, HarperCollins Publishers Inc., 10 East 53rd Street, New York, NY 10022.

First Perennial edition published 2002.

Designed by Deborah Kerner

The Library of Congress has catalogued the hardcover edition as follows:
Dodd, Susan M.
O careless love : stories and a novella / Susan Dodd.—1st ed.
p.   cm.
Contents: So far you can't imagine—The lost art of sleep—
Lady Chatterley's root canal—Ethiopia—I married a space alien—
Lokey man—Adult education—Song-and-dance man—What I
remember now—In France they turn to stone when they die.
ISBN 0-688-16999-6 (acid-free paper)
1. United States—Social life and customs—20th century—Fiction.   I. Title.
PS3554.O318O15   1999
813'.54—dc21   99-11468
CIP

ISBN 0-688-17773-5 (pbk.)

02 03 04 05 06 JT/RRD 10 9 8 7 6 5 4 3 2 1

For Sig Roos and Ruth Rohde

Acknowledgments

I started believing in luck in 1986, when Esther Newberg started making me her business . . . lucky enough to have her for a friend. For an agent? I would buy UConn the NCAA for her if I could. Fortunately, the UConn basketball team decided not to wait around for me to get up the cash.

I started believing I could win the lottery when Claire Wachtel and Michael Murphy started making me their business . . . lucky enough to have them for my editor and my publisher. For friends? I have a bid in on the moon.

And if I ever get hold of it, I hope there's enough of the moon to go around at William Morrow and Company. Special thanks to (and for): Rich Aquan, Jessica Baumgardner, Katherine Beitner, Betty Kelly, Lisa Queen, Sharyn Rosenblum, Marly Rusoff, Linda Stormes, Cissy Tiernan, Bill Wright, Sarina Vetterli, and Jeanette Zwart. A publishing house that feels like *home*? Little wonder I've started believing in miracles.

Contents

So Far
You Can't Imagine

*I*t just goes on and on." Schachter, elegizing the latest tumble of his daredevil heart, shoved his fur hat lower on his perspiring brow. The skull-shaped pelt, souvenir of his diplomat-father's glory days in the Moscow embassy, was snow dampened and spiky. It wreathed Schachter's sorrowing face like a crown of thorns. In the roseate light he might have been sweating blood.

Boston was writhing in the grip of a record-breaking cold spell. Out on Boylston Street, bluebloods succumbed to a contagion of empathy, scattering coins behind them as they ran to waiting cars. The vox populi was a wheeze.

The Japanese restaurant was overheated, but the chill of incompletion lodged in Schachter's dank and salty bones. "Does despair become me, do you think?" he asked.

Melissa, his former therapist, who had been forced to refer him elsewhere when Schachter insisted she was his best friend, leaned forward, her small succulent bosom resting on the edge of the black-lacquered table. Her patterned sweater of salmon and grays matched the sushi on the plate between them.

"Schach, Schach." She shook her head. "May I ask an impertinent question?"

"Does the Mona Lisa ask leave to luminesce?" Schachter had recently made a brief but ambitious expedition through Europe's major museums, where beautiful women with time on their hands were reported to loiter. He'd returned without acquisition, another illusion dashed on fin de siècle rocks. Cultured women were all in offices now, it seemed. Even in Paris.

"Is that a word?" Melissa was asking.

Schachter frowned.

"Luminesce," she said.

"Allow me my superior vocabulary, at least," Schachter said.

Melissa chewed thoughtfully on a shred of tentacle. "What is it you're looking for?" she asked. "I mean, do you know exactly?"

"Shouldn't it be obvious?"

"Who to?" Melissa said.

Schachter winced at her laissez-faire grammar. She knew better. "You *are* impertinent," he said.

"I usually get paid for it." Her inquisitive bosom nosed closer to some yellowtail. Her green eyes glistened. "You didn't use to give me so much lip."

"Budgetary considerations," Schachter said.

"Are you going to answer me?"

"Though it pains me to state the obvious." Schachter sighed. "I am looking, *exactly,* for love."

"Don't be simplistic." Melissa smacked her faux ivory chopsticks down on the table, creating turbulence in the soy sauce. Schachter watched an island of wasabi sink.

"Why not?" he said. "Isn't the desire . . . elemental?"

"I hate it when you whine."

"So do I." He poked the tip of a chopstick into a smear of green paste on his plate, then lifted it to his mouth. His eyes welled up instantly. "My heart may be a little slovenly, but its longing is impeccably intact."

"*Please.*"

Schachter was still sucking on the chopstick. "Is love really so much to ask?"

Melissa drew back, her bosom vacating the table. Her small pale face looked icy. "Maybe it is," she said, "when you've got everything else."

Schachter had the grace to look abashed. The youngest vice president of Boston's largest bank, he owned a three-bedroom condo overlooking the Charles, not to mention a house on the Vineyard his maternal grandparents had left to him. Melissa, still subletting the Somerville studio she'd moved into for graduate school, was entitled to her bitterness.

But she really wasn't, Schachter thought, any great shakes as a therapist.

His friends Grayson and Boyd, being in love, were much more inclined to sympathy. Grayson, a balding man of fifty-two with the body of a high school gymnast, was a CPA. He'd met Boyd English, now twenty-seven, two years ago, when the temp agency Boyd worked for had sent him over to help Grayson through the last few weeks of the tax crush. Grayson had been married at the time, a cordial union of twenty-five years that had produced two sons, a granddaughter, and a painstakingly restored farmhouse in Concord.

"When he turned twenty-six," Grayson had once told Schachter while massaging Boyd's neck, "the worst was over, statistically. I'd never be twice his age again." His fine pale hands lowered to knead Boyd's shoulders. "Quel relief! You can't imagine."

Boyd and Grayson had been living together for less than a month when Schachter had made their acquaintance in the courtyard of the Isabella Stewart Gardner Museum. All the flowers in the atrium were white. Grayson could call each blossom and leaf by name, which was a good conversation starter. (Schachter, in concert with his expansive hopes, was making it a point to be interested in everything then, even when heartbreak was fresh. You never knew what one thing might lead to another.) Boyd and Grayson had captured his attention because they were, without making a public display of it, so palpably in love.

"Grayson and Boyd!" Schachter had said without forethought when, after much botanical chitchat, introductions had come up. "Sounds more like a Beacon Hill law firm than a couple."

This was, as it turned out, the first social acknowledgment of their status, apart from a few comments by the rather seedy divorce lawyer representing Grayson's wife. Schachter's oneliner had seemed to the lovers a blessing upon their union, and they accorded him on its basis pure devotion. And sympathy. Boyd had even introduced Schachter to a couple of the women he worked with. Love made people generous, Schachter observed, though neither of the women had panned out.

Once a week Boyd and Grayson invited Schachter to their Brookline apartment, where they served him a veritable Semitic buffet—knishes and borscht and kugel, tsimmes and half-sours. Their intent was to make him feel at home, of course. Schachter, however, had been raised mostly on hamburgers and frozen french fries by a homebody mother who'd elected to sit out the last plays of the Cold War and the pep rally for détente on the sidelines. If Cleveland could qualify as the sidelines of anything. Schachter's domestic pinings and small streak of parochialism were his mother's doing, he thought. Now he was acquiring new tastes.

He'd arrive in Brookline each week bearing a blood-streaked white parcel of scraps and bones for Farrah Fawcett. The ash blond Afghan had made Grayson and Boyd's conjugal bliss complete. Sometimes, eating at the claw-footed library table Grayson had set with red bandanna napkins, hand-thrown pottery, and calla lilies in a bugle-shaped crystal vase, Schachter would be tempted to weep for longing. The very kitchen walls seeped love, he thought.

"So, boychik." Boyd's slender fingers paid a cool and tender visit to Schachter's steamy jowl. "You getting out? Meeting anybody?"

Schachter, abject, shook his head.

Grayson looked crushed.

"Been busy," Schachter said. "Mortgage activity's picking up."

Boyd slipped two sugary rugelach onto Schachter's dessert plate, which was brown and speckled like a trout. "These things take time, sweetheart."

Grayson, his smile melancholy with memory, nodded.

Boyd touched his lover's wrist. "You've got to look in some unlikely places," he said.

"Not to mention right under your nose." Grayson gave Boyd a deep loving look.

Schachter looked down at his lap. Farrah Fawcett, her narrow chin laced with drool, rested her head on his green wide-wale corduroy knee. Her eyes were liquid with yearning.

"Is it all right to give her one of these cookies?" Schachter said.

The Brookline men's group Schachter had joined in October suspended meetings in late May. Just when he was on the verge of a breakthrough, he thought: the last session he had almost brought himself to tears. Eight of the twelve members and Rob, the "facilitator," were tied up with a softball league. Schachter was lukewarm about sports. He wondered what he should do next, now that his Wednesday nights were about to go begging.

A woman he'd taken out to dinner—once, then never seen again—had told him about a class she'd taken the previous summer at the Harvard Extension School. She'd met a lot of bright, interesting people, she said. Schachter couldn't recall the woman's name—a flower, he thought. Daisy? Rose? No, something less common, like Dahlia or Larkspur. She had not, apart from her availability and a set of bracelets made from knotted elephant hair, been a memorable encounter. But Schachter remembered her when, sitting alone in a Cambridge café, he came upon a schedule of summer classes among the litter on his table.

The course he chose (rather capriciously, he'd have to admit) was "Oral History: A Practicum." Schachter imagined balmy July nights in a dark, cool stone building with wide-open windows, reviewing videotapes of *Roots* as he sat surrounded by serious women in sandals and sundresses and light perfume.

The first class, however, swiftly divested Schachter of this modest accrual of dreams. There were only seven in the class, which met in a stuffy cubicle in the basement of one of Harvard's more obscure libraries. Schachter and the professor, a rather plain, slight woman with a prow-shaped profile and odd ethnic clothes, were the only two in the room much under sixty.

The purpose of the class, Professor Geller explained in a voice Schachter found difficult to hear, was to learn interviewing techniques. Although this was in no way what he'd had in mind, Schachter did not drop the class. He entertained some hope that it might, at the very least, make him a better conversationalist.

By the third week, Schachter was the only student in the class who had not begun interviews for the term project. His failure to so much as select its focus made him feel as if he had infiltrated the hot seminar room under false pretenses.

Professor Geller spoke in a low, rapid voice that sometimes quivered with intensity. Schachter listened desperately to her lectures, hoping for a clue to her incomprehensible zeal, to his own opaque enthusiasms and possibilities. Personal stories were the true repository of human history, she said. "And some-times"—her voice wobbled precariously—"it seems we have little else to leave our children, their children . . . so very little else."

Several of Schachter's classmates nodded sadly.

Looking down, Diane Geller fumbled with a small stack of note cards for a long, awkward moment. When she lifted her head, her dark eyes were skittish and moist.

"Maybe now's a good time for our break," she said.

During the fifteen-minute recess, the professor, who usually stayed to chat, disappeared. Schachter used the time to question his classmates about their projects. Jessica Katz knew an artist who had spent two years of her childhood in Terezin. Mrs. Yuan was writing a biography of her pastor, who had served as a missionary in Seoul. Mr. Grimes was interviewing residents of a local convalescent home about the Depression. Harriet Phillips had already made two trips to Alabama to record the scrambled memories of a hundred-year-old great-aunt, the daughter of slaves, and Martin Tilley had been interviewing homeless Vietnam vets for five years. He'd started out hoping to run across someone who might have known his son, still "missing in action" after nearly thirty years. But "the project got bigger than both of us," Tilley said. He told Schachter he was taking the class because his narrative lacked shape.

"I know what you mean," Schachter said. "I hear you." He turned to Eileen O'Bannon, a plump and bashful woman of eighty or so. "And yourself, madam?"

Mrs. O'Bannon, her blue powder-puff eyes evading Schachter's gaze, blushed mightily. " 'Tis a bit of a rare circumstance, mine," she allowed.

"Oh?" Schachter said. He pictured Mrs. O'Bannon waddling in the wee hours through what was left of the Combat Zone, a mottle-covered composition book in hand, as she pursued fallen women with motherly chiding and a curiosity that wouldn't quit.

Mrs. O'Bannon shrugged, then looked down at the perforated uppers of her white orthopedic shoes. "I looked after the Kennedy youngsters for a time," she said.

Schachter's smile felt arthritic. "Ted and Joan's?"

The old woman shook her head.

Schachter waited.

"Caroline and John-John still stop sometimes," she whispered. "On the way to Hyannis, you know."

"Well, if that isn't something," Schachter said.

Little wonder that Schachter began to view both himself and everyone he knew as . . . well, let's face it, *limited*.

Melissa got all over him, of course. "Christ, you're such a defeatist. Not to mention supercilious. Limited?" The sound she made seemed shockingly crude coming from a mouth that looked like a rosebud.

Schachter sighed. "Thirty-six years of hoping for the best." He shrugged. "So maybe I'm a little jaded."

Melissa's laugh was heartless.

"It's already too late to drop the class."

"You're worried about forfeiting—what, a few hundred bucks?"

"I'm worried," Schachter said, "about having a Harvard transcript that consists of a single F."

"What about your father?"

"He graduated summa."

"And then, unlike certain people, went on to get a *life*. My God, that fabulous career, cooling down all those foreign hot spots . . ."

"Don't rub it in," said Schachter.

"Does the word *interview* ring any chimes in that padded cell that passes for your mind?"

"Please," Schachter groaned. "I'd be listening for years."

"You think it would kill you," Melissa said, "listening for a change?"

"I had a highly infectious childhood," Schachter reminded her. "My hearing is impaired."

"Well, your *listening* is."

"What kind of therapist are you, anyway?"

"Confrontational." She grinned.

"So maybe *you* ought to talk to my father."

"I'd be delighted. He's—"

"Forget it," Schachter said. "Anyway, he's down in Palm Beach. Writing his memoirs."

"So fly down for the weekend."

"This isn't about transportation," Schachter said, "it's

about commerce. You think he's going to give away what Harper and Whosis are willing to pay for? He's already got an advance."

"My God, Schach, he's your *dad*."

"He's in love," Schachter said. "Some goy divorcée. Did you realize Omaha has an upper crust?"

"Don't tell me you're jealous!"

"My mother's remains are still tepid. Remember her—the little woman hanging around Cleveland waiting for him? But hey, what's twenty years?"

"Or six?" Melissa said. "Which is how long your mother's been dead. I remember it was '93 because you were—"

"Tut-tut," Schachter said. "Privileged information. Case records sealed. Besides, my father—"

"Who is, what, seventy-five? How long did you expect him to hold out for the filial blessing?"

"You know, Melissa," Schachter said, "you could seriously start to annoy me."

"Good thing I'm not your therapist, huh?" Melissa said.

In sheer desperation, Schachter spent a day making plans to interview Grayson and Boyd. A love story for the nineties, he thought . . . the changing social fabric of New England . . . *yes!* And those two would love to talk, would never make a mockery of his genuine interest, misconstrue his motives . . .

But when Schachter got down to writing a list of the open-ended questions he would ask, it was just . . . too *personal*. And maybe a little more than he really cared to know. I need a stranger, he thought. I can't go into this with a vested interest.

Professor Geller, who had asked to be called Diane (with the result that no one in the class called her anything), arrived late that week. She looked wan and flustered, and her apologies seemed a little panicky, Schachter thought. He was feeling a little panicky himself. After tonight the course was half over. He was going to have to talk to her.

As always, Professor Geller spent the first half hour lecturing on technique—what she called *craft:* how to gain the subject's confidence, how to handle defensiveness, how to encourage intimacy while maintaining the proper distance, how to regain focus after a digression. "You want to leave room for things to develop," she said, "but not let them get away from you."

"I have a question," Schachter said.

"Yes?" Professor Geller looked distracted.

"What if the person is . . ." Schachter's stubby fingers picked through the air below his chin for the proper word. "I mean, what if they're *boring?*" he said.

The flush that rushed up Diane Geller's neck and engulfed her face filled Schachter with dismay. She thinks I mean *her,* he realized. His own face felt overheated and damp.

"Well." Professor Geller's wounded eyes fluttered around the edges of the seminar table. "Do any of you have suggestions for that?"

Mr. Grimes cleared his throat, opened his mouth, then shut it again.

No one would look at Schachter.

Finally, Mrs. O'Bannon raised a timid hand.

Professor Geller smiled with relief. "Yes, Eileen?"

"Boredom's a thing in the beholder's ear, then, isn't it?" the old lady said sweetly. She gave Schachter a sidewise but scathing glance.

Someone stifled a laugh.

"Yeah," Schachter said humbly, "I guess that's right."

In the second half hour, when they practiced interviewing each other, Schachter got to play the role of a philandering politician. Harriet Phillips's barrage of loaded questions seemed worthy of Geraldo. Schachter wanted to ask if this was history, but he didn't have the nerve. By the time the break arrived, he knew his madras shirt was bleeding, profusely blue, all over his undershirt.

He slumped in the corridor, bathed in accusatory fluorescent light, and waited for Professor Geller to emerge from the ladies' room. Down the hall, in a would-be staff lounge, the others were drinking the sweet iced tea the professor lugged in each week in a huge red plastic thermos. Tonight Mrs. Yuan had brought almond cookies. Schachter, alone in the corridor, felt quarantined by shame.

When the professor finally came out of the rest room, glancing anxiously at her watch, her face looked paler and sharper than ever. She was wearing a black leotard and a gauzy wraparound skirt of some dark Indian material shot with gold threads. She was thinner than Schachter had noticed before, almost frail. A few droplets of water rested in the shallow depressions of her collarbone, as if she'd just bathed her face. He wondered if she might be ill, or troubled by something other than him, but it wasn't really his business.

"Could I . . . detain you for a second?" Schachter said.

She hadn't noticed him leaning against the wall, and her smile was startled. "Of course, Howard."

"My question in there," Schachter said. "I didn't mean—"

"Sha." Her small hushing sound might have been meant to reassure a dreaming child. Its gentleness struck Schachter as almost shocking. Then she smiled again. "Let's face it," she said. "I *am* boring. I get too wrapped up and—"

"My God," Schachter said, "*you* were the last thing on my mind." Then his words rebounded and struck him dumb.

Professor Geller laughed softly. "Never mind. I know what you meant."

"Thank you." He felt like crying.

"Was there something else . . ." She paused for a moment. "Howard?"

"I'm kind of lost," Schachter said.

"Lost?"

"I don't have a subject," he said. "I don't even know how to start trying to find one."

"I see." Her face was sympathetic and much softer full on, Schachter saw, than in profile.

"I wondered, could I come talk to you sometime?" he asked. "Like a conference or something?"

She glanced at her watch. "See me after class?"

"I appreciate it," Schachter said.

The last hour of the class they watched a videotape of Bill Moyers interviewing a famous poet. Diane Geller stopped the tape frequently, pointing out the subtleties of Moyers's skill. She paid a great deal of attention to his facial expressions and posture, leaning in and out of the dark to touch the small rectangular screen. Her hands flew like birds across the light, resting here and there on the journalist's grainy face, touching the corners of his mouth and eyes, hovering over the alert angle of his head, the easy slope of his shoulders.

"Couldn't you just fall in love with someone who *listens* like that?" Diane Geller sounded as if she were talking to herself.

In the darkness the other women murmured like pigeons under the eaves.

———

Late the next afternoon, after work, Schachter made his way, as agreed, to Diane Geller's apartment in Belmont. She lived on the first floor of a homely brown-shingled two-family flat with a porch railing and shutters the color of Dijon mustard. A bright blue plastic recycling basket full of mineral water bottles stood beside the door.

Diane Geller answered the buzzer only seconds after Schachter had pressed it. "It's me," he said. "I'm just disguised as a banker."

"Hello." She held the screen door open for him. "Right on time," she said.

"I wanted to do something right," Schachter said. "Change of pace."

"Relax." She smiled. "We'll get you straightened out."

"In four weeks?" he said. "It's taken me thirty-six years to get like this."

She was dressed, as always, in dark clothes, a black cotton sundress with red-and-purple stitching around the neck and a purple vest that looked like fishnet. Her long brown hair was twisted into a knot at the back of her neck and anchored with two black things that looked like short chopsticks. They formed a dark X just above her nape, where her skin was the translucent white of dogwood petals. Schachter found her suddenly exotic.

The room into which she led him, however, was almost painfully plain: white walls, a bare oak floor, Crate & Barrel furniture the color of sand. An old fireplace was covered with a huge rice-paper fan. Plants in rattan planters hung at each of the three large windows. Schachter, playing for time, gravitated to the nearest window and examined some tangled loops of vine with fuzzy purple leaves.

"Wandering Jew," Diane Geller said.

"That's me," said Schachter.

She smiled. "Me too." She sat down in one corner of the shapeless sofa. Its linen cushions collapsed dejectedly as she leaned back against them. "Please," she said. "Sit down."

Schachter took the other corner of the sofa, leaving room for three people to sit between them.

"You want to tell me what's going on?" Diane Geller said.

"Not much," Schachter said. "That's pretty much the problem."

"Could you give me a little more to go on?"

"Well, like I said last night, I haven't got a subject."

She nodded.

"And I guess I don't really know . . ." Schachter was stumbling. Her eyes were patient and encouraging. He remembered her pale, pliant fingers traveling gently over Bill Moyers's face. "I'm afraid to pick one maybe," Schachter said. "I don't know."

"Why would you be afraid?"

"Getting in over my head?"

A phone rang and Schachter's whole body flinched. The phone was at his elbow, but he hadn't noticed it before. An old-fashioned rotary model, it sat, black and malevolent looking, on a small blond kidney-shaped table next to the sofa. Its ring reminded him of the security alarm on the bank vault.

Diane Geller seemed paralyzed for a moment. Then she stood up stiffly. "I'm afraid I need to answer it," she said.

"Feel free." Schachter wondered if he should offer to leave the room. She looked so tense, almost trapped. But she moved quickly toward the kitchen and picked up an extension there.

Her hello sounded breathless. She stood in the doorway, her back in full view. After a silence he watched her rigid spine soften. "Oh," she said. "Hi." She lowered her voice, but he could still hear her. "I don't really know anything yet."

Schachter got up and examined the plants again. He kept his posture nonchalant.

"I'm in the middle of a . . . sort of student conference. Could I . . . yes, as soon as I know something, okay?"

When she returned to the living room, Schachter was as she had left him, on the sofa. She reclaimed her own place, seating herself with care, like someone with an injury. Her face was very pale. "You were telling me about being afraid," she said.

"Afraid I can't make ordinary people interesting enough, maybe." Schachter sighed. "I don't know anybody famous," he said. "Or . . . you know, remarkable."

"And what about you?" Diane Geller asked softly.

"Interview myself?" Schachter's laugh was rough and dry. "I'm not remarkable."

She leaned forward, her elbows on her knees, slanting toward him. "I'm going to tell you a secret," she said. "The key to the whole thing. I was saving it for the last class, but I think you might need to hear it now."

"What?" Schachter sounded cautious.

"Everyone's remarkable, Howard."

He grimaced.

"You don't like my pet theory?"

"I don't like being called Howard."

"What would you like to be called?"

Schachter looked down. His blunt hands hung like dead things between his knees. He had always hated his hands, the square bluish nails on the stumpy fingers, the tufts of reddish gold hair between the knuckles. His father's were a musician's hands, graceful and competent. He kept them manicured and tanned.

"What would you like me to call you?" Diane Geller insisted quietly.

"Remarkable," Schachter said.

She did not smile.

"I guess I'm getting off the subject," Schachter said.

"Not really." A pale green bottle sat between two glasses on the teak coffee table. Her hands were unsteady as she filled both glasses, then stretched a thin arm down the length of the sofa toward him. Schachter leaned forward to meet her halfway, accepted the glass. The water was scented with lime.

"Thank you."

"You're welcome." She didn't touch her own glass, but clasped her hands tightly in her lap as if to still them. "I'm not very good at this, am I?"

"What?"

"Interviews, conferences . . . teaching." She smiled sadly. "I haven't been doing it long, and right now I—maybe it's me in over her head."

"No," Schachter said. "You've just got a bad subject." He set his glass on the table. "Me, I mean."

Diane Geller's hands flew out suddenly, as if reaching for him. "Ask me something," she said.

"I'm sorry?"

"Listen." She clapped her hands together and Schachter jumped. "Okay, let's say you've got to get to know me. Matter of life and death, right?"

"Whose?" Schachter asked.

Diane Geller cringed, but then waved the question away like a mosquito. "You've got only moments," she said, "to cut to the heart of a lifetime that's making me tick."

"This sounds sort of like open-heart surgery," Schachter said.

"It is." She inched closer on the sofa, straining forward. He thought for a moment that she was getting ready to pounce. "Let's say you've got six questions. Just six strokes to sketch out the contours of my life, the shape of my . . . being." She held up her right hand, fingers spread, and added her left thumb. Then she clapped again. "Six. Let's hear them."

Schachter just stared at her.

"What?" she said. "What's the matter?"

"But who are you supposed to *be*?" he said.

"Isn't that what you've got to find out?"

"You mean a guessing game?" Schachter asked. "Like you're Marie Antoinette or Madonna or something?"

Diane Geller's shoulders sagged just a little. "I thought I could just, you know, be *me*."

Schachter frowned. "Oh." Then he brightened. "Could I be Morley Safer?"

She shook her head. She did not smile.

"You're my professor," Schachter said. "I can't just come barging in here and start asking personal questions."

"*All* questions are personal," she said. "Besides, this is an assignment."

Schachter stood up abruptly. "This is all a big mistake," he said.

"Sit." Her voice was firm. "Start asking."

Schachter, still on his feet, threw her a helpless look. "How old are you?" He felt blood rushing to his face.

"Thirty-two," she said. "That's a waste of one question."

"Where were you born?"

"Pennsylvania. Two down the drain." She smiled grimly.

Schachter began to pace. "I need to think."

"Yes," she said. "You do."

The soles of his wing tips were loud on the floorboards. He loosened his tie as he crossed from the hall entryway to the far windows, from the fireplace to another door, covering the room with a large X. From where he stood he got a good glimpse of the kitchen, gleaming white appliances and pebbly beige linoleum, all out of date. A row of good copper-bottomed pots dangled from an overhead rack of wrought iron.

"You like to cook?" he said.

"I like to feed people," she corrected him. "You're doing better, but not great."

"I don't know where these questions are supposed to *come from*," Schachter said. "Can't you give me a hint?"

He stood in the doorway, his back to her, and continued to study the kitchen. He saw a neon orange tricycle by the back door, a huge pair of filthy running shoes on the floor beside it. She would not answer him. An open box of cinnamon Pop-Tarts sidled up to a smudge-faced chrome toaster, surrounded by more than a dozen amber vials with prescription labels on them. A child's finger painting was clamped to the side of the refrigerator with two magnets that looked like Oreos. So she was married, had a husband and a kid and a life—why ask?

"Sit down for a minute." Behind him her voice sounded tired. Or maybe just tired of him.

Schachter turned around slowly. "I shouldn't be taking up your time like this."

"Sit down," she repeated, patting the sofa seat beside her. "Please."

Schachter, slumping somewhere in the middle of what had been the distance between them, imagined that his body didn't make a dent in the cushions. "Am I hopeless?"

"Just listen to me, all right?" Her face was damp and looked almost bleached. Her stare was irradiating.

Schachter closed his eyes. When Diane Geller started to speak, it sounded as if she were slowly moving away, though he could feel her there beside him still, a suggestion of heat and weight and molecular jostle.

"The questions," she said softly. "They come from your passion. Terror, torture, desire . . . the passion that's within you tapping into the passion in me. If you are full of fear, then that's what you have to work with. Let it guide you to whatever's in me." She hesitated, like someone about to reveal something painful. "It is that simple," she said.

"I'm afraid." There was a hairline fracture in Schachter's voice. "I am."

"Of course you are. We're supposed to be."

Schachter thought he heard the ticking of a clock somewhere. His tongue was parched. He remembered the mineral water on the table, but he did not want to open his eyes. He pictured the drops of moisture caught in the hollows below Diane Geller's throat, and he tasted salt.

"All you have to do is find the . . . the headwaters of that passion," Diane Geller whispered. "Not mine. Just your own. Longing, sorrow . . . they will carry you . . . so far you can't imagine. And nothing will be kept from you. Nothing."

Somewhere above, a baby cried. Then light footsteps crossed a room, a door shut. Schachter waited for stillness.

"But how do you *know*?" he said. "When you're there."

"Shh," she said. "Listen."

He thought a breath glanced his cheek, like warm fingers.

"Take your time," she said. "We need to believe we have all the time in the world."

Schachter, his head bowed, heard the solitary beating of his own heart, frantic and brave. The husband and child would be home soon, and Diane Geller would feed them. The days were growing shorter now, it was nearly August. The air would soon cool, and by eight-thirty it would be fully dark. She would open the windows, drawing frail white curtains over them, against the night. Her fingers would brush the lids of a sleeping child, would caress the first lines at the corners of a man's mouth. The life Schachter craved would be lived, here in this house, without him.

Beside him, her breathing was quick and shallow, and he knew she was waiting, but he didn't know for what.

"Three questions?" Schachter said. "Three left?"

"I'm listening," she said.

Schachter took a deep breath, then let it go. "I want to ask you about love," he said. "How did you find it, or know when you did?"

His eyes were sealed, he was falling in the dark, he knew no fear at all.

A phone rang, and a small broken sound came from the throat of the woman beside him, but Schachter didn't hear.

"If you didn't already love someone," he said, "could you love somebody like me? Am I doing everything wrong?"

The Lost Art
of Sleep

In the city, a man and a woman have renounced sleep. The nights are cooling, days coming up short. The man and the woman have vowed they will never again close their eyes, and they have been so faithful to that vow that their eyes have become holy stigmata and their feet spread low blue flame wherever they walk.

They look, this man and woman, like brother and sister: Both are tall and lean, graceful and dark. But they are not brother and sister. Once they were lovers. Now they are husband and wife. The skin of each is shaped to the other's flesh; the scent of one seeps from the other's pores. In a time when sleep was still possible, the man held his wife and dreamed they would, soon again, be lovers. But the woman had by then renounced dreams. Lying in the dark, she transforms the man in her arms into children she holds safe against her through the keen, unremitting nights.

Rain bounces off the street, sputtering like grease, as the overnight guests are spun out into the morning. It is seven o'clock and the welfare hotel is being cleared out for the day. The departing women, children bundled in their arms and bunched around their legs, look stunned. Daylight bruises their faces and blackens their eyes.

A woman in tan shorts and a sleeveless blouse glances back over her shoulder at the sign above the revolving door:

BLYTHE HOUSE FAMILY RESIDENCE

NO MEN ALLOWED

BOYS UNDER 12 ONLY

NO EXCEPTIONS!

The woman pulls a section of newspaper from her shoulder bag and holds it, folded in quarters, above her head. She stands by the curb looking up and down the drenched street. The rain quickly soaks through her thin white blouse, making it transparent. The woman looks down, then lowers the sodden newspaper and holds it like a fan in front of her breasts.

Near the corner, a woman with long elegant bones and powder white hair clipped close to her skull kneels on the sidewalk. She is surrounded by seven children and holds an infant in her arms.

"Grandmère—" The largest child, a boy perhaps seven, stretches out sapling arms for the baby. "Let me." The woman smiles as she watches the boy button the infant inside his oversized red shirt. Then she trains her attention on the street. A man in a faded blue raincoat is moving toward them. The woman watches him, craning her black swan's neck and beckoning with fingers like wands. She waits until she can see the man's eyes, though he is looking away from her. "Please . . . the children got to eat and the babies got to grow. . . ." The lilt of Haiti moves in her voice.

She spreads her arms wide, enclosing the children, as her eyes bore into the man. "We sing for the gentleman, eh?"

The children open their mouths like dark fledglings about to be fed.

The man stops, holding out a hand to silence the children, to stay their song. He keeps his eyes slanted away from the woman. "Sorry," he says. "You got the wrong guy."

The woman tucks her head down like a swan. Her arms curtail their embrace. The children, huddling nearer the old woman, close their mouths. Their voodoo eyes follow the man down the rain-spattered street.

When the afternoon begins to lose its heat, Lisabet starts back toward the river, taking a long looping way out of the city. Her spine is plumb, her shoulders square and narrow, but occasionally she twists around to look back over the distance she has covered. She regards the city skyline through eyes tapered by disdain: a mean place, clamorous with danger and incivility. Lisabet would like to keep the city at her back, at a distance. But most days before the light rises to the river's edge, she rushes back to the city streets alone, leaving her grandchildren to fend for themselves in a cave. For though the sky is still white with heat at noon, the days are foreshortened and the children slow her down. Also, begging is an art at which she does not wish them to grow adept. So she mostly leaves them behind, Gabrial, her oldest grandson, looking after the littlest ones. The middle ones must look after themselves. Each afternoon, exhausted and parched, Lisabet returns to the river on legs gone flimsy with fear. Each day she's amazed all over again to find the children just where she left them.

Most days she returns with a little food, but never with anything else. The children's eyes, alight at her approach, absorb the shame of her day's failing, and dull as she draws near. At the edge of the river they circle her, gentle as ripples around a dropped stone. But they do not ask, *Where is our mother? Our father?* The children have by now stopped asking, learning for her sake to hide their hope.

Lisabet walks slowly, running once when she must cross a highway, then pausing briefly in the coolness of an underpass. A rat skitters near her sandaled feet, carrying something large in its mouth. The rat's eyes are yellow in the shadows, scathing. Lisabet picks up her step. An empty factory with shattered windows looms behind a spiked iron fence where she reenters daylight. Lisabet breathes the names of the children, a litany for their safety. "Gabrial, Charlène, Isaac," she says. "Antony-Daniel . . . Noelle . . ." Her breath quickens. "Brébeuf . . . Lalande . . ." She inhales, drawing deep, then raises her face to the sun. "Goupil." Lisabet nods in a satisfied way and murmurs, "Ainsi soit-il."

In the sparsely wooded apron that scallops the river, the air cools a fraction. Hulks of abandoned cars lie ambushed by tall and tangled weeds. Lisabet spots a snake, greenish brown and harmless, as it slithers under a bush whose branches hang low with purple berries. Lisabet smiles. She likes snakes. The land was full of them when she was a girl, serpents dangling from trees like lucky charms. There are snakes in the cave, but Lisabet does not call attention to them for she knows the children would take fright. Snakes are, as God's creatures go, poorly treated and painfully misunderstood, Lisabet thinks. The children's fear would be better spent on friendly strangers, speeding cars, needles scattered in schoolyards like playthings.

Lisabet picks three purple berries from the bush, but their taste is so bitter that she spits them out on the ground. Her arm tightens around the dark bundle slung against her hip: two worm-scarred apples, a cellophane bag with a sprinkling of coarse salt from the pretzels it once held, a loaf of moldy bread. Her findings are tied inside a ruined black sweater. Provisions. Something to bring the children.

But Madeleine and Simon . . . Lisabet lowers her head as if the late-day sun is pressing it down. She hasn't turned up sign or rumor of the children's parents, her daughter and son-in-law. They may truly be gone, she thinks, gone for good. Could be in prison or hospital or dead . . . just *gone*.

Lisabet no longer knows how many of her children are alive. Three infant girls taken by fevers, two boys drowned . . . two more simply vanished at the threshold of manhood. By the time Lisabet thought to leave Haiti, only François and Madeleine remained within sight, bickering over what was left of their mother's cut-down heart. Perhaps François still haunts the famished lanes of Port-au-Prince. Sometimes Lisabet can almost see him, stretching out his beautiful long-fingered hands to passing tourists outside the Iron Market. François has not aged. His mother sees the wily slender boy who stayed behind years ago, stayed for some need Lisabet could not fathom because she was blinded by faith in a more hospitable world across the fathomless blue-green sea. François, his eyes reddened from midnight quorums his lips never alluded to, said he could not bear to leave Haiti just when everything was about to change. Lisabet told her son she could not bear to stay, not in a country that had made a widow of her when she was scarcely more than a girl. Haiti would *never* change. The men who came for her husband, a carpenter, had blended in with night, their eyes concealed by black glass. They had cut off both of Jules's hands before ushering him out into the hot darkness.

François grew silent. His one indomitable argument was to remain behind when his mother and sister left. Now Lisabet can no longer calculate the sum of her surviving children, nor conjure a memory of her husband's face. Sometimes late at night, when Madeleine's children are sleeping, Lisabet hears Jules wailing deep within the cave. The bats, flying home one step ahead of dawn, scream. And the stones shudder. She hears nothing of François, however. Now nothing of Madeleine.

Lisabet, walking toward the river, fixes her thoughts on the little ones, reminding herself that she, an old white-headed woman with no more than a fistful of greenish bread and a sprinkling of salt, might be the whole world left to the children now. And she thrusts out her chin at the sun and walks faster toward the dark sidewinder river.

The man and the woman have—small miracle—a home on the other side of the river. In order to find and make this home, they left their children in the city with only an old woman, slender as a reed, to watch over them. The man and woman did not want to leave their children. They did so before they had come to understand that sleep and dreams could be renounced. They knew only that, like a reed, the old woman might bend but she would not break. So they gave their children into her care and crossed the river, seeking a place to sleep.

Their home is made of rotting wood and moss-covered stones and it wants for a new roof. But it has an ancient hearth with two blackened iron cooking pots, a stream almost within sight, and many trees for the fires they will live on. The house is owned by a farmer who says they may stay if the man will work for him and if the woman will keep the children quiet.

"I will work like a dog," the man has told the farmer.

"I will watch them like a hawk," the woman has promised. "The children are quiet as mice."

The farmer is quite old, but he has a boy's laugh. "The wife gets nervous as a cat around noisy youngsters," he says.

The man and woman have swept the house, cut wood, carried water. They have patched the roof and sealed the single window with mud. They have acquired—small miracles—several blankets, two bars of soap, a few dishes, and an oil lamp from the farmer's nervous but kindly wife.

The man, a wreath of sweat slipping down his brow, has built a fence and painted a barn and weeded a garden. The woman, her eyes stinging with salt and swimming in the noonday heat, has worked beside her husband to make up to the farmer for the time they will be gone. For with the start of summer's decline they must return to the city to find the old woman and to bring the children to their new home on the far side of the river.

The candle has melted into a crooked thumb. Its small flame is fickle.

Lisabet lies on a pallet of rock and listens to the singing of the bats and watches the children sleep. Their eyes are closed, their expressions rapt. Lisabet is fascinated, for to her sleep is a lost art. It has been so for many years.

The night is chilly. Lisabet sits up, shivering, and wraps herself in arms like long dark vines.

Deep in the cave, far from the reach of light, the snakes move. Though she expects them, the snakes unsettle Lisabet's blood. She disentangles herself from her arms' cool embrace, stands up, then stoops for a willow switch that lies at her feet. Three rats skulk outside the circle of sickly light, watching her.

The rats are drawn to the sweet scent of sleeping children. Each night they nose out of the darkness, their small hot eyes spattering the cave's shadows with light.

Lisabet raises the willow switch above her head, then slices through the air.

The rats scramble off, their feet scraping sound from stone.

Lisabet glances at the sleeping children. Not a hair has been turned in the circle of small dark heads. Lisabet looks away from the children then and waits, her blood writhing.

The snakes, their skins patterned with all the colors of darkness, slip from the cave's slick orifices and come to her. Their brazen tongues tease her feet, and Lisabet tickles their bellies with the tip at the willow switch until they coil around it, letting her swoop them up into the air. Their phosphorescent skins write fleeting messages on the walls of swarthy stone.

Lisabet's eyes are wide open, deciphering, until dawn.

The season, though late, was still mild when the man and woman returned to the city. The farmer's blessing was upon them: "Just get back quick as you can."

"It shouldn't be more than a week," the man said.

His wife, her face beautiful with craving, nodded. The flavor of her children's skin was making her mouth water.

But now it has been ten weeks, and the man and woman have renounced sleep and their feet have spread blue flame all through the city, and still they have no word of the children and the reedlike old woman whose breaking has become a possibility they must allow.

"Maman—" The woman can barely speak, so strong is the taste of ash in her mouth.

"We'll find them." The man embraces his wife as if they are lovers. "We will, soon."

The woman nods and gathers the man to her body, but her bleeding eyes see children, only children, all around in the dark.

No one has seen them anywhere.

Misericordia Women's Shelter is a converted warehouse, a three-story brick building the color of a bloodstain. In its heyday, the place was stacked to the rafters with imported toys. Later, in wartime, it served as an annex to the state armory. The large square windows are covered with plywood and metal bands. The doors are sheeted with steel. The ramp to the loading dock has been chained off, but the women never hesitate to duck under the chains. The loading dock is as good a place as any to wait for the shelter's door to be unlocked.

When Lisabet arrives at Misericordia, it is late afternoon, and a dozen women, most of them old, are already settled in to wait. Lisabet walks past the ramp, her eyes cast straight ahead, and starts hammering on the door. Her slender hand, cramped into a fist, barely makes a sound against the steel, but Lisabet keeps pounding, prepared to devote hours to the task of raising someone.

"It don't open until eight," one of the women calls out to her. "Might as well come sit down."

Lisabet shakes her head and keeps pounding. Her lips are stitched together in one tight straight seam.

Finally a gaunt woman leaves the ramp and limps over to Lisabet on swollen legs. She wears sunglasses with purple heart-shaped frames that make her pale face look ghostly. "The door don't crack open for nobody, not a minute before eight."

Lisabet slams the side of her fist into the door's impervious steel face. "I need only to inquire of someone," she says through clenched teeth. She pounds again.

"Even if you could get somebody to hear your story, they wouldn't care what it was." The woman touches Lisabet's arm with a bashful hand. "Don't wear yourself out."

Lisabet pulls from the touch and kicks at the door.

"Suit yourself." The woman shrugs and goes back to the ramp, where the other women are laughing.

The flesh at the side of Lisabet's hand splits open. She keeps hammering.

Inside the shelter, Doña Alicia Luz Caudron ignores the muffled thumps at the door as she goes about distributing bed linen. Monday is the day for clean sheets. She drops a plastic-wrapped package on the foot of each cot. The women who come on Mondays make up the beds themselves; the Sunday women tear the sheets off and drop them in bins in the hall when they leave Monday morning. By then the bedding is blackened and often bloodied. The corridor crawls with bugs.

The line is always longest on Mondays. The women like clean sheets. Alicia wonders how many are already out there. The pounding doesn't surprise her. It happens all the time. As the pounding at the door keeps up, though, Doña Alicia starts to get curious. What would make a person do something so useless for such a long time? Finished distributing the sheets, she goes to check on supplies in the room they call the Welcome Center. The women are offered tea when they come in at night, coffee before they leave in the morning. Sometimes cookies or crullers are donated by a local baking company, but not so often. Pies were given out once. They'd made such a mess, with no plates or anything, that now the director always says no to pie. Doña Alicia thinks it's a shame, turning down free food when so many are hungry. But nobody asks what she thinks. Her job is to enforce the rules others make. That's fine with her. She'd hate to be the one who had to think up rules against everything that could go wrong in a place like this.

Alicia fills two tin basins with packets of sugar, Sweet 'n Low, and powdered creamer. The women with little ones filch handfuls of the creamer, later mixing it with water and feeding it to their kids like it was real milk. Alicia has heard the white powder is the same stuff they use to make shoe polish. Maybe, maybe not. But no milk in it for sure.

When the pounding has gone on for twenty minutes, curiosity gets the best of Alicia. She keeps the safety chain fastened. "What is it?" Alicia squints through the gap with her better eye, the right one. "We don't open, lady. Not yet."

The woman at the door is very tall, but old and frail. Her white hair, short and fluffy, reminds Alicia of the fuzz on a milky dandelion stem.

"Have you not heard me?" The old lady's fist is still raised, but it doesn't seem like a threat, just a habit. Alicia sees that the pounding has left her hand bloody and swollen.

"I hear you, sure. Come back at eight, I let you in," Alicia says, sounding sympathetic.

"I have no wish to come in."

The haughtiness, the nerve . . . Alicia's seen enough of that Haitian pride back in Santo Domingo to last a lifetime and she surely isn't about to swallow another dose of it, not here. "Good. I got no wish to *let* you in, either, so maybe you just go away."

"I am trying to find someone," the woman says, just as if she hasn't heard Alicia at all.

"Nobody in here but me." Alicia starts to shut the door,

but the woman is leaning against it now, almost collapsed, not a trace of haughtiness left.

"Please," she whispers. "I beg of you . . . my daughter."

"Lady," Alicia says gently. "I don't lie. Not a soul in here but me."

"But tell me only if you have her name on a list or—"

"List? We got no list."

"But it may be that you have seen her . . ." The woman pulls a snapshot, faded and creased, from her pocket. "Madeleine," she says, pushing it through the crack in the door. "And Simon, her husband."

Alicia looks at the photograph: a handsome young couple in bright clothes and sunshine. The woman looks tall and thin like her mother. Two white flowers are pinned in her hair.

Alicia smiles. She remembers their smell, those very flowers. "You got a beautiful girl there."

"Eight grandchildren." The woman's voice is faint. "And only myself to see to them. You have perhaps seen her?"

Alicia looks again, shaking her head sadly. "I got more than a hundred beds," she says. "Full every night. Who sleeps in them I can't know."

For an instant the woman looks as if she will weep. Then she straightens, her haughtiness and height almost like a costume she steps into. Her long dark fingers slip inside the door to retrieve the photograph. She uses her less damaged left hand.

"I'm sorry, lady."

The woman nods, holding her head high.

"She's a beauty," Alicia says. "I would remember if I see, I think."

"This was the last place," the woman says. "Thank you."

Doña Alicia's left eye watches as the woman moves down the steps, the photograph in her hand. From the back she looks slender, but strong. As she passes the ramp her outline blurs, then blends in with the other women, and Alicia closes and bolts the door. For the rest of the evening, the hallways of the women's shelter will smell of nameless white flowers.

A late Indian summer goads the city to improvisation. Midnight jumps with taxis and the scat songs of addled birds. The sidewalk cafés have unchained their chairs, umbrellas bloom above tables like riotous blossoms.

Corazon, a soup kitchen near the Bolivar public housing project, served beans and rice and fried plantains for supper. Salsa and reggae were pulsing from an old boom box someone had donated or dropped there. A young nun spoke kindly to Madeleine and Simon as they went out into the balmy night. She knew nothing of Lisabet and the children, she said, but she would keep them in her prayers. *Keep them.* The words filled Madeleine with wild and perilous hope. Summer in late November, good things were occurring, maybe prayers were being heard.

But now, going on one A.M., the shelters and welfare hotels have been checked out and closed up, the street musicians Simon used to play with before his flute was stolen are packing up to leave. Simon and Madeleine sit on the downwind side of the Lincoln Plaza fountain, soaking their feet as a cool spray blows down on them. A man in an orange shirt waves to Simon. Then he slings his congas onto his back and heads for the street. An old woman on a nearby bench wraps herself in two plastic trash bags and stretches out to sleep. "Sweet dreams," she says. Simon smiles at her.

Madeleine lowers her face into her hands.

Simon, without touching her, feels her quake. "She is someplace," he says. "She's got to be."

Madeleine shakes her head without looking up.

"If something happened to her we would have found the children by now." Simon puts his arm around his wife's shoulders. "City Welfare would have some record . . . foster homes, something."

Madeleine raises her head and knuckles the tears from under her eyes. "Maybe we should go back," she says. "Maybe he'd still let us come back."

Simon's stern face starts her crying again.

"Will we look forever?"

"If we have to." He touches her face. "Yah, we will."

A young couple walks past, arm in arm. The girl's short black dress is scattered with tiny jet beads that shimmer in the fountain's lights. The boy murmurs something in her ear and the girl lays her head on his shoulder, laughing softly. Simon sees her dress tremble.

"Let's go down by the river," he says.

"The river? What for?"

"Maybe we'll sleep where it's quiet," he says. "It's warm enough."

When they reach the street, they stop to put on their shoes. A police cruiser slows down as it passes them, then continues toward the corner, where five boys in black tank tops are smoking and making noise.

Madeleine and Simon walk toward the river in silence, holding hands when they cross the highway. In the warehouse district the streets are black and deserted. Once, a guard dog hurls itself against a chain-link fence, snarling. They run, Simon trying to keep his arm around his wife, but she is faster than he is.

Then they come to the scrub land, a feeble barricade between the river and the city. They know this ground well. They often slept here on the late-summer nights when they'd still thought each day would be the one to end their search. They slept well here.

"Maman must know we're looking for her," Madeleine says. "Do you think she knows?"

"The kids know, too," says Simon. "They wouldn't think we'd just—"

"We should never have gone."

There is no breeze and only a faint glow from the lights downtown. The hum and rumble of highway traffic have grown distant. Simon moves ahead, feeling around the ground for sharp rocks, glass splinters, the remains of animals. The dry brush is almost like a mattress when he pats it down. He unslings a canvas bag from his shoulder and takes out a light blanket, two sweaters, and four slices of bread saved from the soup kitchen. Then he puts the bread back inside the bag.

"Seems all right." Simon spreads the blanket over the tamped-down brush and rolls the sweaters into pillows. He guides Madeleine onto the blanket and lies down beside her. "Damned if this ain't August," he says.

"A month to Christmas," Madeleine says.

Simon thinks about Christmas . . . the year before last, when they lived in the project, had a place of their own. They didn't have Goupil yet, Lalande was just a few months old and what a baby, always laughing. Simon had a job working in a body shop. But nobody could find out about that, it would have meant the end of food stamps, the project, everything. Madeleine kept aloof from the neighbors and Simon even moved out for a while, to make it look like he'd split. Late at night he'd come sneaking in for a few hours, to be with his wife, to watch his kids' faces animated with dreams and longings from which even he, their father, was barred.

Then Madeleine's mother got put out of her apartment across town. It was nothing she had done. Lisabet had lived there quietly for more than seven years. But her neighborhood had started getting valuable and her building was going to be knocked down to make room for some fancy town houses. The same thing was happening all over the city. Waiting lists for the subsidized places for old folks were half a lifetime long.

Lisabet's last night in her apartment, Simon had come for her late, nearly midnight. He could tell it crushed something in the old woman, having to leave most of her things behind. Not that what she had was so much. But nine people now in four rooms . . . where in hell were they going to put the remnants of a tenth life?

Simon made two trips to the car, moving her clothes and a few mementos. He still remembers a drinking gourd from Haiti and a big bright-painted plate covered with birds. Lisabet kept the plate on her lap, her hand on his shoulder, all the way across town. Then they tiptoed into the project and Lisabet took his place in the bed beside Madeleine.

It wasn't two weeks later when the eviction notice was slipped under their door. Forty-eight hours. Lisabet blamed herself. She had mentioned Simon's job to the lady across the hall, an old acquaintance. Madeleine was sure one of the kids talked too much, bragging. The worst thing for Simon, even now, is that it could have been anybody and he'll never know, never be able to stop wondering. No benefits, no overtime . . . who would have betrayed them for something so poor as that?

He glances at Madeleine. Her face is turned away, toward the city.

"We'll find them way before Christmas," Simon says.

Madeleine doesn't answer.

Simon lies on his back, his eyes navigating the mottled amethyst sky, trying to discern the stars he knows must be there. The reflection of the city's lights makes the heavens disappear, he thinks. Madeleine's shoulder is barely touching his arm. Her eyes are closed now. Simon knows she is not sleeping. Still, his skin jumps when she speaks.

"Don't think about it anymore," she says.

"How do you know what I'm thinking about?"

She offers no reply. Simon turns his head in time to catch the fleeting suggestion of a smile on his wife's exhausted face. He wants, even now, to make love to her. He imagines a fusion of bodies that could somehow redeem their souls. But when Madeleine reaches over and touches his chest, he cannot feel her fingers on his skin. He is numb.

"You wind up this way you're bound to wonder . . ." Simon closes his eyes, conceiving of himself as a different man, a man so quick and canny and ruthless that fate's nets could never trip or entangle him. "Do you know?" he whispers. "What I should not have done?"

Madeleine is silent, staring off into the darkness on the other side of the river. Her eyes burn holes in the fabric of the night.

Lisabet lies flat, her face tipped up, and gazes through dense eyelashes at the cave's low overhang. The rock is pitted, made plain by daylight pouring in through the snaggletoothed opening nearby. Open my eyes a thread more the children will stop believing I still sleep, she thinks.

Lalande is chirping. Charlène and Noelle chatter. Brébeuf sings to himself in a high sweet voice full of air. Like birds, Lisabet thinks. She closes her eyes tighter, snipping off the thread of light between her lashes. I should be gone by now.

The baby, Goupil, whimpers.

"Ssh, bébé, you wake grandmère." Gabrial sounds worried. He has never caught me at sleep, Lisabet thinks. Perhaps he fears I have died in the night. She opens her eyes and smiles at the boy. "Bonjour, bonjour, mes enfants!" She rises and dusts off her hands.

The children flock to her side, pecking at her with small hands and mouths, with sharp eyes. Lisabet shooes them away with a few sweeps of her dusty gray skirt. Her eyes take inventory, counting noses that resemble small buttons of polished horn. Six. The twins are not there. "Where are Isaac and Antony-Daniel?"

"They have gone out just to wash," Gabrial says.

Lisabet shakes her head. That filthy river, brown and fatty as a good bouillon. She hears the little boys splashing and laughing outside in the light. Suddenly, with a force that thins her breath, Lisabet longs to lie down again, simply let go and fall. She imagines a stone bolster cushioning her head, the snakes weaving a coverlet over her. And sleep is sucked like marrow from the memory of her bones.

The twins race inside the cave, their hides and heads dripping. Lisabet watches droplets of oily water scatter at her feet like dropped coins. Her grandchildren's eyes, watchful, expectant, pin her where she stands. They are waiting, all of them, to be fed. Even Gabrial, so subtle for a child, cannot conceal his hunger and his hope.

Lisabet lowers her head, tucking in her chin, deflating her chest. She does not need to look beyond the mouth of the cave. She has already seen the sun touching the peaked skyline of the city. She should be long gone.

Lisabet shuts her eyes, imagining the din, the glare, the long walk to and fro. She feels her spine bending, bending so low that it feels as if something inside her must surely give way.

"Grandmère?" The children flap about in her skirt. Gabrial is touching her hand.

Lisabet does not look down. She is asleep on her feet.

Lady Chatterley's
Root Canal

My name is Margaret Chatterley, so my friends call me Lady, of course. You'd think a person working at the most famous university in the world, even as a secretary (people always seem surprised I went to college, like correcting the Chair's terrible spelling and collating course descriptions is my dream come true, right?), would have found friends with a little more imagination. And this is a story about imagination, really—his, the old man's I mean, and my own. If I hadn't imagined all those heartaches and dreams to fill in the blank spaces in Bailey Randall's clueless blue eyes, I wouldn't have got my heart broken, again. And if that hadn't happened, who knows what the old man—Dr. Scheetz—might have sniffed out in me when I dropped like a pile of dirty laundry into his cruddy little waiting room on the morning after my hallucinatory heart had been smashed to smithereens for the fifth and final time.

I woke up that morning wrecked, my heart, in shards, redundant. A root canal seemed as good a way as any to celebrate. I'd already put off two appointments. I was going to have to go through with it some-time. It was because I was feeling so lousy that I tried to look so good. I admit it. It's always been kind of a fetish with me, since I first came to Harvard—psych major from Wellesley, MSW dropout from Simmons, your average statistic—to dress like I don't belong here. I spend about a third of my salary on clothes. Cheaper than therapy is what I tell myself, though that's maybe not quite true. Anyway, I'm just going to the dentist, but I slither into a short suede skirt and the silk blouse that matches it, ankle boots with Cuban heels, and tights with a fine little stripe I think makes my legs look longer. Everything's burgundy, a color that, depending on your mood, could remind you of expensive wine or raw meat. I probably don't need to mention which way my imagination happened to be leaning.

As I walked up Mass. Ave. toward Porter Square, I felt needles of sleet stitching lines in my face. In another two blocks, I figure, I'll look seventy. The hem of my dragass black coat snatched at the piles of frozen slush that lined the sidewalk. A homeless woman was standing in front of the health food store, one sleeve gone from her pink parka. I gave her a dollar before she could ask and made sure to look into her eyes and smile when I did it. It's one thing to feel shitty, something else to feel sorry for yourself.

Bailey had told me he was busy the night before, Friday night, reading sophomore tutorial projects. Undergraduate deadlines put a lot more fear and loathing in junior faculty than in the students, believe me. And if poor Bailey was any lower on the Department totem pole, his incisors would be digging up night crawlers.

So Bailey was tied up with a shitload of papers—again. And I'd gone to the Brattle alone to see *Harold and Maude*—

again. (Which should have been enough to tip me off, I guess, that my life was tiptoeing toward desolation. Again.)

It was almost midnight when I got home. The wind was tearing into the trees like a loan shark's goon. I walked up the driveway to the sound of breaking bones. Before I reached the back of the house where I pay $950 a month to live in the basement, though, I spotted Bailey's pitiful Pinto, wedged into the dent in the bushes that, in Cambridge, passes for off-street parking. The motor was coughing, the parking lights were on. And Bailey was in the car. Not alone. Waiting for me? Not hardly.

The lights were out in my apartment, of course, and it was so late they must have imagined they were safe, that I'd already be asleep. I wouldn't have seen them, either, if the car lights had been off, the driver's window up. I guess Bailey had opened it because of all the steam on the windshield.

Andrea, my landlady, is almost fifty and looks bulimic. She got this house, where she and I and four students live, in a manhandling divorce settlement. Her ex-husband writes about pop culture, screws nearly everybody he interviews, and apparently gets paid handsomely to do it. Being married to him for twenty years couldn't have been any joyride.

But blessed with a steady income, Andrea is nursing her self-esteem back to health. She goes to modern dance classes every day, like she's going to be Martha Graham when she grows up. She flies off to Taos or Sedona every few months for workshops on healing with crystals, deep-breathing, and macrobiotic tacos. She's invited me upstairs to a few parties— sorry, *salons*. Dinner usually involves tofu in deep cover. Andrea cultivates women who wear what look like wall hangings, batiked and hand-loomed. The men generally have published something about which they manage to be both self-deprecating and pompous. Andrea provides me with photocopied reviews and contributors' notes in advance, in case I want to fawn.

The wind was bullying the bushes. The bushes started taking it out on the Pinto. I sidled up to the driver's side window and just stood there, looking in. A Suzanne Vega tape was playing, something about domestic violence. Lipstick was smeared past Andrea's stingy lip line and her bony hands were busy in Bailey's lap, like they were maybe working on a jammed zipper. My God, the man is *forty*. Maybe they never got a chance to do it in a car in high school, I thought. The first thing I wanted to do was laugh. I imagine that's what it's like to get shot, or stabbed: you'd find yourself having this completely inappropriate reaction before the pain got through to you and clued you in: Hey, you're dying.

"We were going to tell you, Lady." Bailey didn't even try to look me in the eye.

Andrea had no such compunction. "I suppose you'll want your security deposit back." Her laugh was brittle, a little hysterical. Her shriveled face and colorless Dutch boy hair reminded me of those Appalachian dolls made of dried apples and corn husks. I looked at Bailey like there was bound to be a rational explanation and he'd be the one to give it to me.

"It just sort of happened," he said.

Andrea appeared to be doing deep-breathing exercises. Suzanne Vega sounded like she was, too. "Why don't we all go inside?" Andrea said. "I'll make some chamomile tea."

One of the grad students had told me a joke that week, something about anal geodes. Crystals you could shove up your ass. But the setup would have taken too long, the punch line seemed predictable, and I was just plain tired. I turned and walked away without saying a word.

"I'll call you, okay?" Bailey said.

The office was on the street level of a dignified, down-at-the-heels apartment building. A spattered square of glass was lettered in gold: Solomon H. Scheetz, Endodontist. The building had always kind of intrigued me because, though I passed it at least a couple of times each day, I never saw anyone going in or out of there. I imagined a full occupancy of ancient ladies in wheelchairs, their wealth and sanity slowly being pilfered by unscrupulous nieces with lurid fantasy lives and unbridled lust for rent-controlled apartments in Cambridge.

Seeing a wiry old guy in a bloodstained white smock with a drill in his hand didn't do much to temper my own lurid fantasies. He was wearing goggles.

"The drill is broken and I've got a hole in my finger the size of goddamn Fresh Pond," the old man said. As if in corroboration, a drop of blood made a dime-sized splat on the algae-colored linoleum.

"Well," he said, "am I going to get some sympathy here? A little goddamn *concern?*"

"I'm sorry," I said, starting to back out into the cryptlike marble lobby.

"We're *all* sorry," Dr. Scheetz said. "Sick and sorry as sin." He turned around in a waiting room so small that the two of us, both thin, barely fit in it together. Then he disappeared into what I assumed must be his office. "Take off your coat. You can leave it on the chair. Nobody else is coming in until after lunch."

I sneaked a look at my watch. It was two minutes past nine.

He was back in the doorway again, staring at me. "The goddamn coat's still on," he said. "Makes you look like some pathetic widow."

By now, of course, I was afraid to take my coat off—my coat which by the way was a Comme des Garçons I got on sale at the end of last winter and definitely had nothing pathetic about it.

The old man was slouching against the door frame, a wad of toilet paper twisted around his bleeding finger. He looked avid and impatient. "Let's see what you got," he said.

I looked around the office as if it were considerably more expansive and complex than a double closet. "Where's your nurse?"

"You think you're at the goddamn gynecologist?" Scheetz laughed, a short playful bark. "I had a nurse once. She killed herself, beat me to the punch."

Then it got through to me—he was going to keep this up as long as I let him. "Okay," I said. "That's it. Enough."

He looked pleased and not the least bit apologetic. "You sure?"

I fixed him with the flash-freeze glare I was working on for Andrea and Bailey, who were going to be in my face every day unless I was willing to move, quit my job.

"Goddamn positive," I said. "Let's get on with it."

Dr. Scheetz didn't say a word. He just looked at me for the briefest instant, then turned away with something on his face that for all the world resembled sorrow, fresh and well fastened.

The door closed softly. His voice sounded muffled on the other side of it. "Be with you any day now," he said. "Just let me see if I can get my breathing restarted."

Right, I thought. Me, too.

———

His office was the color of Band-Aids and had—I swear I'm not making this up—one picture on the wall, the one where a bunch of dogs are smoking cigars and playing poker. I was numb to the eyebrow on the right side and choking on my own saliva, and bleeding internally besides, but I kept wanting to laugh. The unfortunate form my giddiness took, with my lips and throat out of commission, was that my eyes kept filling with tears.

"We're not even to the part that hurts yet, goddamn it," Scheetz said.

I tried to nod just as he was jamming the drill into my mouth, and the sucking hook that was supposed to keep me from drowning in spit slipped onto my shoulder, hissing like a snake.

"What—" Scheetz said. "You want me to ventilate that sweet mug while I'm at it, it's not enough I'm going after your nerves with a drill?"

I opened my mouth. "I wasn't—" It came out *Ah-wudjun,* or something like that. I clamped my lips together. Why give him the satisfaction? Next thing I know, I've got tears streaming down my face and my shoulders are heaving so hard I'm afraid I might break his old dinosaur chair.

Dr. Scheetz just stood there for a minute or two and stared at me. His arms hung limp at his sides, the drill dangling so near his thigh that even in my condition I was worried. "Can't you be careful?" I sobbed.

The expression on his face was absolutely zip—not surprise or sympathy, not even irritation. It looked like he was off somewhere having an out-of-body experience.

"Sorry," I said.

He just kept looking at me.

My mouth felt like sandpaper. "It isn't you," I said.

"Goddamn right it isn't."

I nodded.

"You know how big those nerves are?" he said. "No bigger around than the finest needle your grandmother'd use to sew a baby's underpants."

I opened my mouth, docile as a nestling.

"Little bastards," he said, going in.

After that, neither of said anything for a while. My eyes felt dry and hard and steady as dominoes. Dr. Scheetz grunted every now and then, and once he muttered, "Where *are* you, you little sonofabitch?" But there was no bite in it.

After an hour, he looked at his watch. His short-sleeved white smock exposed pale skinny arms, dark veins writhing under tangles of silver hair, like a black-and-white photograph of snakes in weeds. His face was completely hidden by safety goggles and a sanitary mask, and his hands were coated with thin gloves of yellowish rubber. But there was something about those arms, brushing so near my face and neck and shoulders . . . I wondered how it would feel to be held in them, tight and desperate, the way a man would hold on to a woman he feared might disappear on him any second.

"A goddamn whole hour," he said, "and I just got the first one. You want to call it a day?"

He stepped back and I watched his arms pulling away from me, letting me go. The drain was still in my mouth, sucking. "Huh-uh," I said.

"A trouper," he said. "Hah."

I think I sort of knew that behind the mask and goggles the old man was smiling.

After another half hour or so, Dr. Scheetz turned on an old Philco radio with a gold mesh front. It sat on a piece of plywood laid across the radiator below the window. With a string orchestra playing, it took me a second to recognize "Hotel California." Then the lyrics came back to me. My eyes started to tear up and the corners of my mouth were twitching. I'd checked myself in. Would I ever be allowed to leave?

"Easy," Scheetz said.

A glissando into "Peaceful, Easy Feeling" yanked me back from the edge of hysteria.

"I love this goddamn tune," Scheetz said. "What's it—the Pips, some fool bunch like that?"

I tried to say Eagles. It came out EEE-UHZ.

"Save it." Scheetz grinned close to my face. "What do you know, anyhow?"

I sighed, then realized my breath must smell like a chicken coop by now.

"Thought I had the little bastard for a second there." He sounded strangely content. I let my back and shoulders relax. He was talking to himself. I closed my eyes.

I was practically asleep when the fuzzy back of his forearm grazed my cheek. I shivered and opened my eyes. His brow, close to mine, was glazed with sweat.

"Almost there," he whispered. "Next year . . . year after that at the latest."

I closed my eyes again. And then what—married to a professor and a couple little prodigies in hand-sewn underpants?

"I've seen you, you know it?" Scheetz said. "Oh, yeah, you'd be surprised what I take in from this grimy little goddamn window."

I kept my eyes closed.

"You pass by here at least a couple times most days." His voice was low and sounded distracted. He was working with some kind of pick now. A twinge shot up the right side of my face. "Right?" The numbness was running out.

"Those gorgeous legs and always some kind of silly stockings. How old are you, anyway? You look like a goddamn kid."

If I didn't let my expression change, didn't open my eyes and look at him, maybe he'd think I was asleep.

"I figure you got to be thirty, thirty-five . . . somewhere in there. But you don't look it most days. Don't act it, either."

His hand came to rest on the top of my head and startled me into opening my eyes.

"Are you listening?"

I nodded.

"Just wondered. You don't need to look at me. No point. But I want to know if you can hear me."

My eyes must have shown alarm or something, because he touched my eyelids with his thumbs, closing them. "You haven't got a goddamn thing to worry about," he said. "I'm all talk."

And maybe I shouldn't have, I still don't know. But I believed him.

"Your life's a goddamn mess, right? Never mind, don't tell me. Maybe you bring it all on yourself, maybe you don't. It's not up to me to say."

The drill made a brief foray back into my mouth, shrieked once, then pulled back.

"You know why I watch you so much?"

I didn't move a muscle.

"It's not what you think, I bet. Doesn't have a goddamn thing to do with those showgirl legs, those Raggedy Ann stockings. That funeral coat blowing out behind you like a set of wings . . . hasn't got a goddamn thing to do with the price of tea in China, trust me."

He was hurting me now, grasping my chin too tightly, slamming the drill into me like a jackhammer. He hit the nerve. I moaned softly. He was leaning down so close that his chest was nearly touching mine, he was covering me.

"Don't move," he said.

I thought of Bailey slamming into Andrea, the rustle and scratch of dried corn husks, her quickened breath stale with starvation and bitterness. I didn't even breathe.

"There," Scheetz said triumphantly. "Oh, yes, goddamn it, I've got you now."

I lay back exhausted, spent. My lips felt swollen and parched. It was 11:45.

"Drink this." Scheetz held a tiny pleated paper cup to my mouth. The water was tepid and tasted coppery. "You are really something," he said.

I looked up at him, blotted my caked lips with the paper bib he'd hung around my neck on a little chain. "Are you done?"

"Three out of four," he said. "Not bad. You got no idea how slippery those little bastards can be."

"I'm beginning to get the picture," I said.

Scheetz smiled.

"So," I said. "One more to go?"

"You want to come back next week?" he said. "A little luck, I could finish you off in half an hour."

He had taken off the mask and goggles and was wiping his face with a coarse brown paper towel. The man had to be at least sixty-five. His cheeks were hollow and the flesh under his eyes sagged.

"I want you to do it now," I said.

"Goddamn," he said. "You might look like a kid, but you're a woman and a half."

"I'm thirty-six," I said.

He blinked. His eyes were the kind of gray you see on the Charles in early spring, before all the ice has melted.

"You still gotta come back," he said. He tossed the paper towel in the wastebasket. "Another ten days or so, let anything drain that needs to. Then if they're clean I cap off all those pinholes I yanked the nerves out of."

"Piece of cake," I said.

"Goddamn right." He smiled. "You want another shot," he asked, "before we go back in?"

"Hell, no," I said. "What I want is not to traipse out of here with an exposed nerve, all right?"

He raised his hands in some gesture between surrender and salute. "As you wish, princess," he said. "Open wide."

"Wait," I said. "I want to ask you something."

"It's your nickel," Scheetz said.

I hadn't thought of that. Did he charge by the hour or the nerve? I hoped he took credit cards.

"You never finished telling me," I said.

"What?" he said.

Outside the window a pigeon that looked like it had the start of alopecia was marching in place on the rusty air conditioner that hung out over the sidewalk. It was lunchtime. The traffic on Mass. Ave. had worked itself into a snarl.

"Why you watch me," I said "What is it?"

"Oh, that." Scheetz slapped on his goggles. "Let me ask *you* something," he said. "You ever hear of crossing at the corner? Maybe *with* the goddamn light?"

He slipped the mask over his mouth.

"Do I strike you as a cautious kind of person?" I said, closing my eyes.

He leaned down close and peered into my face. I could smell his aftershave—Royal Lime.

"No comment," he said.

It was well after one. I wondered when the next unsuspecting patient would wander in. "After lunch" could mean five o'clock. I imagined my head on an iron spike, mouth open in a permanent soundless howl, in some museum of the freakish. "Scheetz's Folly" would be the caption on the little plaque below my chin.

The radio was still on. Fred Waring's Pennsylvanians were singing the theme from *Doctor Zhivago*.

"Goddamn," said Scheetz. Pure filler.

Outside on Mass. Ave. the grind and groan of metal announced a desperate parallel parker's miscalculation. The top of my head felt like it was about to blow off. I wondered how the old man felt. At least I hadn't been on my feet all this time. And at his age.

"You've been pretty game," he said suddenly. "Makes me feel kind of guilty that I wasn't exactly honest with you."

He was going to come clean now, confess that he didn't have a license, had never gone to dental school. The *real* Dr. Scheetz was scuba-diving off Tortola this week and . . . my eyes snapped open.

"Still there, huh?" he said.

I nodded.

"You're a fine-looking woman," he said. "But a kid you don't look like." He lifted his chin and looked into my eyes. "No offense," he said.

I yanked the drain out of my mouth. "Since when?" My consonants were sludgy.

He smiled. "You might want to close your eyes for this next part."

I did, then opened my mouth, waiting for the drill.

The rubber-gloved hand, soft and fragrant as talcum along my jaw, tenderly closed my mouth. Then a soundless moment passed, as if time stopped even out on the street.

"What I think of when I see you . . ." The old man's voice sounded impossibly distant in the small cubicle. I opened one eye, just a sliver. He was standing at the window, gazing through spattered slush and pigeon droppings out onto the winter-ruined avenue.

"I think of that woman in the movie," he said softly. "You ever see it? *Zorba the Greek*?"

I gave no sign of reply. His back was turned to me and I knew from his voice that he was talking to himself again. I listened.

"There's this woman, anyway," he said. "A widow. And it isn't exactly that she's so goddamn beautiful, although maybe she is . . . I'm no judge."

He reached down and shut off the radio. Sleet lisped against the glass.

"There's just something about her," Scheetz said. "Any fool can see it. The other women in the village—they stone her, see, because whatever it is about her, she's the kind of woman who can drive a man mad just by walking down the street."

Something unbearably heavy was pressing down on my chest, harder and harder, until my lungs were starved for air. Scheetz was still in front of the window.

"The other women . . ." he said dreamily. "They're all

skinny and sour-mouthed and dressed in black." He slanted his head just slightly toward me and smiled. "Just like your goddamn coat."

I waited, not breathing.

"Bunch of goddamn crows." I heard the old man sigh. Then he came back and stood beside the chair, his hands empty at his sides.

"I watch you to make sure nobody's throwing any stones," he said. "So sue me."

I waited a few minutes before opening my eyes. Then I blinked a few times and made a big show of stretching. I felt my suede skirt sliding up my thighs, my silk shirt pulling taut across my breasts, and quickly straightened up.

"All done," Scheetz said. "Have a nice snooze?"

I tried to smile. "Did I miss anything?"

The old man tossed his mask and goggles into a chipped enamel sink. "Not a goddamn thing," he said.

We could work out the billing at the next appointment, Scheetz said. Not to worry. He walked me to the door, helped me on with my coat. Then, his knotty hands bared, he reached under the back of my collar and lifted up my hair, settling it on my shoulders. "Next time buy yourself a red one," he said.

Out on the avenue I turned and faced into the wind, heading away from my apartment. The weather was vicious, the day was shot, and so was I. But I wanted to walk around for a while, stretch my legs, maybe stop for a cappuccino. It was going to be hard, for a while, going home.

I glanced back at Scheetz's office window once, quickly. I might have seen his white smock centered under the curve of gold lettering. But the window was so filthy and the air was full of needles and I was too far away, really, to be sure he was actually there.

Still, just in case, I waited until I got to the corner before I ran my usual ragged line between the wheezing buses and speeding cars, leaping from one pile of ice to another. Like a kid with nothing to lose, like a woman with someplace to go.

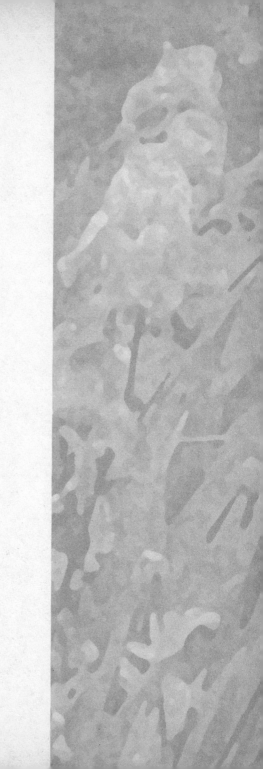

Ethiopia

I

*I*n the first blue press of morning, a transparent shaving of moon still pasted to the sky, he had lost his place in her mind.

Her tiny cottage was hemmed in by ragged winds. Brittle leaves crackled against laggard window screens. He did not, in the morning's first terrible moment, exist for her. And the day ahead looked desolate and dangerous as a storm-stacked horizon.

"Marcus."

She seemed to have spoken his name aloud before he had occurred to her. As if there were no here to there, no then to now. He suddenly, simply *was*. And with his return to the world, though he was hundreds of miles distant, the bright cold day grew into something that suited her, fit her like a glove.

He had never—apart from a comradely arm across her shoulders as they crossed a city street—touched her.

Nola sat up quickly and looked through the row of colored glass bottles lining the windowsill above her bed.

The sky over the marsh was the color of a pilot light flame, the white moon flimsy as ash.

"Marcus."

The small brown-and-white spaniel curled at the foot of the bed looked up as if the name were his.

"Here, love," Nola said. "Come here." She heard urgency in her voice. Isaac heard it, too. The dog scrambled across the thready quilt and slid down the slope of her knees to fill the barren space her arms implied.

Nola rested her cheek for a moment on the dog's head, letting the tangled covers, the faded hooked rug, the soft pine planks of the floor soak up the echo. *Marcus.* He had never held her, barely touched her.

The bottles on the window ledge were cobalt and amethyst, garnet and citrine. A peridot decanter, curvaceous as a mermaid, towered over a potbellied cruet of carnival glass. Nola imagined the bottles filling up with the sound of his name until they overflowed.

"I'm getting whimsical," she told the dog. "Look out."

The first day's meetings had been contentious, exhausting. Many of the writers, moving fluidly between art and politics, had earned international reputations. Nola, feeling outclassed, took refuge in silence as a barrage of vociferously informed opinion flew over her head. Copyright laws, First Amendment rights, disturbing trends in publishing were debated. A letter was drafted protesting the arrest of a prominent Chilean poet. Nola listened, anguish and awe usurping her face, as rumors of torture and resistance circulated through the conference room.

The major business of the day's last session was the awarding of a prestigious (not to mention lucrative) prize for a literary work that made a singular contribution to world social justice. Five years earlier, a book of Nola's, a slender novel about the Triangle Shirtwaist Factory fire, had been nominated for the prize before disappearing without a trace. She had been appointed to the prize committee this year, she knew, to redress its embarrassing gender imbalance.

For months now she had been reading the year's entries, a whole crate of books. Most showed a dispiriting lean toward the ponderous and the grim. But among them Nola had found a remarkable memoir, a book whose clarity and simplicity seemed somehow sacred and even shocking, Nola thought.

She had read *While the Angel Laughs* three times, her admiration for the author deepening to devotion. Vera Villa-Hermosa, a migrant farmworker, had bent her back to the soil of more than half the States, her sons and daughters toiling beside her. Now ninety-three years old, she had outlived three husbands and all but one of her fourteen children. Her account of her lifetime illuminated moments of humor, hope, and startling beauty among decades of inhuman labor and oppression. The face on the back of the book's stark black-and-white jacket portrayed a kind of saint, Nola thought, miraculous innocence preserved behind a skein of deep lines, an intaglio of scars. For weeks now, Vera Villa-Hermosa's face had been dominating Nola's dreams.

Attendance at the day's earlier meetings had been sporadic, as interest and controversy had ebbed and flowed. Now, though, the hotel conference room was packed. There were not enough chairs and a dozen distinguished delegates were forced to stand in back by the door.

It was a closed session. Beyond the tufted leather doors reporters waited for an announcement. Each time a door opened, they pressed forward, attempting to peer inside. Several minicams lurched on shoulders that leaned into the doorway. Nola wondered whether any of the reporters had ever heard of Vera Villa-Hermosa.

The prize committee had already narrowed the field to five entries. Nominations were a formality. Nola, sitting off to the side of the room, was outside the Chair's peripheral vision. She tried to pay attention as four of her colleagues, all men, praised other books: an African novel, the autobiography of a Central American diplomat . . . She kept seeing Vera Villa-Hermosa's etched face. The old woman already looked disappointed, Nola thought.

Finally, she was recognized by the Chair. When she placed *While the Angel Laughs* in nomination, Nola spoke too softly and was asked to repeat the book's title and the author's name. She did so in a voice that sounded tinny and harried.

"Here are a woman's life and soul laid bare." Nola's voice steadied with conviction as she outlined the old woman's suffering and survival, attempted to describe her indomitable spirit. "This book is about injustice, yes. But beyond that, it is a rare document of forgiveness, of courage and faith. And to pay tribute to those . . ." Nola drew a deep breath. "To accord honor to this book and the extraordinary woman who lived and wrote it can only add a measure of grace to a world that is starved for it."

Nola sat down, her knees watery, her damp shirt stuck to her back. A moment of silence malingered. Beyond the door someone laughed. Nola felt stripped, exposed.

A snippy young critic from Yale stood up, clearing his throat. "It's awfully . . . Steinbeck, isn't it." He had nervous hands and a receding hairline. "Aside from chance variants of gender and culture, of course?"

Nola's hands clenched. The stillness in the room was like a slap.

"I mean, *The Grapes of Wrath* has been *done*," the critic said. "Hasn't it." His tie paraded a silkscreened likeness of the Mona Lisa in black and gray. "I don't find here the subtlety, the . . . *discretion* of true art. With all due respect to Señora Villa-Hermosa and"—he nodded at Nola—"her zealous votary, I fear there is more than a trace of the didactic and derivative . . ." He smiled his regrets. "Ma Joad Revisited," he said, and sat down.

Nola rose from her chair before she could stop herself. "If the similarity's less than subtle," she said, "maybe that's because the abuse of migrant farm labor hasn't changed much in fifty years." She turned from the critic to the Chair, an elderly Canadian biographer and journalist. "Exactly how *discreet* are we supposed to be about exploitation?"

A few delegates shifted uneasily. Metal folding chairs creaked and ticked. The biographer looked at Nola with neutral blue eyes.

"Does discretion address starvation, disease, the stunting of the spirit?" Nola's eyes stung. "If that is art's response to injustice and suffering, maybe art is something we just can't afford anymore."

The critic rolled his eyes above a pointedly tolerant smile. The Chairman blinked.

Then, from the doorway at the back of the room, Nola heard the modest ovation of a single pair of hands. "Let those who have ears hear." Marcus Turner. The gentle irony in his voice freighted the room. Nola sank down in her chair. The hush seemed to go on forever.

Twenty minutes later, by secret ballot, the coveted Cheney

Prize was awarded to a collection of short stories from the Ukraine. Their author was still in his twenties, their slant decidedly postmodern.

As the meeting broke up, Nola eased past the knot of reporters and threaded her way through the crowded corridor. She wanted only to disappear and so was dismayed when Marcus Turner followed her to the elevators.

"You might not want to hear this right now, but you did her justice," he said.

"Thank you," Nola murmured. "I—" She stopped, finding it difficult to speak.

"I wasn't much help, I'm afraid."

"'Ma Joad Revisited.'" Nola's voice was tight. "My God. And those clever little stories—"

"The princeling has no clothes." Marcus shrugged. "So what else is new? The Soviet republics are all the rage this year."

Nola stabbed at the elevator button. "I've got no business here. I'm no good at this."

"Delivering the truth is a thankless job." Marcus Turner's smile was sympathetic. "But somebody's got to do it."

Marcus Turner had landed in the literary limelight before he was thirty with the publication of a novel about the Underground Railroad. His work had been praised for its erudite passion, its passionate erudition. He had, for more than a decade now, held a position on literature's fickle center stage. Known as a gifted and generous teacher, as well as a stringent critic, Marcus seemed slightly bemused by the adulation that followed him.

Nola had fallen in love with her idea of him, she knew,

years ago, when first reading his work. Since then, they'd
met half a dozen times, at literary and academic gatherings,
had served on a panel together. Nola's idea of Marcus had
fleshed out some, but was little altered. He remained a hero
to her. On more than one occasion she'd seen his wit and
courtesy save others from embarrassment. He had a flair for
drawing hostile factions toward compromise. He'd once
praised Nola for her clarity of mind—the issue of debate
now long forgotten. What stayed with her, though, was the
way he'd looked at her, as if his eyes were holding her close,
holding her up to the light . . . *as if*, she thought, *I were
someone interesting*. Still, each time they met again, she was
amazed he remembered her name.

Earlier in the day, at the opening luncheon, Nola had
watched from a distance as Marcus charmed the head table and
picked around the edges of his salade Niçoise. His darkness
appeared vivid against the hotel dining room's insipid white
decor.

He'd been seated between a venerable Chinese novelist
with lushly hooded eyes and a Senegalese poet whose turbaned
head swayed on a serpentine neck collared with hammered
gold. As Nola watched, Marcus said something, his arms rising
in an expansive gesture that seemed to embrace the entire room.
The novelist's impassive face crinkled, then collapsed with
laughter like parchment in flame.

The poet, also laughing, leaned toward Marcus, the beauty
of her face like a gift she seemed to be offering him. Then,
with wandlike fingers, she plucked something, a bread crumb
perhaps, from his unruly beard. Nola's admiration and envy
had felt like an ache.

Now sagging by a bank of steel-faced elevators, Nola took

a closer look at Marcus. His vividness seemed to have faded in the course of the afternoon. Creases bracketed his mouth and something like misgiving showed in his eyes.

A bellhop sidled up to them, a pyramid of matching tapestry luggage balanced on a two-wheeled cart. Nola imagined the bags toppling to the marble floor, springing open, utterly empty.

"All for show," she said, realizing it for the first time. She should have been lobbying all these weeks, not rereading, dreaming. Her own naïveté astonished her.

Marcus said something, but she didn't hear him.

"Nola?"

"I'm sorry," she said.

"I wondered if you had plans for dinner," he said.

Nola glanced at him with some alarm. "Dinner?"

"Don't tell me you were planning a hunger strike?" He smiled.

The invitation is clearly a kindness, she told herself. Accept it at face value. Still, Nola couldn't help wondering if it suggested some flaw in him, that hers was the company he'd seek.

"Face value"—the phrase loitered at the back of Nola's mind, resounding with defeat. Even as a child she had grasped how far her face fell short of any value she might possess or acquire. Tall, she thought of herself as gawky. And plain: Her light brown hair was too fine to make anything of. It hung straight to her jawline and ended there, curt and tidy. Her eyes, too large for her face, had a wounded look. Even, the man she was once married to had pointed out, when she laughed. *Especially then*, he'd say. Surrounded by the discouraging loveliness of her mother and sisters, Nola had learned early not to read gratuity into good manners or simple goodwill.

"I'd be glad of some company," Marcus was saying. "Especially yours, if you're free."

"I might be cranky," Nola warned him.

"Feel free." He smiled again. "Seven-thirty?"

Nola took her time with a bath, listening to the evening news. She was prone to tunnel vision where the world at large was concerned. Both politics and economics stymied her. She also had trouble remembering the names of movies and who had starred in them. Her ex-husband, a journalist, had found her lack of worldliness enervating. She hoped Marcus would not manage to stumble across her ignorance in some awful way.

Dressing, Nola chose colors and jewelry as if they possessed talismanic powers—topaz earrings a man had once told her winked like fireflies in her hair, a necklace of bloodstones and voodoo charms. Her blouse was gold silk, her jacket amber. Her skirt was short and simple and black. Diamond-patterned stockings and lace-up leather boots would deflect attention from her face. The boots had high thin heels. Nola's legs were much envied by her sisters.

Before leaving the glistening white-tiled bathroom, Nola lingered for a moment, her face off-center in the oval mirror over the sink. The light was unsparing. She saw the lines around her eyes, the softness starting to undermine her mouth and jaw. Soon I will be forty, she thought with a kind of wonderment. She was afraid to leave her hotel room.

Marcus Turner's tired eyes looked full of kindness as he watched her step from the elevator and cross the lobby. Though Nola had tried to ban all speculation from her mind, she was surprised to find Marcus alone, without a retinue, without so much as a protégé or sidekick. She wondered if he had a wife somewhere, a terse and independent beauty who would not permit him to flaunt her, who took little interest in his professional life.

"It's just us?" She looked down at the lobby carpet, malachite green busy with birds and vines. He would be bored with her.

"I wanted to talk," Marcus said. "With you. We're in a crowd all day."

Nola lifted her eyes. "You're very kind," she said.

Marcus reared up his head and laughed. A chandelier rained down drops of light on his full black beard, his strong white teeth. She wondered how old he was . . . a few years older, anyway, than she. She'd read his first book when she was still in college. His face looked wild and very beautiful. "Kindness doesn't have a lot to do with it," he said.

She had lived in the city years before, when it was a different city—without subways or a symphony hall, without panhandlers, without shame. The neighborhood where the taxi dropped them was unfamiliar, but Nola knew she was in a part of the city her ex-husband would have warned her to steer clear of, even in daylight, fifteen years ago.

The street was bright and loud and lined with restaurants—Cajun, Cambodian, Cuban. Below a persimmon-colored canopy, "Cafe Addis Ababa" emblazoned on it in a Moorish-looking script, young and fashionably dressed couples pressed together, waiting to get in. Two boys, not more than eight or nine years old, were working the crowd. One was doing some sort of acrobatic dancing, flattened beer cans affixed to the soles of his ragged blue hightops. His feet were a marvel of percussion on the pavement. A slightly smaller boy with topiary hair was passing a limp purple cap, keeping up a rapid patter as he moved through the crowd. Neither of the children was drawing much attention. They need some music, Nola thought.

The air around the doorway smelled spicy and fat. Nola tried to glimpse something of the menu in the restaurant's opaque window, for she couldn't imagine the cuisine of a region known for famine. She failed to make out the words but saw numbers. The prices were exorbitant.

The expensive restaurant seemed like a tasteless joke, and Nola wanted to say so to Marcus. But he veered away from her just then, ducking under the edge of the awning. Then she lost sight of him. Was this where they were going? Something in Nola cringed. Then she caught sight of Marcus again. He was dropping a crumpled bill into the purple cap. The slight boy looked up, grinning, and said something Nola couldn't hear. Then Marcus was moving back toward her, a strangely private smile on his face. Two emaciated young women in jeans and spangled toreador jackets were watching him with famished eyes, but he seemed unaware of them.

"Was this where you wanted to go?" Nola asked.

"Here?" Marcus glanced up at the scalloped awning. "It's noisy and overpriced," he said. "Unless you had a big craving for lentils."

Nola smiled. Outrage lodged in her throat, a hard sharp thing that tasted of rust.

They were poised on a corner, waiting for the light to change. Marcus touched her elbow, lightly, and Nola stepped from the curb before realizing the light was still red.

"What is it?" he said.

"I'm sorry?" She stepped back up on the curb.

The light changed, but suddenly they weren't going any-where. His jacket, a soft gray wool, looked like rough stone in the harsh neon light that burst from every corner of the intersection.

"Something buried you like an avalanche just now," he said. "You want to give me a holler so I can figure out where to start digging?"

Nola shook her head, reassembled her smile. "That won't be necessary," she said.

The light was red again. Marcus draped his arm across her shoulders in a comradely way. "I can see I'm going to have my work cut out with you," he said. Then he dodged out in front of a limousine, Nola tucked under his arm like something fragile.

The restaurant he chose was Tuscan, its windows covered with trellises and vines.

"You're partial to the classical?" Nola glanced back out to the street. "I thought we were in the Third World."

"Third World, maybe." Marcus smiled. "But like the song says, maybe it's my first time around."

As the headwaiter led them to a table, Nola noticed how many people turned to look at Marcus, how frequently they smiled. His ease made the world seem pliant and tame, eager to please. She wondered if he were aware of this gift, if he had any idea how the illusions he created might endanger those around him. At his side Nola felt timid and wan.

They were led to a small alcove that looked like a grape arbor. Their ornate wrought-iron chairs were softened with cushions of Chianti-colored suede. Nola shrugged off her jacket and shook out the full sleeves of her blouse. Its silk looked like honey in the restaurant's generous candlelight.

Marcus suggested a bottle of wine, an appetizer of roasted

baby eggplants and fennel. "The rest," he told the waiter, "can wait. We'd like to take our time."

Nola found herself thinking of the protagonist of Marcus's latest novel, a man slightly bewildered by the world but one who seemed to understand women perfectly.

Nola, given a sabbatical year, was living on a slip of an island, a wind-bitten nubbin of sand where shorebirds whooped it up as the human species struggled to keep a toehold. It was mid-autumn. Pelicans congregated on fly-by-night sandbars. Whip-cracks of geese lashed the sky.

The cold came without warning, like the tornadoes of Nola's childhood, impetuous and fraught. On Halloween she'd been to the beach to swim, a sheen of oil on her faintly bronzed skin. When she awoke on All Saints' Day her bathing suit was frozen on the porch clothesline.

Only a week earlier she'd been in the city, with Marcus, candlelit, balanced on spindle-thin heels. The world at large. In the metal lockbox in the shed out back Nola found her long underwear, tossed there in spring, as if she'd never again have need of such qualmish protection.

Time was of such little consequence on the island that it scarcely seemed necessary to turn back the clocks on the ap-pointed Saturday night. But in the days that followed, the deficit of daylight was somehow cordial to Nola's work, a novel about a sixth-century Irish saint. The girl was martyred by her wid-owed father for declining to replace her mother in his bed. Her father was of royal blood and placed great stock in unspoiled beauty.

For several years the saint's voice had defied Nola, clinging stubbornly to an earnest girlish tone. What was needed was an ecstatic lilt, Nola felt, a tongue as quirky and overwrought as the girl's visions, as extravagant as her mettle.

With the change of season, Nola succumbed to a sudden mistrust of the skittish typewriter that had borne the brunt of her ambitions since high school. She took up with an antique fountain pen instead, filling the lines on cheap notebook paper with long elegant strokes, with thoughts that seemed to crystallize as the temperature dropped. The saint, perhaps for the first time, seemed within her grasp.

At night Nola drove herself through the works of the venerable Chinese novelist, for he had seemed a holy man to her, as if all struggle had been laid to rest in him. She was forced to rely on what she suspected was a poor translation. Filaments of story and character split and separated, and the novelist's syntax seemed surprisingly turbulent for a man of such fierce quiescence. When Nola finished one novel, a paperback edition, its pages were fluted with her frustration. She picked up another, an earlier work. The Chinese novelist was a shoo-in for a Nobel Prize, Marcus said.

"Literature?" Nola had asked. "Or Peace?"

"Hell of a choice, ain't it," he had said.

Each morning Nola grappled with words, but gently, like a lepidopterist pinning wings. At certain charmed moments her prose seemed iridescent and, when the day's work was done, left traces fine as moth dust in her mind. She imagined herself before a scathing fire, reading aloud to Marcus, the saint's voice forged with her own.

"Ethiopia," he said.

Marcus had waited only until their salads were delivered.

Nola was studying the composition of oiled radicchio, arugula, and pine nuts before her, suggestive and exacting as haiku.

"I'm sorry?"

"No, I am."

Nola looked up. She could not decode the intensity of his gaze.

"I knew exactly what you were thinking back there," he said. "I don't know why I acted like I didn't." He leaned back in his chair, drawing away from the light cast by the candle in the center of their table. "No, that's not true, either," he said.

"It doesn't—" Nola shrugged, at a loss.

"I hope you weren't going to say *matter*," Marcus said.

"I don't know what I was going to say." Nola's face felt hot.

"I had a chance to go there last year," Marcus said. "I couldn't do it."

"Ethiopia?"

He nodded. "The State Department was sending a few writers." He closed his eyes. " 'To lend the power of our voices,' they said . . . so maybe the American people could begin to understand. . . ."

"That must have been hard to turn down," Nola said.

Marcus, his eyes still closed, shook his head. He looked pained. "I just couldn't face it." He opened his eyes and looked steadily at Nola. "You'd have gone," he said.

Nola was quiet for a moment. "You don't know that," she said.

"You'd have gone," he repeated. "A couple of years ago, so would I. But now?" He sighed and the candle between them flared brighter for an instant, then steadied.

"A person knows how much he can bear," Nola said. "It's pointless—"

"It's hardly pointless," Marcus said. "The terrible part was how easy it was to say no." He shook his head. "I barely even thought about it."

"Then you ought to trust that," Nola said. "Your instincts—"

"Instincts." Marcus leaned across the table, bringing his face close to hers. "I didn't feel anything," he said. "I had no shame."

"I can understand that," Nola said.

"I don't believe you." His voice was low and severe. "Your capacity for feeling, Nola . . . when you see something that's wrong it's like your whole being hurls itself against it."

"What good does it do?" Nola said softly.

"In concrete terms? Maybe none at all." Marcus bent his head and blew out the candle. The flame's afterimage danced on Nola's eyes, a scrim of misleading light. "You get bruised. But you don't look away. And you don't let anybody else do it, either."

"This isn't exactly a social skill that's prized." Nola smiled. "I can ruin a perfectly pleasant evening like nobody's business."

"Perfectly pleasant evenings are overrated." Marcus reached across the table, his hands dark against the white damask cloth. He is going to touch me, Nola thought.

The waiter breezed by with a loaded tray. "Your entrées will be out any second," he said, glancing with disapproval at their untouched salads.

"We're not ready." Marcus's hands retreated. His eyes did not leave Nola's. "You don't know your own strength," he said.

Nola shook her head. "I take things too hard," she said. "It's always been like that with me."

" 'Too,' " Marcus said. "What's *too*?"

Nola was staring past him, at the restaurant's front door. She wondered if the two children were still out on the sidewalk, trying to charm a tough audience out of its indifference, dancing with a noise that, no matter how they tried, would never pass for music.

"Nola?" Marcus was holding out her wineglass, refilled. The wine, deprived of the candle's light, looked like ink.

"Thank you." The first sip tasted bitter, the second less so. "I'm trying to rid myself of a penchant for stating the obvious," Nola said. "It leaves gaps in my conversation sometimes."

"Real obvious stuff," Marcus said. "Right. Like 'the emperor has no clothes'?"

"Marcus, you can't—"

"Which of you had the fettuccine?" The waiter rested his tray on the edge of the table, pulled a book of matches from his pocket, and relit their candle. "Mustn't lose our ambience," he said.

"The fettuccine's for me." Nola sounded abject.

"Please take it back to the kitchen," Marcus said. Nola saw a slight tremor in his hands. "Would you see that it's kept warm until we're ready?"

The waiter, a slender young man in tight black clothing, froze in position, already half turned away. His profile was edgy and touched with disdain. He slowly swiveled his head and stared at Marcus.

Marcus stared back.

After a moment, the waiter nodded, removed Nola's plate from the table, and disappeared into the kitchen. The swinging door flapped behind him.

"We could leave." Marcus's voice was low and strained. "Would you rather?"

Nola shook her head. The fragrances of garlic and cheese

lingered around her face, making her feel queasy. She picked up her salad fork. "Maybe we ought to try to settle down here," she said.

The Chinese novelist wrote of his hunger as an enemy with whom he lived on intimate terms. His attentiveness to its nuances and demands bordered on obsession. His first novel, to which Nola came last, was lyrical and clear, electric with anger, elastic with hope. The book was called *Rice*. For days after she read it, Nola ate from a single bowl, its yellow sides austere with three lotus blossoms, its shallow pearl interior inscrutable.

In the late afternoon, at the first lowering of premature darkness, Nola would place a small pot on the stove's back burner, adding rice when the salted water had come to a boil. She always watched the clock, never the rice. She was not permitted to lift the lid until a quarter past six, when the sky was dark. Each night the moon had filled out a little more as Nola sat before her back window, eating a bowl of rice, hot and pristine.

In the mornings she ate leftover rice, cold, with milk and honey and cinnamon on it. This was not, she told herself, about deprivation, but merely a craving. At noon she would gently heat what was left of the rice in a cupful of vegetable broth scented with ginger. Sometimes she ate a bit more for lunch than she cared to, to finish the batch. For it seemed essential that she honor each twilight by cooking a fresh portion, and she could not abide waste. Millions of people were starving. She did not know one of them. She had been too shy to speak to the Chinese novelist even when, once, she had found herself seated right beside him.

Isaac, her dog, spoiled on a tradition of treats and table scraps, saddened under her abstemious regimen. Nola dug bits of cheese and broken cookies out of the back of the refrigerator to comfort him; she missed the way he used to prop his chin on her knee while she ate.

The night the letter came, Nola could not swallow. Even plain rice. He had enjoyed her company, Marcus said, and he thought of her often now, envying her a solitude so luxurious he could scarcely imagine it. His own existence (he suggested, obliquely) was frenetic and shadowed. His mother, dying a little bit at a time, no longer knew him. He was doing too much traveling, too much teaching and lecturing, too little writing. He wasn't complaining, he said, just trying to fill in a backdrop to the fact that Nola preoccupied him, creating a serene corner in an otherwise fractious and foggy mind.

"When," he wrote, "not to mention how on earth, can I finagle us into the same spot at the same time again? And soon. I am prepared to lie, to extort, to leap a gorge to see you. Your contumacy is good for my soul."

Nola could not eat. She could not work or even read. Her sleep was a commotion of dreams, and when she woke the morning light scorched her eyes.

The restaurant, half emptied, seemed hushed. Now and then an espresso machine hissed behind the small bar. The wick of their candle floated in what looked like a pool of butter.

"You know what we need?" Marcus rolled the stem of his empty wineglass between his palms. "Some chocolate." He looked up at the waiter. "How's the chocolate-raspberry torte?"

"Obscene." The waiter's smile was ingratiating. "Two?"

"Forks," Nola said. "Two forks." She turned to Marcus. "Are you always this . . . profligate?"

"Rarely," he said, "Too rarely. And you, are you always this circumspect?"

She laughed.

"Well, are you?"

"I'm afraid so," Nola said.

"A shame." Marcus shook his head. "I'd love to see you really throw some weight around."

"You don't think I was sufficiently obstreperous this afternoon? For my weight class, I mean."

He nodded. "Must be damn tricky, though, trying to keep all that furious conviction within polite bounds."

"I don't always," Nola said. "You saw—"

"What I saw," Marcus said. ". . . forgive me, but what I think I saw was one hell of a fighter keeping one hand behind her back. That guy from Yale, you could have taken him down."

"The knock-down-drag-out's hardly my style."

He smiled. "That's not to say you couldn't whip some ass, though, is it?"

"I don't know," Nola said. "Is it?"

"Have you ever tried?"

She looked down at the table.

"The giving-a-damn in you, Nola, it's . . . you blurt out the truth like Pavarotti sings." He snapped his fingers. "Nothing to it."

"What good is truth?"

"Not much," Marcus admitted, "if you just leave it at that."

"I don't think—"

"Exactly." Marcus leaned forward, the sputtering flame

sparking in his eyes. "To get to the truth you don't even *have* to think. It just erupts from you like a force of nature."

"A natural disaster." Nola laughed.

"A natural *weapon*." He looked into her eyes. "You act like passion's something to be afraid of."

"Sometimes passion's . . . unseemly," she said. "You've survived universities. For God's sake, Marcus, you've *thrived*. Don't pretend you don't know what I'm talking about." With effort Nola lowered her voice. "Besides, what makes you think you've got me all figured out?"

"I don't," Marcus said. "But I'm trying."

"Women are constantly accused of that, pulling punches. It's facile."

"If I touched a sore spot I'm sorry."

Nola looked into his eyes, troubled and tired and kind. "I can take it," she said.

"You know what's going on here, don't you?"

Somewhere in the back of the restaurant a busboy dropped a tray of glasses. Someone applauded.

"Envy," Marcus said. "Plain and simple."

She'd envied Marcus Turner from the first moment she'd seen him, she knew, envied his confidence and brilliance and power, his charm and even his beauty. She'd read his books and envied each of them, envied his passion and erudition. Now he had apprehended her—coveting not all he had, but worse, all he was.

Marcus was staring at her intently. Nola had to force herself not to look away. When he finally spoke, his voice was so low she could barely hear him. "Of course I envy you, Nola. Have you got any idea what I'd give for those instincts of yours?"

For a moment Nola was too shocked to speak. "I don't understand," she said at last. "You're—"

"I'm no singer," Marcus said. "At least not anymore. Do

you know how long it takes me to drag myself to places where you land as natural as rain?" He shook his head. "And that's if I ever get there," he said.

"I don't know what you're talking about." Nola sounded frightened.

"I'm talking about confusing famine with fashion, and being entertained by little kids singing for their supper. I'm talking about getting taken in."

Nola shook her head.

"But mostly," Marcus said, "I'm talking about letting things *pass*."

"It sounds like you're talking about somebody else," Nola said. "Not you."

"I'm the local expert." He smiled sadly. "On this subject, at least."

"How about listening to your own advice then? All this power . . . you act like you're ashamed of it."

"The emperor's clothes." Marcus shrugged. "And they're not even new anymore."

"I'm supposedly the one with the unerring instincts," Nola said. "Why aren't you listening to me?"

"I hear you," Marcus said. "Good enough?"

"Not nearly."

"You want to know something pitiful?"

"Probably not." Nola's smile was tentative.

"In the interest of truth?" Marcus said.

"I'm listening."

"That meeting this afternoon, the prize thing . . . I came in half-assed ready to go with the Ukrainian princeling," he said. "Float with the tide. Until I heard you." Marcus lowered his head. "Jesus. I just didn't care."

"Big disgrace. So you'd have wound up in the same corner

with a Nobel laureate, a couple of Pulitzers, and the most influential literary critic in France. Not to mention Yale," Nola said. "Stayed put, you'd have *won*."

"Talk about your Pyrrhic victories." Marcus closed his eyes a moment. "I've gone a little cloudy, Nola. I need somebody to help me see straight."

The waiter set down a gold-rimmed dessert plate, two forks counterbalanced on its edges. A black slab of cake lay in a pool of raspberry sauce bright as arterial blood. "Enjoy," he said.

Marcus took a long look at the plate. "I'm going to need a lot of help here," he said.

"Contumacy." It meant something like heresy, Nola thought. She looked it up. *Insubordination*. Close enough.

The saint's voice, like autumn, seemed to vanish overnight and Nola was always freezing. Marcus's letter lay on her bedside table, sandwiched between Brother Lawrence's *The Practice of the Presence of God* and a first edition, grown quite valuable, of Marcus's first novel. One edge of the envelope protruded a scant inch from between the books. His stationery was the color of coffee ice cream. He wrote in a large, loose hand. Nola did not reread the letter after the day it arrived. She did not need to. With a modicum of concentration she could reassemble it, word for word, in her mind.

Your contumacy is good for my soul.

He thought he had her pegged. I have never been insubordinate in my life, Nola thought. I wouldn't know how. The truth he believed he saw in her was ignorance, only that. *He should be taking me at face value.*

The marshes were spangled with frost at dawn and the sunset, night after night, looked like a blood blister framed in Nola's window. Combative winds ripped the weaker limbs from the trees. The island seemed to shrink. The saint was gone and Nola could not manage, no matter what she did, to keep warm. My blood must be thin, she thought. She imagined Marcus's beard, wild and warm as a nest and smelling of earth freshly turned. He had never even touched her.

Morning upon severe morning, Nola tried to coax the saint's song from icy silence, tried to pursue her fevered visions through darkness. She drank scalding tea all day and stopped cooking rice at dusk, eating instead root vegetables that tasted bitter and left her hungering.

Finally, with a keen and impassable sorrow, Nola set the novel aside. She needed a respite. Or the saint did, perhaps. Marcus was a liquid presence in the small house, overfilling the jewel-colored bottles on the windowsill, opaquing the panes with steam. This will evaporate, Nola thought, I'll find my way back by spring. Little wonder the Irish beauty had fled. The dead of winter was too perilous a time for asceticism, for visions fallible and skewed. Nola tried not to entertain the notion that she had lost her feel for sanctity.

Two weeks after receiving Marcus's letter, one week after sending him a cautiously worded reply, Nola began writing a story. The words seemed to fall to the paper now with a fluency the saint had never, in the most blessed moments, indulged.

The story was a contemporary treatment of the myth of Semele, a minor goddess who, spying Zeus in his unbridled glory, was consumed by lightning. This was, to Nola's mind, a way of perishing entirely too spectacular. The man in her story was an astronomer, recently gone blind. The woman, no goddess, scalded her retinas by staring directly into the sun in order to describe to her lover the minute progressions of a solar eclipse. They were vacationing in a village high in the Andes. The man left the woman, of course, once her eyes were no longer of use to him.

Nola finished the story in a single week. It ended on a note of perfect restraint, she felt, leaving the reader to decide whether the woman would manage to find her way out of the mountains, whether her eyes, given time, would heal.

It was close to midnight when Nola and Marcus left the restaurant. Across the street the line in front of Cafe Addis Ababa was longer than it had been at eight. The two small boys had been replaced by a steel drum band. The pavement seemed to vibrate under Nola's feet.

"Could you stand a walk?" Marcus asked. "There's a lot I still need to ask you."

"The exercise would do me good," Nola said. "The interrogation I'm not so sure about."

Marcus, his fingertips on her elbow, steered her around a trash can in which something was smoldering. "I only want to know . . . the way you live, I guess. All that time and nobody to answer to. How does a person put . . . shape to days that are all her own?"

Were her days shapely? It wasn't something she'd ever really thought about. "The shape comes mostly from the working," Nola said. "If you'd call that shape. My work pushes me around and I try not to fight it. Or to panic."

"Sometimes I think I'd give anything to—" Marcus shook his head. "I doubt I could do what you do."

His face seemed touched with sorrow. "What is it you think I do?" Nola said.

"You live with yourself."

"You don't?"

"I live alone," Marcus said. "It's not the same."

"How is it different?" My ignorance is showing, Nola thought.

Marcus sighed. "I manage to keep pretty much on the run. It keeps me from having to face myself day in and day out."

Nola was quiet for a few minutes. The short fashionable span of the street fell behind them, absorbing all the light. Dark derelict buildings squeezed the sidewalk and the curbs were crumbling. Nola felt foolhardy in her imprudent heels.

"What about your days?" she said. "Their shape?"

"You're taking over the interrogation?" Marcus smiled. "I'm a churlish old bachelor with a neat but musty apartment. Saturday nights when I'm not on the road, I'm usually to be found hunched over, cackling with glee, as I pick holes in tender dissertations. You're welcome to greater detail, but you'll risk extinction by boredom."

"I think I've been immunized. Remember that colloquium on cyberfiction in Phoenix last fall?"

Marcus and Nola both laughed.

"So, have you always been?" Nola did not look at him.

"What?"

"A churlish old bachelor."

"Only since I stopped being a churlish young bachelor," Marcus said.

Nola sneaked a quick sideways glance at him. "Are you telling me, nicely, to stop prying?"

He smiled. "Only insofar as it might head off the inevitable question."

"Which is—"

"Why not?" He shrugged. "I prefer to avoid questions I have no answer for, that's all."

"Could have fooled me," Nola said.

"This one isn't exactly . . . academic, is it?" He sounded wistful. "Had a friend used to say I'd need to slow down if I hoped somebody might catch me."

"But you didn't?"

"Didn't slow down, anyway . . . the hope, I don't know. I suppose an answer's implicit in there somewhere."

"I doubt you're missing much." The second she said it, Nola wanted to take it back. "I sound jaded," she said.

Marcus smiled again. "You just sound a little . . . divorced, maybe."

"A *lot* divorced," said Nola. "I was just a little married." She hoped her eyes did not look wounded. "Way back when," she said.

"You think alone is something a person can get the hang of?"

"Definitely."

"Figured as much."

Did Marcus really sound sad, Nola wondered, or was that just her idea of him talking? "And what about family?" she said.

"Only child of two only children," Marcus said. "It makes for a fairly minimalist genealogy. My father died when I was thirteen, working in a steel mill. My mother had a stroke last year and is in a nursing home. She—"

A pizza delivery van without a muffler roared past. Marcus waited until it peeled around a corner.

"I'm trying to figure out how to complete that sentence without taking refuge behind irony," he said. "I seem to do that a lot lately."

"It's like morphine," Nola said. "Sometimes you can't do without it."

"Right," Marcus said. "And while you're not paying attention you turn into an addict."

"Tell me about her."

"My mother? She's a sad old lady with a cloudy mind," Marcus said. "God's truth. No irony."

"But before she got old——?"

"Something like you," Marcus said, "now that I think about it. 'A pistol,' my dad used to call her. I think 'pisser' was what he meant. But we'd never talk like that in front of her." He smiled. "Ma, though . . . no minced words there. She was quiet-spoken, gracious even. But that tongue of hers could wrap itself around some mighty truth."

They came to a wide avenue, a blitzkrieg of sodium-vapor light and bus exhaust, and made it halfway across, then were stranded on a traffic island. The wind from passing cars plastered their clothes to their bodies as they waited for the light to change. Nola shivered.

"I see her nearly every day," Marcus said. "The nursing home's not a mile from my place. She's just this dark little face now, sort of scrunched up in the middle of a huge white pillow . . . reminds me of a lamb."

Nola touched his arm.

"She just doesn't remind me much of my mother."

Marcus looked up and Nola's eyes followed his. "God, what she's *wanted* for me," he said. "All my life. So I didn't ask a lot of questions, I just went and got it, got it all. And she doesn't even know." The sky, purple and light-mottled, looked bruised. "What about you?" he said.

"Lucky." They stepped off the island and Nola's hand slipped from his arm. "I've got three sisters, a dozen nieces and nephews, a whole tribe of cousins and uncles and aunts. Just about everybody but me's still in Kansas, near Emporia, in a town called Admire. My folks are nearly eighty but still on their feet, still looking after each other and convinced they've got to keep looking after the rest of us."

"Sounds like a lot to lean on," Marcus said.

Nola nodded. "And run away from."

"You go back, though."

"I go back." Nola took a deep breath. "At Christmas and every summer. And they love me to pieces for a week or so. Then I crawl back into my life and spend a couple of months trying to sort the pieces back into some kind of order."

"What do they make of you?" He sounded genuinely curious.

"Besides a mess? I wish I knew." Nola's slight heel caught in a seam in the sidewalk and she stumbled but caught her balance before Marcus could reach out to steady her. "I'm probably better off not knowing," she said. "They love me. My father thinks I should get paid more. My mother wishes I'd get a telephone and wear red lipstick to give me some color."

"You don't have a phone?" Marcus said. "That's pretty colorful."

They passed a travel agency window, crowded with silver planes and lurid seacoasts, palm trees and gaudy tropical meals.

"Admire, Kansas," Marcus said. "You ever run into the Wizard of Oz?"

"Not unless he's disguised as a critic from Yale," Nola said.

"Nasty," said Marcus. "I like that in a woman."

"Is that a sexist remark?"

"Nope. I like it in a man, too. So are you going to tell me the secret of your exemplary existence?"

"There's no secret." Nola thought for a moment. "Or

maybe there is." She slanted her face away from Marcus. "You think I'm facing myself every day, but all I'm really doing is refusing to face anything else."

"You don't believe in making things easy, do you?"

Nola glanced at him. His eyes were glistening under a streetlamp. "That's not a talent everyone has," she said.

"Touché," said Marcus softly. "The great gift of sliding by."

"I didn't mean anything the least bit like that," Nola said.

"Still, there you are, landing on the truth, natural as rain."

"It's so strange here." Nola's eyes scanned the sky. "With all this light the stars might just as well not exist."

"It's what I'm used to," Marcus said. "I hardly even look anymore."

"I'll tell you the truth now if you want."

Marcus stopped and turned toward her. After a moment he nodded.

"I don't like what you're doing," Nola said. "Using me as a stick to beat yourself with." She jammed her hands into her jacket pockets and began to walk again.

"You're right," Marcus said from behind her. "You didn't ask for the job."

They walked for half a block without speaking. Nola, for once, felt no compulsion to fill or bridge the silence. Her anger was oddly pleasing to her, an accomplishment.

Their hotel came into sight, a marquee blazing above the sidewalk with a galaxy of tiny yellow lights. Two taxis and a limousine idled beneath it. Then a man and a woman in dark clothes got into the limousine and it drove away.

"I'm sorry," Marcus said.

"It's all right." Nola smiled. "Takes one to know one," she said.

"I can get pretty self-absorbed."

Nola laughed softly. "Maybe I just got feeling . . . proprietary," she said. "Everything you pin on yourself belongs on me."

Marcus opened his mouth to object, but Nola cut him off.

"It's . . . unsettling," she said, "having someone I admire so extravagantly—"

"I don't want you to admire me, Nola. I'll just fall flat on my face when you know me."

Nola stopped smiling. "I don't want you to admire me, either," she said.

"Do you suppose we could figure out a way to . . . you know, just *like* each other?"

Marcus looked grave and doubtful. Nola wanted to reach out and stroke his face, to comfort him somehow. But he seemed suddenly beyond her reach, as if she had missed the one possible moment. She clasped her hands behind her back.

"I'll try to curb my extravagance," she said. "But you shouldn't blame me if it doesn't happen overnight."

"When can I see you?" he wrote. "And where? And why in God's name do you refuse to get a telephone?"

Nola imagined how the nights would elongate, their shapeliness (she could see it now) disfigured by yearning as she waited for his voice to confirm her. She forecast a silence grown excruciating once he'd forgotten her, the loss become a cacophony, the saint's voice forever drowned out. Marcus wanted to rearrange the fragments of her existence into a pattern conforming to his misconceptions, the things he needed to believe about her for reasons of his own. He had never even touched her.

Why in God's name do you refuse . . . The question, Nola decided, could be treated as rhetorical.

"Couldn't we meet somewhere?" he asked. He ran through a litany of idyllic and ridiculous spots that lay between them, colorful cities and quiet resorts and popular tourist attractions. Nola pictured the two of them crawling like ticks across the granite profiles of Mount Rushmore, like Cary Grant and that beautiful blond actress with the don't-touch-me look. *There are still so many things I want to ask you.*

"I'm quite involved with work at the moment," Nola wrote. "Not a good time to get away." She couldn't remember the name of the movie, nor what it was Cary Grant and the ice princess were so frantic to escape . . . only how tiny they were, up there on George Washington's forehead.

The lobby chandelier had been dimmed. Its muted light fell on the thick green carpet like late-afternoon sunlight filtering through jungle fronds. Desultory piano music drifted from the bar. After a moment, Nola recognized the song: "Mr. Wonderful."

"I'd better check for messages," Marcus said.

Nola's smile felt slightly giddy.

The clusters of wingback chairs and settees were all unoccupied, invitations to intimate conversation declined. In the bar the piano made a lazy slide into "Time After Time." Nola stood beside a huge ficus in an elephant's-foot planter and watched as the young man at the registration desk handed Marcus four or five pink message slips.

The clerk looked sprightly as a game show host in his green linen blazer. Marcus stuffed the messages into his pocket without looking at them.

"I don't suppose I could talk you into a nightcap?"

"It's late," Nola said.

"Right."

Marcus pressed the up button and the elevator doors slid open with a hum.

"Ma'am?" Marcus said.

"I'm sorry?"

"Your floor," he said.

"Twelve," Nola said. "Sorry."

"Mine, too," Marcus said.

Wings fluttered in Nola's stomach as the car swooped them up.

They stepped off the elevator into a gray silence. Three corridors spoked out from the elevator, dim and deserted as dawn.

"I'm down there." Marcus pointed left. "About a mile and a half."

"I'm just here." Nola gestured to the middle corridor.

"I'll see you to your room."

"Oh, you don't need to—"

Marcus smiled. "I'll stand here and watch then, all right? Until you're safely inside."

"Thank you." Nola wondered what dangers could penetrate these endless corridors. "It was—"

Marcus reached out with both hands, as if he were going to take hold of her shoulders. Then, his eyes on Nola's, he let his arms drop to his sides. "I'd better let you go," he said. "You're tired."

"Good night, Marcus."

Nola turned and started down the long gray hallway. Her stride felt graceless, unnatural. She thought of the slips of pink paper in his pocket, imagining women's names on them, fluid exotic names like Sabine and Elektra and Anneliese. The insistence of their devotion and desire would be marked with heavy black Xs: PLEASE CALL . . . WANTS TO SEE YOU . . . URGENT.

"Nola?" Marcus's half whisper carried easily down the carpet-muffled corridor.

Nola stopped and turned around.

His two hands, again, seemed to be reaching for her. But now he was far away. "You ever decide to go," he said, "I'd like to tag along."

"Go?"

"Ethiopia."

Nola laughed softly. "I thought we were going to start curbing our extravagance," she said.

This year she was not going home. The Monday before Christmas, as the island cowered under a tantrum of northeasterly winds, the UPS truck pulled up in front of Nola's cottage. She held on to Isaac's collar—he was unaccustomed to visitors—as she accepted a small parcel from a slight freckled man in a brown uniform. "Have a good one," the man said. Nola wondered if perhaps she ought to tip someone who'd come so far to find her, but her hands were full and the man didn't linger. "You too," she called out as he jumped into his truck.

The tiny box inside the padded envelope was wrapped in silver paper with a lacy white snowflake design on it. The design reminded Nola of how, as a child, she had loved decorating the schoolroom windows for Christmas, using stencils and sponges and that bottled white stuff she hadn't seen or thought about in years. It was probably toxic. Suddenly she wished she were going home. A ten-day break would scarcely have mattered, the way her work was going.

A thin gold bracelet lay between two layers of cotton. Three charms dangled from it: a telephone, a pair of boxing gloves, and a tiny map of Africa. Not quite halfway down the eastern edge of the continent, at the foot of its upper curve, a red stone the size of a pinhead glittered. Ethiopia? Geography was not Nola's strong suit. There was no card.

That afternoon, though the wind was bitter, Nola roamed the beach at the island's deserted northern tip, searching for something to send him. As Isaac ran ebullient circles around her, looping from the shore to the tops of the dunes, she gathered shells and stones and shards of seaglass frosted and smoothed by the ocean's strife. In a tangle of seaweed she found a whelk's egg case that looked like a desiccated lei from some long-ago luau. The pockets of her heavy canvas jacket were stuffed with feathers, the discarded finery of gulls and loons, egrets and pelicans.

It wasn't until she was nearly back at her car that she found the heron's skull, perfectly intact and bleached white by the sun. The membrane of an eyeball, dried and translucent, still lay in one socket. But the wind snatched it as Nola picked up the skull. It sailed away like a bubble.

At home Nola soaked the skull briefly in Clorox and water, then gingerly patted it dry. She wrapped it in countless layers of pale blue tissue. The next morning she mailed it to Marcus in a wooden cigar box that had a tiny brass clasp on it. If the gift was not to his liking, perhaps its container would please him.

He had slipped into the vacant chair beside hers half an hour after the morning's first session began. The conference was to end that day, after lunch. The floor was now open for nominations to the Policy Committee. The Chairman's peaceable blue eyes were half closed as the Secretary, a shy novelist from Brisbane in outdated tweeds, labored over the spelling of eastern European names.

"The usual hotbed of apathy?" Marcus raised his eyebrows.

"Wait," Nola whispered, "fund-raising comes next."

"I can't," Marcus said. "I've got to leave early."

"Is everything all right?" Nola thought of his mother, docile as a lamb among clouds of white bedding.

"There's a noon flight," Marcus said. The Chairman opened his eyes and sent them a look of chastisement. "I wanted to see you first."

Nola's face was full of heat. She waited until the Chairman looked away before she nodded.

"I've got to go," Marcus said.

He had never touched her.

Nola closed her eyes. When she opened them again, the chair beside her was empty. She looked down at her lap. Her hands, white at the knuckle, were clenched. She opened her fingers slowly, until her hands lay spread open, palm up, across her thighs.

It had never been so cold. By the end of January the island was trapped in an embrace of ice. For more than a week the ferry stopped running, no mail came in or went out. The power went off a dozen times a day, pipes froze and car engines died. The shelves in the village store began to look pillaged. Fresh produce, meager in the best of times, vanished. There was no rice.

Nola started eating things she found exiled at the back of the cupboard, imported luxuries reserved for occasions that never arose—Greek olives and mandarin oranges, pear butter and marrons glacés. When the dog food ran out she fed Isaac Cheerios.

After the coast guard broke through the ice and the ferry was running again, the islanders crowded the post office, anxious as if awaiting casualty lists. Nola's slot was stuffed—lingerie catalogs and literary journals, requests for letters of recommendation from former students whose features had blurred. Christmas had not been the same without her, her mother said. She wrote on stationery whose scalloped edge was bordered with pansies, like a well-kept yard. Her script was slanted and infirm.

Another month went by with no word from Marcus. Imperceptibly the days were lengthening, but the cold held on. The saint's voice returned, pestering Nola awake at ungodly hours. Pages inked with prayer and exhortation began to pile up beside the unused typewriter. The girl had not, Nola realized, gone willingly to God. She had died in a rage, grasping in her final moments that virginity was nothing to die for, what she should have fought to preserve was her life.

But by the time this epiphany broke upon her she was a saint, awash in blood, no beauty about her. The strangled sound of her thwarted vengeance chilled Nola to the bone.

II

Spring came in a rush to the island. The lengthening days displayed a wild moodiness. Frostbitten mornings melted into almost tropical afternoons. One night a heat wave skulked in, setting off a barrage of hail. Storm fronts appeared out of nowhere, hostile hordes of cloud amassing on the northeasterly horizon and swooping in on havoc-bent winds.

Nola rose earlier and earlier, studying the sky like a soothsayer as she left her bed. She dressed before sunrise in odd layers of clothing, discarding and replacing garments at the whim of volatile air currents and a faithless sun.

By the start of April the beaches were littered with thousands of dead seagulls. An insidious strain of bird cholera was cutting its way down the southern Atlantic coast. The diseased corpses were reported to be highly poisonous to dogs. Nola left Isaac at home when she walked on the beach, but she soon stopped going at all. Wings, broken and matted, spiked the sand. The wreckage of all that bird life was unbearable to witness, and Nola felt as if she were somehow implicated in the creatures' suffering. There was nothing anyone could do, the county conservation officer said.

Most days Nola wrote all morning and into the afternoon, often forgetting to eat. Then, if the day was warm and the wind not too obstreperous, she would climb the ladder affixed to the side of her house to lie in the sun on her roof.

The end of the saint's abbreviated life was careening into view, and though the work made Nola's days exhausting, the final push also kept her wakeful at night. Once the girl's holy rage had been tapped, it seemed it could not be contained or tempered. Nola felt herself too small and fragile a vessel for what was pouring into her. Her dreams were of torture, dismemberment, burning.

And her house felt overcrowded, cramped. The closest she came to true rest was when she lay, her limbs carefully arranged on the diagonal at the downwind side of her modestly pitched roof, in the sunlight. Her skin began to turn a rosy brown shade that disguised the violet shadows under her eyes.

She was losing weight and could feel the edges of the asphalt roofing tiles cutting into her spine. Sometimes she fell asleep, invariably dreaming she was rolling off the roof. She'd start awake to find her fingers digging into the rough tiles. Time after time, Nola witnessed her own fall in precise and dispassionate detail. Then, looking down from the edge of the roof, she'd see the crumpled mass of her body in the weeds below. She looked like the dead seagulls scattered on the beach, flattened and shapeless and already stiff.

Nola scarcely thought of Marcus at all, except by way of noting, with a certain degree of self-approval, how very little she thought of him. The bottles on the window ledge, their vibrant colors dulled, looked empty and dry. One day she would have to replace them with something less troublesome, Nola thought, they were like magnets to dust.

It was only by the most insubstantial of accidents that Nola learned, in late April, about Marcus. She was tossing away, unread, the program of one more professional meeting when a strip of photocopied paper fell out of the brochure and floated to the floor beside the wastebasket. When Nola picked up the scrap, his name caught her eye under the heading "Addenda & Errata": "Due to the unfortunate illness of Professor Marcus Turner, the symposium on the Literature of Emerging Nations is to be chaired by . . ." A well-known Southern novelist was named.

It was a warm overcast day without a breath of breeze. The sky looked yellowish. Nola stood outside a restaurant, still boarded up for a winter that now seemed long past, and fed piles of quarters and dimes into a pay telephone.

His home number was unlisted. She had to call information several times and go through the university's main switchboard before getting the number for his office. She let the phone ring fifteen times, counting, before she gave up. Then she made a second call to the main university number and spent several minutes on hold.

"English department?"

"Yes," Nola said hesitantly. "I'm trying to reach Professor Marcus Turner?"

"Professor Turner's on leave. I'd be happy to take a message, though."

"He's ill?" Nola's hands were trembling.

"I'm sorry," the young woman said. "I can't provide any information."

The sun gouged through a bank of clouds and poured down, dizzying, on Nola's head. "I'm a friend," she said. "Is there someone who could—?"

"The Chair's in a meeting right now. If you could leave your name and number, maybe he—"

"I don't have a phone," Nola said. "I just want to know how I can reach him."

"No phone? I guess you'd need to call back." The young woman sounded miserable over her failure to be helpful.

"It's not your fault," Nola said. "I just—"

"Why don't you leave your name?" the young woman said. "I can at least tell the Chair you'll be calling back."

Nola offered her name in a low, unsteady voice. In the hush that followed, she thought she'd been disconnected. Her eyes were watering.

"Maze of Fire?" the young woman said. "You . . . wow, we read that in my women's studies seminar. It was awesome."

Nola blinked. "Thank you."

"I can't believe I'm talking to you." The girl laughed self-consciously. "I'm not very businesslike," she said.

"Neither am I," said Nola.

"Listen." The young voice sounded muffled. "I'm really not supposed to know this."

A drop of sweat ran down Nola's back. "I'm here," she said.

"Professor Turner's at this place called the Greenvale Psychiatric Institute. It's up in Connecticut somewhere."

For a moment Nola couldn't breathe.

"I took Afro-Am Lit with him last term," the girl said softly. "He's such a great guy."

"Yes," Nola whispered.

Before she could thank the young woman, the operator had cut into the line. By the time Nola had dropped five more quarters into the phone, her informant had hung up.

She flew into Hartford the next afternoon, renting a car at Bradley. The Avis clerk provided her with a map and directions to the hospital. The drive, through postcard towns with tidy greens, quaint shops, and steepled white churches, took an hour. The whole way, Nola thought about the spontaneous and poorly conceived ventures she'd undertaken in her life. They had been few, and none, it seemed, as risky or impulsive as this. She might, she realized, be the last person on earth Marcus would care to see. It amazed her that she didn't care. She could not imagine Marcus broken, impaired in any way. She intended to see him.

Nola reached the hospital at five-thirty. The patients were at dinner, the woman at the reception desk said. Visiting hours didn't start until seven and ended promptly at nine. She gave Nola a visitor's pass and directed her to a lounge where she could wait until the proper time.

The reception lounge looked like the drawing room of a wealthy and erratic patron of the arts. The carpets were Turkish, the furniture English, the flowers fresh. Nearly everything else in the room had been made, a plaque by the door informed her, by the patients. Vivid, unruly paintings and drawings of obsessive detail crowded the walls. Sculptures that looked like nightmares rendered permanent in clay and wood and metal overwhelmed the gleaming surfaces of mahogany tables and a carved marble mantelpiece. Although no smoking was allowed (the notice done in crewel embroidery), there were misshapen ashtrays everywhere, and several mobiles hung from the ceiling. Baroque music drifted softly from unseen speakers. The air was scented with lemon oil.

The room was unoccupied. Nola sank into a wingback chair, letting her head rest against its rose velvet back. The setting sun, lowering in the long window she faced, looked like a blood orange. When it reached the center of the window, Nola closed her eyes. She felt strangely at home here, invisible in the stillness. The sun's dying light seeped red through her eyelids.

When Nola awoke, the window was dark and a pleasant woman's voice, faintly accented with Spanish, was announcing that it was seven o'clock and visitors might proceed to the various floors. In a far corner of the room, an elderly couple rose silently from a brocade settee. The woman, wearing a purple tweed coat and carrying a white bakery box by its flimsy string, smiled apologetically at Nola, as if for intruding on her private preserve. Nola smiled back. The man, the rims of his eyes red, looked away from Nola and took the woman's arm.

As directed, Nola took an elevator to the third floor. A bewildering trail of signs and turns delivered her to the east wing. She pictured Marcus there in a monastic cell of a room in a narrow iron bed. He was dressed in a hospital gown and robe of the palest blue, and a thin white blanket was pulled up to the middle of his chest. Although she seemed to see him clearly, when Nola tried to bring his face into focus, Marcus's features melted into a flat dark shape against the whiteness of the bedding.

Marcus sat in a bright orange beanbag chair near a service elevator. He was wearing faded jeans and a red T-shirt, black high-top sneakers with the laces removed from them. An unopened book lay on his lap. He seemed to be staring at a red fire exit sign above a gray metal door marked EMERGENCY USE ONLY.

His face was puffy and his dark skin had a dusty look. The wildness had been trimmed from his hair and beard. Nola stood off to the side, a dozen feet away, and just stared for a moment. He looked oddly young and subdued, but his knees were jumping up and down. As she watched, Marcus leaned forward and rested his arms on his knees, forcing stillness on them. His book fell to the floor. He seemed not to notice. His hands hung limp in the space between his thighs. He lowered his head and studied the gray linoleum floor.

"Marcus?" Nola said.

He did not move.

"Hey," Nola said. She walked over and squatted down in front of him, where he could not help but see her. "Hey, pal." Her purse slipped from her shoulder and dropped to the floor with a small dull thud.

Marcus lifted his head slightly and looked into her eyes. His expression didn't change, but Nola somehow knew that he recognized her.

Clumsy, off balance, she sank down to sit cross-legged on the floor, wrapping her arms around her knees. "What's going on?" she said.

His shoulders might have lifted in the slightest shrug, she couldn't be sure. Then he drew back into the chair, as if he found her closeness distasteful. His knees were jumping again.

"Okay, so you couldn't call me," she said. "But you owe me a letter, you know."

He looked into her eyes again, just for a moment, as if he might ask her something. Then his lids closed and Nola felt like a door had slammed in her face.

Impatiently, she rubbed tears away with the backs of her hands. "Be that way," she said.

Then she just sat there, on the floor at his feet, looking at him for what seemed like a very long time.

He did not open his eyes, but after a while his knees went still and his breathing became slow and regular. He might have been asleep. His breath had a faintly metallic smell and the corners of his mouth were cracked with dryness.

After perhaps an hour, Nola, without raising herself from the floor, scooted around until her back was to him. Then she fit herself between his knees and rested her back against the bottom of his chair. "I'll be here," she said. "Just in case you've got anything to say for yourself."

She raised her right arm and rested it on his leg. Her pale hand hung down beside his, her small gold bracelet dangling from her wrist. His thigh muscles tightened for a moment, then relaxed again.

"Anytime you're ready, pal," Nola said.

For three days, Nola came to the hospital at three o'clock, left at four-thirty, returned at seven, and left at nine. The patients' days, she learned, were long and full, with individual and group and occupational therapy, exercise and organized recreation, medical procedures. Blood pressure was checked twice a day. Medications were distributed according to a strictly supervised regimen in which the patients lined up at the nurses' station.

Outside visiting hours, Nola's time was spent mainly in her Spartan room in the reasonable and nondescript motel she'd found near the hospital. The motel had a coffee shop and there was a Wendy's just across the road. After one dinner in the coffee shop, where everything seemed to be fried, she became a regular patron of the Wendy's salad bar. For breakfast she went to a McDonald's drive-thru near the highway and carried coffee back to her room. Its window overlooked an empty swimming pool, a concrete pit with brown sludge at the bottom, set off by a chain-link fence. There was not a tree or a bird in sight and the sky was sliced into pieces by power lines and telephone wires. Nola developed an unhealthy interest in daytime television. When she tried to read, she would fall asleep.

The visits were all the same. Marcus never spoke or responded to her in any meaningful way. And Nola felt less and less compelled to speak herself, sensing that words were not what he wanted or needed from her, if he wanted or needed her at all. She brought him nothing, dressed in plain everyday clothes—jeans, sweaters, her heavy jacket. On the first of May, it was thirty-four degrees in Connecticut and a light snow fell in the morning. Nola had stopped putting on makeup after the first day. Marcus never really looked at her. No one did. Once each afternoon, once each evening, she slipped into the hospital like a shadow trailing other visitors, those whose rights and reasons for being there were more valid than her own. She would find Marcus then and sit with him wherever he was, as close as he would let her.

She learned that he'd allow her to come closer if she wouldn't look at him, so Nola often kept her back to him, their bodies touching in some slight way as her few words trailed off into empty space. One afternoon she'd held his hand for a moment. But his fingers were cold and lifeless and his eyes had taken on a frantic look, as if she were causing him pain. Nola quickly let go of his hand and kept her face slanted away from him. She did not cry until she was back in her car, returning to the motel to wait for seven o'clock.

On the fourth morning, terrified by her lack of purpose, Nola called the hospital and requested an appointment with Marcus's doctor.

"It's a team," the woman in Patient Services told her. "Doctors, social workers, a psychologist, other trained professional—"

"I just need to talk to someone," Nola said, "who's familiar with his case."

"You're a family member?"

"Not exactly," Nola said.

"Well, no one would be authorized to discuss a patient with anyone other than a close relative . . . confidentiality . . . I'm sure you can understand."

"I'm a close friend," Nola said. "He has no family."

"I see." The woman sounded both sympathetic and dubious.

"I'm not trying to pry," Nola said. "I just thought there might be somebody who could tell me if there's some way to get him to talk." Her voice broke. "Why won't he talk to me?" she whispered.

The woman was silent for a moment.

"I'm sorry," Nola said.

"Are you all right?" the woman asked gently.

"Yes," Nola said. "But he's not."

"I know," the woman said. "I know, dear." Nola could hear another phone ringing in the background. "Give me a number," the woman said. "I'll get someone to call you."

Nola released a long, unsteady breath. "You're very kind," she said.

———

Dr. Brockton Hsu, the psychiatrist heading Marcus's "team," looked about sixteen years old, Nola thought. He had an appealing gap between his front teeth and a long fringe of silky hair that brushed the gold wire rims of his oval eyeglasses. His office, the size of a closet, had two framed Escher posters on the walls. There was no window. A stuffed iguana, highly shellacked, crouched on the corner of a scarred metal desk beside a ceramic lamp that looked like a gargoyle.

Dr. Hsu's glance followed Nola's to the iguana and lamp. "We try to discourage patient gifts," he said, "but sometimes they are irresistible." He grinned.

"I understand pets can be very . . . therapeutic," Nola said.

The young doctor laughed. He motioned Nola to the one visitor's chair, then sat down behind his desk. "How may I help you?"

"I want to know . . . anything you can tell me," Nola said.

"About Marcus Turner," Dr. Hsu said. "Yes. You've seen him?"

"Twice a day for three days," Nola said.

"So you've talked with him?"

"If you mean has he talked to me," Nola said, "no."

The doctor nodded. "You understand there is much I'm not . . . authorized to discuss?"

"He has no family. His mother—"

He nodded again. "Passed away in January, yes."

"Oh," Nola said.

"You didn't know?"

Nola, realizing it was too late to lie, shook her head.

"Might I ask . . ." The doctor folded his hands, precise and delicate as origami. "The nature of your relationship with Marcus?"

"We're friends," Nola said.

"Not lovers?" He blushed faintly.

"We might have been," Nola said. "But no."

The doctor waited.

"That has no bearing on anything now," Nola said. "I want to know how . . . *if* I can help him. As a friend."

"We, all of us here, want to know that," Dr. Hsu said.

"Does he talk to you?"

"Occasionally."

"If he doesn't talk to me, does that mean he wants me to go away?"

"I wouldn't assume that."

Nola stared at Dr. Hsu for a moment, amazed that a face so young and smooth could look so grave.

"Then I won't," Nola said. "Assume that. It's one of the main things I wanted to know."

"Marcus Turner is a brilliant man," Dr. Hsu said. "It makes him . . . difficult to help. He is suffering from a deep and complex depression. And there is, as you may know, a great deal we don't yet understand about depression."

Nola nodded.

"It has, nearly always, a chemical component. We now have a number of antidepressants that are quite effective. But even the medications have their mysteries." He sighed. "I'm not at liberty, really, to go into all that."

"I understand." Nola leaned forward, her fingers lined up in the edge of his desk. "His mother dying . . . is that what . . ."

"Triggered the depression?" The young doctor shrugged. "It played some part, certainly."

Nola was silent for a moment, her hands pressing into the desk.

"Yes?" Dr. Hsu said.

"I don't know what I'm allowed to ask."

Dr. Hsu smiled. "You are allowed to ask anything," he said. "There are just some things I'm not allowed to answer."

"How did he get here?"

"He admitted himself."

She shook her head impatiently. "I mean——"

"I see," he said, then sighed again. "Who knows? If you asked me what single factor tipped the balance, I'd have to say exhaustion. There is nearly always a genetic component, of course, what you might call a predisposition. And stress. And loss. There may be a million elements to it. But your friend is——" He smiled. "To put it in rigorous and highly scientific terms, Marcus is thoroughly worn out. He has been for a long time. And that's why silence is so appealing to him right now, I think. He just hasn't got the energy to engage."

"So I shouldn't try?"

"I'm not saying that. I'm suggesting you shouldn't take it personally if he doesn't seem to respond to you."

"I'm working on that." Nola smiled sadly. "Has anyone else been to see him?"

"I'm not permitted to say," Dr. Hsu said. "But no." He grinned, then glanced at his watch.

"One last question," Nola said.

"Of course."

"Will Marcus get better?"

The doctor looked intently into Nola's eyes. His pupils, behind the polished lenses of his glasses, were huge and lively.

"If I have anything to say about it?" he said. "Definitely." There was a catch in Nola's breath.

"Better," Dr. Hsu said softly. "Stronger. But no one must expect him to be unchanged."

————

When Nola came for visiting hours that evening, Marcus could not be found. She looked, on the way to his room, in all the places where she'd found him before: in several lounge areas, in the small kitchen where the patients could help themselves to tea and juice and snacks, in the television room, the reading room, the beanbag chair near the fire exit.

She had never been in his room before. His roommate, who looked about eighteen, sat on the edge of the bed near the window, reading a *Star Wars* paperback. The boy, enormously fat, was wearing a voluminous white T-shirt with blue and silver stars on it, and a halo of springy gold ringlets circled his head. He looked like a monstrous cherub, Nola thought.

The second bed, nearer the door, was neatly made, unindented. Beside it, on a gray metal nightstand, Nola saw the heron skull resting on a stack of books.

"Excuse me," she said.

The boy looked up from his book. His eyes, pinched in pouches of pink flesh, were pale blue and dreamy-looking. "I've already told them everything I know," he said. His voice was dreamy, too.

"I'm looking for Marcus," Nola said.

"Figures." He looked down at his book again.

Nola walked over to the nightstand and picked up the bird skull, cupping it in both hands. It seemed to weigh nothing at all. She remembered the eye membrane, floating off in the air like a small bubble.

"Better leave his stuff alone," the kid said without looking up.

Nola replaced the skull, positioning it exactly as she'd found it. "Right," she said. "I guess you don't know where he is?"

After a moment, when he didn't reply or look at her, Nola turned to leave.

"Cool earrings."

Nola reached up and touched her earlobe. She wasn't wearing earrings. "Thanks," she said.

"Whatever," the fat angel said.

She was on her way to the nurses' station to ask for help finding Marcus when she passed the solarium. The large glass box of a room was in semidarkness. A standing sign in the doorway said CAUTION—WET FLOOR.

Marcus, all but invisible in shapeless black canvas pants and a black sweatshirt, was suddenly illuminated by a flash of lightning. The wall of black glass he faced was lashed with rain. His hands hung at his sides. When Nola drew near, she saw that his forehead was resting on the glass.

"Hey," she said softly, trying not to startle him.

The sound of her voice made him flinch a little, but he didn't turn around.

Nola stood beside him, just slightly further back from the window. One small lamp had been left burning in a far corner of the wide, greenery-strewn room. The air in the solarium was steamy and smelled of damp earth.

Far down the corridor, something shattered. Angry voices erupted, were quickly quelled.

"Heart of darkness," Nola said.

From the corner of her eye she thought she saw Marcus's lips twitch in a pained fragment of a smile. "Do you know how I miss you?" she said.

Marcus sighed. A steamy cloud formed around his mouth

on the glass. Nola watched the steam evaporate before she spoke again.

"I saw your doctor today," she said. "Dr. Hsu. I hope you don't mind."

Someone hurried past the solarium. Rubber soles squeaked on the linoleum.

"He says that just because you don't talk to me doesn't mean you don't want me here. I'm trying to believe him." Her eyes were watering and she blinked. "Marcus?"

He did not answer or look at her.

"I've *decided* to believe him," Nola said. She moved a step closer, her shoulder barely touching up against his arm. "If you want me to go, you'll have to tell me." He felt still and hard and cold as stone against her shoulder.

"You remember what you said that time, about how when I see something I think's not right my whole being just kind of . . . how did you say it? *Hurls itself* against it, was what you said, I think."

Nola covered her eyes with her hands.

"I know you're tired, pal," she said. "And very sad." Her hands dropped away from her face. "So I'm trying not to get too noisy about it. But I am hurling myself against you . . . against what is wrong with you. I'm not going to *let* you be this way, Marcus."

A ragged seam of light ripped the sky, then the glass was dark again. The sleet looked like frozen tears.

"Your mother . . ." Nola said. "I'm sorry."

He seemed to hold his breath for a moment, then slowly let it go.

"I'm sorry for everything that's ever hurt you," Nola said. "For everything I don't know."

Slowly, Marcus raised his hands and placed them, palms flattened, against the glass, as if he were trying to push back the darkness.

"Good," Nola whispered. "That's good."

After a minute she took a step closer to the glass, then another, until her hot forehead rested against it. The glass was cold. Nola lifted her hands and laid them flat beside Marcus's, as if she could help him hold the night and the cold at bay.

"Do you know how I miss you?" she asked him again.

"Yes," Marcus whispered. "I know."

It was nearly June by the time Nola went home. She had been gone for four weeks. When she left Hartford, spring had just begun to stake a tentative claim on the land along the Connecticut River. Some eight hours later, reaching the island, Nola ran head-long into full-fledged summer. It knocked the breath out of her.

She had stopped on the way down from the Norfolk Air-port to pick up Isaac, who'd been exiled to a kennel for nearly a month, their first separation. The puppy, who had filled out some, held no grudges. As she made the ferry crossing, Nola sat on the deck with Isaac on her lap, amazed at the weight of him and the intensity of the late-afternoon sun. Her jacket was stowed in the trunk of the car. Her jeans stuck to her legs and she had to roll up the sleeves of her cotton shirt. Her arms looked pallid and bluish in the strong sunlight. Isaac licked the salt from her skin.

The water was Wedgwood blue. Pelicans flew low along-side the ferry, skimming for fish, and an escort of gulls hovered above, snatching torn bread from the fingers of indulgent tour-ists. Nola stared at the water until its brightness hurt her eyes. She felt like she'd been gone for years.

She needed, she told herself, to set her feet on the ground, settle down, make plans. The month in Connecticut had been, financially, ruinous: twenty-four dollars a day for the motel room, twelve dollars a day to keep Isaac at the kennel, forty dollars a week for airport parking . . . not to mention the plane tickets, car rental, restaurant meals. Either she'd have to pick up some summer teaching or ask her family for a loan to make it to fall. Nola tried to muster up some alarm, but found she could not. Things would somehow work out.

There would be a month's worth of mail to answer. Her modest bills were all in arrears. But none of it seemed to matter very much, not even the lost work time. I am getting *profligate*, she thought, as her car bumped off the ferry and onto the sand-strewn road.

Ahead of her, in a small red convertible, two college-age couples in neon-bright shorts and tank tops whooped and raised brown bottles to the lowering sun. Nola smiled. Profligate, she thought, and contumacious. They seemed to her marvelous words.

Isaac put his front paws on her knee and stretched. "We're almost there," Nola said.

Two days ago she had not been able to imagine herself at home because she had not been able to imagine leaving Marcus. Though he seemed a little sturdier, spoke a little more each day, he was likely to remain in the hospital for weeks yet, perhaps even months. It was, Dr. Hsu said, "counterproductive" to try to make predictions. But Marcus was healing, the doctor told Nola. She need have no doubt about that.

And as he had begun healing, slowly, Marcus had allowed Nola to come closer. His silences often, especially in the evening, were still prolonged. But he didn't seem to mind as much when Nola looked directly at him. And sometimes, unable to break through wordlessness, he would lean against her, or touch her hand.

Although she tried unceasingly to imagine what Marcus was thinking and feeling, Nola could not. Still, his silences grew less troubling to her as she sensed, more and more, that they were starting to come from peace rather than pure despair. She told herself he was resting.

There was only one time when he actually tried to explain to Nola what had happened to him, and his explanation then had been oblique and almost incidental. Marcus had taken up painting in occupational therapy. One afternoon he showed Nola a small watercolor he'd done that morning.

"An assignment," he said. "They told us to paint 'the abyss'—" He tucked down his head and laughed softly. " 'Our personal look into the abyss.' " When he raised his head, his eyes for an instant looked full of light.

"Are you sure I'm ready for this?" Nola asked.

Marcus turned the picture around.

Nola felt the blood drain from her face.

The painting, all grays and browns and dull blues, was a cityscape, unpeopled. Off to the side, dominating the foreground, stood a phone booth, empty, its door ajar.

"You couldn't reach me," Nola whispered.

Marcus's smile vanished. "No." He took hold of her wrist gently, then tightened his grasp. "It's not about that, Nola, not anything like that."

She looked into his eyes. "I don't understand."

He kept hold of her wrists. "Listen to me."

"I am." She closed her eyes.

"It's about . . . there was this day I ducked into the handy phone booth and found out my cape wasn't there anymore."

Nola opened her eyes. "Superman?"

Marcus nodded. His smile was wistful. "Just standing out there on the corner in his underpants," he said.

Nola waited for more, but Marcus only shook his head. "Imagine," he said.

They were sitting in his room, he at the foot of his bed, Nola in the chair beside it. Marcus's newest roommate, an elderly man with a Yiddish accent, was down the hall playing chess with one of the counselors.

"So are you trying to find it?" Nola asked after a moment.

"What?" Marcus dropped the painting on his pillow, facedown.

"Your cape," Nola said.

"No way." Marcus picked up the heron skull, studied it for a moment, then set it gently on a book. "No, ma'am," he said. "Just contemplating my own skinny backside and trying to figure out how to get by from here on without the costume."

"You don't need it," Nola said. "You never did."

"So they tell me." His smile was uncertain. "And what about you?" he said.

"Me?" Nola said. "I'm not into costumes."

Marcus shook his head. "Wouldn't be caught dead near a phone booth. But how about going out on limbs in your underwear?"

Nola smiled.

"Why did you come out here?" Marcus asked.

Nola thought for a moment. "To see you." The simple words were the closest she could come to truth.

Marcus gazed at her briefly, then lowered his head. "Skinny butt and all," he said.

"That's not how it looks to me," Nola said.

He sighed. "I know it." When he raised his head, his face was troubled. "But maybe I'm going to need someone . . . need *you*," he said, "to see me like I am. Just that."

Nola nodded slowly. "I guess I'll just have to keep trying," she said.

"There's something else," said Marcus.

"What?"

"You ought to be getting on home."

Nola struggled to keep her face impassive "Is that what you want?"

Marcus slipped from the bed and went to stand looking out the room's single window. The light outside at four o'clock was pale and lemony, slightly hazy. On a hillside beyond the hospital parking lot a man in dark clothes stood alone against a tangle of gimlet-colored shrubbery just beginning to bud.

"There's a lot of this I've got to face down by myself," Marcus said. "You know that."

Nola's hands twisted into a knot. "How alone is somebody supposed to be?" she said.

When she looked up, Marcus had turned around. He stood bathed in weak golden light.

"Why are you smiling like that?" she said.

"I didn't know you were such an existentialist," he said.

"It's a sideline." Nola tried to smile. "I don't want to leave you," she said. "Not yet."

"It's time," Marcus said. "We've both got work to do. And I'll be coming along after a while."

He could have meant a million things. Or nothing.

The next morning Nola booked a return flight on her open ticket.

The morning after that she flew south, toward home, where it was already summer.

Behind the barricade of unpaid bills, unanswered letters, and the demands of a neglected house, the saint awaited Nola's attention. The girl, her demands strident now, lacked the patience of a saint.

Nola thirsted first for sleep and sun. In a week of rigorous mornings, she cleared her desk, cleaned her house, washed her winter clothes and stowed them, stuffed into plastic bags, in the lockbox in the shed. She filled her refrigerator with fruit and vegetables, eggs and cheese, stocked the cupboard with staples. Twice she bathed Isaac, who had imported from the kennel a stubborn and expensive accompaniment of fleas.

High winds must have visited the island in her absence. The yard around her house was strewn with broken branches and somebody's trash, and a small sickly pine at the side of the shed had come down. Nola gathered the debris into a tidy pile in one corner of the yard, then hired a man with a chain saw and truck to dismantle the fallen tree and haul everything away.

A spate of jonquils had emerged along the driveway. Fiddler crabs did their off-balance dance in the sun, then coyly sidled under the stepping-stones that led to her front door. The restaurants and motels, all open now, began to fill with tourists, and the island, strange and standoffish in winter, seemed familiar again. Nola got up each morning knowing exactly where she was and what she was supposed to be doing.

Despite the ruckus-raising winds, the ladder still clung to the south side of the house. After lunch, a full morning of chores and obligations under her belt, Nola would climb to the roof to lie in the sun. If it was warm enough, she'd strip off all her clothes, for she was hidden there. She rubbed oil into her skin.

Later in the day she would jump in the car with Isaac and drive out to the beach. The dead gulls had all been cleared or washed away. Nola wondered whether the mysterious epidemic had died out or simply moved on to spoil some other place. If the island's bird population was decimated, it wasn't evident. The air was overwrought with wings and a racket of scolding.

After a full week of industrious mornings, idle afternoons, and sleep-nourished nights, Nola took stock of herself and her surroundings. Her desk was clear, her house spotless and well ordered. Her skin was the color of brown sugar. She had written Marcus twice, received two letters from him, and also spoken to him once on the phone. He was beginning to sound more like himself all the time.

The shadows were gone from under Nola's eyes—she could see that herself when she looked in the mirror. Her eyes looked more thoughtful than wounded, she thought. Just maybe a little worried. The saint's voice, peckish and haughty, was growing boisterous. It refused Nola all mercy. She craved stillness, yet dreaded what she knew she must do to bring it about.

Each day she procrastinated, prolonged the girl's life.

And her suffering.

On the second Monday in June, just after dawn, Nola pulled a fresh tablet of lined paper from the shelf above her desk. The day was going to be hot. She opened a window. The trees were full of bickering birds.

Her antique fountain pen, a stubby tortoiseshell finger, lay inside an old wooden pencil box in the desk drawer. The thin silver rim around the edge of its cap reminded Nola of the bands affixed to the legs of birds, carrier pigeons, and dwindling species deemed worth keeping track of. But there were, she recalled reading, no carrier pigeons anymore. The species may have died out before she was even born.

Nola filled the pen with a fresh supply of black ink. Its odor, faintly antiseptic, brought back the hospital. She wondered if Marcus loved his silences, or if he would learn to. She wondered if he missed her solid, intrusive presence leaning into him. She wondered if, in Connecticut, summer seemed any closer.

Gently, with a kind of wordless prayer caught in her throat,

Nola set Marcus to the side of the empty sheet of paper before her. The girl was there, ruining stillness with her anguish and fury, needing her now, needing Nola this one last time.

"Shh," Nola said. "I'm here."

She closed her eyes for a moment. She had lost her feel for sanctity, she knew that now. It was an inhuman thing, holiness, rare or perhaps even extinct, and no business, surely, of hers. Yet she, clumsy, unknowing, profligate, and contumacious, had forced this suffering soul back to life. Nola could not abandon the girl-martyr now, not without first laying her to rest.

The pen, uncapped, lay on the empty page. *Forgive me my ignorance*, Nola thought. She opened her eyes and looked down. The faint blue lines looked deeply etched into the paper and the paper was like skin, naked without the words to cover it properly. She closed her eyes again. Behind them the pure white pages, deeply cut, began to bleed.

The girl-saint fell silent then. Nola knew she was there, though, waiting. The air was too imperious to breathe.

"Just a minute," Nola whispered. "Hold on."

Outside the window the birds, too, went still. She had lost her feel for sanctity. Everything she knew now was human, merely that. It would have to do.

Nola opened her eyes and picked up her pen. As her fingers accepted and enclosed it, her hands stopped shaking. There wasn't anything to wait for.

Nola saw the girl clearly then, all torn flesh and terror, quirk and mettle. *I will be with you*, she thought. *I am here*.

Then, wrapped in silence, Nola hurled herself once more against everything she knew she could not remit or revise, could never emend, could only begin to imagine.

I Married
a Space Alien

*M*y neighbor goose-steps down the dew-slick road wearing headphones and hot pink sweatpants. OLD AGE AIN'T FOR SISSIES, her T-shirt says. When she spots me snipping dahlias out in my yard, Belinda yanks the yellow plugs out of her ears and hikes up the sagging seat of her pants.

"Nice morning," I call out to her.

"Here on earth." She keeps moving toward me, her legs pumping, her feet pummeling the asphalt. "Who knows what goes on in other galaxies?"

Belinda is a retired school nurse. At seventy, she is trim and energetic and practical. She is also nothing if not direct. I recognize a segue when I see one.

"On earth?" I say.

Reeboks spinning out on the gravel, Belinda makes a sharp turn into my driveway without missing a beat. She skids to a stop so close under my chin that my nose feels like a hood ornament. Rusted shears and brilliant flowers fall at my feet.

"How are you, Grace?" Belinda is breathing

hard. Inside the headphones looped around her neck, the Bee Gees are wailing. "*Really*, I mean?"

"Stayin' alive," I say.

Her pitying look seems uncalled for. At six-thirty in the morning, what level of wit can she expect?

"I gather you've already seen the papers then," she says.

"The papers."

"Well, Edgar and I for one won't be talking to any confounded reporters, so that's one worry you can forget about," she says.

Next thing I know, Andy Gibb is screeching about the wind of change and my next-door neighbor of nine summers is breaking the news to me, sympathetic and concerned as if the culture's just come back with strep written all over it.

"Your ex," she says.

"A space alien?"

"Right there on page one," she says. "And the headlines swelled up something fierce . . . Grace, honey, are you all right?"

I sit down fast on the soggy grass. Belinda is faster, kicking the shears out of harm's way. "Try putting your head between your knees," she says.

"I thought you didn't even know I was ever married," I say.

Belinda is clearly affronted. "I'll try to give you some advance notice when I start losing my faculties," she says.

The summer I left Bryan had just been reelected. By a landslide. He was everywhere I looked—on billboards and bumper stickers, giveaway pens and pocket combs and shoehorns. His face had even been silkscreened on pot holders, tempting me to imagine scalding metals branding his cheeks and nose and chin.

I'd promised myself I would bypass divorce's bitter phase. *No-fault:* I tried to make a mantra of the phrase. But it is hard not to blame someone who just stands there looking helpless while your dreams are sucked noisily down the drain.

I moved one small state away—to evade my husband's likeness, to avoid the press. I rented a garage apartment near the sea. I craved peace and quiet and anonymity. The long march to mandate had left me bedraggled. Bryan had what he wanted. Now I needed to find out what, if anything, was left of me.

On my way out of Bryan's constituency, I had dropped off my public wifely wardrobe at a thrift shop—five basic black trash bags filled with pert suits and demure dresses, silk blouses and simple pumps. There were even, God help me, a few hats. Those are the pictures I can least bear to see now—me wearing hats. I suppose it doesn't seem like much, and I didn't look half-bad. Reminders of my willingness to become a different woman then are just bound to mortify the woman I am now. I mustn't entirely blame *him* for that.

Anyway, I'd cut the labels out of all the clothes, thankful that at least the media consultants had steered me clear of anything too memorable or showy. I hoped the shoes wouldn't betray me. Their soles were worn thin with stumping, their toes mashed by receiving lines and dutiful foxtrots with precinct captains and contributors. My footwear revealed, at the very least, our party affiliation—everyone knows Republicans resole their shoes, keep them forever. And while I'd stopped reading the papers by then, I was pretty sure I was the only high-visibility Democratic wife to leap off the bandwagon that year.

I parked in the narrow alley behind Resuscitations, the hospital auxiliary thrift shop, and hefted the overstuffed sacks from my trunk. It was five in the morning and still dark. The black bags mounded up around the door, making something like a bunker. The last sack, holding my two wool coats and most of the shoes, was unwieldy. I imagined for a moment that it was my own body I was disposing of, in pieces. I had a real flair for the dramatic, Bryan said.

By the time I crossed the state line, the sun was beaming into my eyes like a searchlight, white and hot. My mouth tasted ocean salt. I showed no regard for speed limits. If I got arrested now, it probably wouldn't even make the news.

When I got to the beach I saw women carrying canvas tote bags with Bryan's name, Kirk—my name—on them. And the campaign slogan: LEADERSHIP TOWARD A NEW CENTURY. The staff had started calling my husband "Captain Kirk," and the press picked up on it, of course. At night his voice, amplified and distorted by distance, floated to me on the airwaves. The tote bags, midnight blue, faded quickly in the sun. By the end of that summer, I'd still see women wandering along the beach and through the market with my husband's name slung over their tan shoulders. The letters were getting harder to read, though, the little clusters of stars around them scarcely more than shadows.

"So," Kitty says. "Where is it?"

"What?" My friend's turquoise eyes, ringed with last night's makeup, distract me. Her hair, radically streaked, hangs in a bushy tail over one shoulder. She looks like Andy Warhol's version of a raccoon.

"The paper, Miss Babe-in-the-Woods. The rag in question. The scandal sheet." Kitty holds out one hand, her magenta-tipped fingers making a gimme-gimme motion. "Show-and-tell time, kid. You're on."

"I haven't got it."

"You woke me up at seven-thirty A.M. on the basis of hearsay? My God."

"Why would Belinda lie?"

"Belinda might be working on a case of Alzheimer's."

"Very nice."

"But not far-fetched," Kitty says. "Not like, say, your ex tracing his roots back to Saturn." She tosses back the sleeve of her purple kimono and glances at a huge tank watch with a red rubber band. Her wrist is corded and yellowish and brittle-looking like a sheaf of uncooked spaghetti. "Shit, the store doesn't open for twenty minutes yet," she says. "I hope I don't dampen my drawers."

"I'll drive you, okay?"

"Say what?"

"You don't think *I'm* going in there?"

"Who knows what you might do?" Kitty's teeth are small and sharp. I try not to look at them when she laughs, which is mostly at all the wrong times. "You married a space alien, didn't you?"

"What if somebody recognizes me?"

"Pshh." Kitty waves her arms and purple silk wings flap. "There aren't a thousand people in this town and you've lived here ten years. Somebody recognizing you's a pretty safe bet."

"You know what I mean."

"Grace, nobody here knows you were married to . . ." She mercifully covers her mouth with both hands. "E.T.," she sputters behind them.

Kitty and I go back about as far as Nancy Reagan and Mr. T. And the friendship's just about as likely. "You're a riot," I say. "Belinda knew, didn't she?"

"Belinda's a nosy old fart."

"Right. Like the town's not full of them."

"You're getting paranoid, Grace."

"Having the tabloids tail you can do that."

The rings around Belinda's eyes get even bigger. "God," she says. "You might get your picture in—"

"Go get dressed," I tell her.

She clutches her hair and groans. "Paparazzi."

"Try a hat," I say. "I'll pay you back."

"With what, your alimony?" Kitty doesn't bother to hide her mouth this time. "We take Visa and Discover," she says. "No moon rocks."

When Kitty comes back she is wearing a black spandex catsuit with a plunging neckline and silver sandals laced up to the knee. A headband with springy antennae shoots two tinfoil balls into orbit above her ears.

I watch with a horrified sort of fascination as she completes the ensemble with meteorite earrings. "What the hell do you think you're doing?"

Kitty puts on a pair of glasses and stares at me through cobalt prism lenses. "Just trying to throw the earthlings off your scent," she says. "Let's launch it."

The general store, ten minutes after opening, is already swarming. Fishermen cluster in the parking lot, their weathered hands warped to the shape of Styrofoam coffee cups and cinnamon doughnuts. Winnebagos circle like a wagon train in hostile territory. Tourists with coffin-sized coolers are lined up at the ice machine.

I spot Edgar Eccles, Belinda's husband, over by the gas pumps and I scrunch down behind the steering wheel. I think Edgar spotted me, too, but is pretending not to see me. I wonder if there's such a thing as alien-by-marriage and a shunning ritual for it. I've broken a sweat by the time Kitty gets back in the car, her arms full of newsprint.

"Good God," I say, "how many papers are carrying this crap?"

"Well, we won't know that, Grace, will we, until we read them." She picks up the thick paper on the top of the pile, her antennae quivering.

"*The New York Times?*" I say. "Please."

"We might as well start at the top." Kitty gives me a haughty look. "If we want a reliable account."

I sigh. "What do I owe you?"

She doesn't glance up from the front page. "A blind date with Mr. Spock ought to do it," she says.

I've only been on one blind date in my life, and that was with Bryan.

D.C. back in the early seventies was a depressing place to work. Vietnam was dying out too slowly, Watergate heating up too fast. Whole city blocks, still charred from the riots a few years earlier, reeked of stale smoke. Freshly haunted by Bobby Kennedy and Dr. King, the place, for all the frantic maneuvering, felt a little like a ghost town.

I was less than two years out of college, though, with a poly-sci degree, and the glamour-tinged grunt work on the Hill seemed exciting and hopeful to me. I thrived on my convictions.

Bryan had a postgrad fellowship at Georgetown, working for the D.C. Public Defender's Office. He spent most of his time trying to interview people who'd done unspeakable things. He'd also just flunked the bar exam and was kind of shell-shocked, my roommate, Audrey Gulick, said. Audrey was dating Bryan's best friend.

"Just one simple date, Grace," she said. "I'll make you dinner every night for a month. You guys'd make a great couple."

"Gee, thanks. I want to see a picture," I said. "In color and not just a head shot."

"I'll even do the dishes," Audrey said.

"No Swanson TV dinners," I said. "No Banquet beef-and-gravy sandwiches."

"Besides," said Audrey, "he's gorgeous."

"Uh-huh," I said. "And your damn meat loaf with the hard-boiled eggs hiding in the middle will not be acceptable."

"Jesus, Grace, I'm trying to do you a favor!"

"I expect the vegetables to be fresh," I said. "And not a lima bean in or near *anything*."

Bryan Kirk was—no lie—drop-dead gorgeous: a tall fair-haired boy with the long, lean limbs of a long-distance runner and eyelashes you could dust Venetian blinds with. Our first date was a textbook case of what gives blind dates their rotten name.

He picked me up on a Sunday afternoon in mid-November. The day was rainy and raw and he didn't have a car. He took me to, of all things, a Buster Keaton film festival. We sat in a rank-smelling basement theater off Dupont Circle, through three silent movies in a row. Hardly anybody laughed. Certainly not me. The only thing that kept me awake was the challenge of unsticking Jujubes from my teeth without using my fingers.

Afterward we walked through pouring rain to a little Greek restaurant on M Street. I didn't know much about Greek food beyond feta cheese, which I didn't like, so I asked Bryan to order for me. Then I ducked into the putrid ladies room and tried to dry my hair with brittle brown paper towels.

"I decided to go exotic," Bryan said, when I got back to the table.

"Me, too," I said. I'd wound my Peter Max scarf around my head. I knew the Maya Angelou thing wasn't really working on me, but at least my scalp was warm.

A surly waiter slapped two plates on the table. The aroma that rose from them reminded me of the ladies room. "What is this?" I asked, trying to sound game.

"I believe in trying new things," Bryan said.

The squid, afloat in oily pools of tomato sauce, was like rubber tubing. It was good to have a lot of chewing to do, though, because our conversation only slightly outdid Buster Keaton's. Ouzo, I discovered, tasted exactly like rubbing alcohol.

It wasn't quite nine o'clock when Bryan took me home. It was still pouring. "Thanks for a terrific time," I said, "I didn't know those old movies could be so . . . relaxing."

Bryan, hunched deep inside what I couldn't help noticing was a real Burberry coat, groaned softly and kind of doubled over. All of a sudden he was the same height as I was. His eyes were closed. His lashes trimmed his pale cheeks like dark embroidery.

"No, really," I said. "It was—"

"Awful!" He shuddered, showering me with secondhand raindrops. I thought he was crying, or maybe having a violent delayed reaction to the squid. I touched one of his soggy epaulets. "Oh, God," he said, "I'm sorry."

"It doesn't matter," I said.

"Ordinarily," he said, "it wouldn't." When he looked up, his eyes really did look shell-shocked. "The problem is, I like you."

"Oh," I said.

"Maybe I could meet you again," he said. "When I get back to normal."

My smile felt bleak. "Yeah, maybe,"

"You'd probably be married by then, though." He sighed. "Or famous and living in Europe."

Bryan straightened up slowly, pulling his collar up close around his neck. Then, his eyes closed, his lashes fluttering slightly, he leaned over and touched his lips to mine. "Just in case we miss each other and wind up on different planets," he said.

Standing in a circle of streetlamp light, I watched Bryan Kirk's face transform itself. Delicate color flooded his throat and he looked heartbreakingly young, though he was a few years older than I was, and a little scared. Then, like time-lapse photography run backward, his face a flower, its petals so frag- ile I would have to fear for them in any earthly climate, closed back into a tight hard bud.

I wanted to run for my life. But it was early and how could I leave him standing there in a downpour all alone?

"If you're going to Mars and me to Europe," I said softly, "maybe we ought to have a cup of coffee for the road?"

Bryan stared at me. I was twisting my heavy ring of keys in both hands. I probably had two or three dozen—keys to storerooms in the Rayburn Building, to bicycle locks, to lockers and closets, apartments and mailboxes and storage bins where my leases and memberships had long since lapsed, keys to an old Austin-Healey sold for parts six months ago. I had, for a twenty-three-year-old, already left quite a lot behind.

Bryan pried my fingers, one by one, from the keys. His fingers were colder than mine. I will never know how he knew exactly which one would open the door to the building, which two would fit my apartment locks, but he got us in out of the rain.

After that, Bryan Kirk turned out to be quite a conversationalist. We sat up half the night for several years. He told me about the parents and little brother who were killed in a car accident one summer when Bryan was nine and away at camp, about the dutiful aunt who took on his rearing because she'd given her word. He told me about the high school sweetheart who'd loved him right through law school, then married somebody else the weekend before the D.C. bar exam, and how he'd never failed or lost at anything before and never would again.

We were married for a dozen years, Bryan and I. I hung on his every syllable for a good long time. But somewhere back between the first and second campaigns, I began to get the feeling it wasn't me Bryan was talking to anymore.

He ran in odd-numbered years. Along about the fourth campaign, I guess it was, I pretty much stopped listening to him. But I never stopped watching the people who did. There were hundreds of them, then thousands. They raised their faces and looked at my husband with a kind of shock. His words hovered just above them, shimmering, and filled their eyes with a glow you'd have to call otherworldly.

Kitty starts at the top of the stack of newspapers. I pull a tabloid from the bottom of the heap. Politics teaches you to be pragmatic, to do the expedient thing.

The story appears in only one of the $12.78 worth of newspapers and it's one I've never even heard of before. *The American Inquisitor*, according to its masthead, is published in Hammond, Indiana, and has an international readership of 850,000 inquiring minds. TOP U.S. POLICYMAKERS ARE (ILLEGAL?) ALIENS!! the front-page headline says.

At least he isn't alone. Bryan's picture is flanked by two cabinet members. A Supreme Court justice, a prominent western governor, and a powerful southern senator make up the second tier.

"God," I say. "Bryan got old."

Kitty drops the "Style" section of *The Washington Post* and lunges, knocking a coffee mug off the wicker table between us. A sluggish brown stain creeps across the raffia rug.

I swing the tabloid beyond her reach. "His antennae are a lot bigger than yours." My smile is pitying.

"Size is a male myth, Grace." She jumps up and snatches the paper out of my hands. "Ew," she says, "*really* old. You're probably better off, Grace."

Then Kitty starts reading the story aloud, interrupting herself with shrieks of laughter. I lean back in my wicker chair, close my eyes, and rock slowly back and forth. A mourning dove perches in an azalea on the other side of the screen, adding an eerie descant to Kitty's big solo.

"Omigod. Wait till you hear this."

"I'm listening." I don't open my eyes.

" 'Contacted at his subterranean office at the White House, where Kirk has been serving as Special Counsel to the President since'—blah-blah-blah—'the granite-jawed former Majority Whip of the Senate said, "The truth is, I'm relieved." ' "

I snicker.

"Relieved!" Kitty screams. "Can you stand it?"

I grip the scrolled arms of the wicker chair. "Keep your voice down!" I hiss. Who knows if Belinda is still listening to the Bee Gees?

"Sorry." Kitty resumes reading. " ' "It's been a great burden," Kirk said, "having to keep my history and my true nature a secret. Now that the air's been cleared, I just want to get on with the business of helping the President get America back on its feet." ' "

"Yeah," I say. "That sounds like Bryan."

"It does?"

I open my eyes. Kitty is staring at me the way I used to see crowds stare at Bryan: avid and credulous, hungry for more.

"You don't have to be seventy to get Alzheimer's, you know," I say.

Kitty closes her mouth, tightening her jaw a little. Her eyes still look mesmerized, though. "But how could they print it, Grace, if he never said it?"

"Just finish the reading," I say. "The panel discussion on freedom of the press comes later."

Kitty puts on her blue prism glasses, looks down at the paper, then takes the glasses off again. "Blah-blah . . . it's about all this stuff he used to be . . . human rights, international trade, blah . . . doesn't so much as *mention* you, Grace."

"You know my motto, 'Forgotten, not gone.' " My eyes are closed again. The mourning dove has called it quits on backup.

" 'Kirk, known for his cool judgment and poise under public fire, seemed unruffled when contacted by the *Inquisitor* Friday. But sources close to the private man indicate Kirk now fears his hope of running for the highest office in the land may be constitutionally thwarted.' "

"Oh, brother," I say.

"What do they mean?"

When I look at Kitty her turquoise eyes are murky with confusion. "You have to be born here to run for President," I explain.

"On earth?"

"In the United States," I say.

"Bummer," says Kitty.

There was one night when I almost didn't leave him. Bryan doesn't know that. He doesn't need to. It was just a moment, really, and not one anything even happened in. Still, it is there, small and dark and definite as a punctuation mark in the paragraph my life will come down to.

I had already told him I'd be going. It had become inevitable, he knew that, Bryan said. My books, packed in heavy cartons, lined the back hallway where nobody but us and the once-a-week cleaning lady would need to see them. It was a Saturday night in the middle of April. Bryan had flown home for the weekend. He'd brought along our tax return, prepared by his accountant and double-checked by his staff. It was half an inch thick. Bryan had already signed it. The places where I was supposed to add my signature below his were marked with a yellow highlighter pen, faintly glowing Xs. I wrote my name, and the date, six or eight times without reading what I was attesting to or signing away.

Bryan looked sober and relieved when I handed back the sheaf of papers. I think he always expected me to make waves, though I never really did. Maybe I should have, for both our sakes.

"Hey, big spender," I said. It was a song I used to sing sometimes, back when he was in his first term in Congress and wouldn't get home, even to sleep, for weeks on end: *Hey, big spender, spend a little time with me.*

"Thank you, Grace." Bryan's gaze held steady and deep.

I felt as if he were looking at me, really seeing me, for the first time in years. I wondered if he still liked me.

"No problem," I said. "If anything's off base, we could get reunited at Lewisburg."

"Isaacs doesn't cut corners," Bryan said. "And I had Rodney and Fred go over it. I have every confidence in them."

I sighed. "I know."

After a moment he nodded. "I guess there's not going to be any refund," he said. "I'm sorry."

"I'll be okay," I said. "We both will."

Bryan closed his eyes for a minute. He looked exhausted. The thick fringe of his lashes nearly got lost in the deep shadows under his eyes, but I could still see them. I remembered how, when we were first married, he used bring his face up close to mine, keeping his eyes closed. Then, his eye socket fitted to the curve of my cheek, he'd begin to blink. Slowly, then faster, his lashes would move back and forth against my skin with the lightest touch. It was something his mother taught him when he was very small. Butterfly kisses, Bryan called them. I tried to return them, but mine weren't much good. I just didn't have the eyelashes for it. And he didn't have the cheekbones.

A phone started ringing in the back of the house. Bryan opened his eyes, but he made no move to go answer. "Sure," he said. "We'll be fine." He didn't sound quite like himself. There is a difference—I saw it then, or heard it—between determination and conviction. It's a nuance I've never forgotten.

I found it hard to look at Bryan those last few weeks. I'd already signed a lease on the apartment at the beach. We both knew I'd be moving the first of May. The phone continued to ring. He just stood there looking at me, looking lost. I turned away, scanning the living room shelves. I had to make sure I wasn't leaving behind anything I couldn't live without.

"Want a cup of coffee?" Bryan said.

"No, thanks." I kept my back to him.

After a little while the kettle whined out in the kitchen. A couple minutes later I heard the sliding glass door to the deck at the back of the house ease open, then closed.

After an hour, busy sorting and packing, I'd almost forgotten him. I was used to being alone in the house, to keeping myself occupied. I went out to the kitchen to get the cup of coffee I felt like I needed now, though I knew it was so late the caffeine would keep me up for hours.

The lights were off in the kitchen, the deck floodlights, too. On the other side of the spotless glass the night sky was black and moonless and perforated with sharp stars. There was nothing, really, to see, just all those stars and the broad back of Bryan's white shirt standing out among them, faint and solitary and somehow frail.

My hand went to the door, fingers probing for the handhold to slide it aside. It would have been the most natural thing in the world to go out, to stand beside him in the dark. For a moment I imagined myself leaning into the light of his thin shirt as I listened, once more, for the sound of his heart. But change was a conviction I had lost by then, I suppose. And so it was easier to stay where I was.

Tonight the sea sounds restless and a little out of sorts. It is August and the papers are full of a hurricane that's starting to hint at its ambitions down in the Caribbean somewhere. But it hasn't been given a name yet. It's still just a tropical storm.

My place is a squat and sturdy little cottage tucked back

behind the dunes in a snarl of beach grass and wild plum. That it's my own still amazes me. I've kept things simple here. When hurricane season comes around I just have to remember to take down the bird feeders and carry the two porch chairs inside. The first couple of years, I'd tape the windows at the first warning, shut off the water main the moment the light began to fail. But after a few storms, when nothing really happens, you start to take them in stride.

I'm not actually afraid, anyway, of getting swept out to sea or carried off on gale-force winds. My flair for the dramatic isn't what it used to be. The only thing I really dread, the nightmare that won't quit, is waking up to find out this little place I found for myself has been blown away during the night by something I can't quite understand. I don't know where I'd find the heart to start all over again.

Kitty says I ought to give Bryan a call, see how he's holding up—as if this little tempest of wacko publicity is a crisis or something. I can't seem to convince her that public figures deal with stuff like this every day . . . or that papers catering to lunatics who spend their lives on the lookout for alien spaceships don't preoccupy those with a whole troubled country on their minds.

"A whole troubled universe, you mean," Kitty says. "Would it kill you just to let him know you're here?"

Bryan knows where I am, of course. Last I heard he'd moved into a condo up by Embassy Row, but I doubt he'd be there at the moment. He never stayed at home much, or certainly not with me. In a way, Bryan never seemed quite at home anywhere. Anyway, an ordinary person doesn't just call up the White House switchboard at ten-thirty at night and ask for somebody she used to know.

"There's an 800 number, I bet," Kitty said.

"And an answering machine with a huge menu," I speculated. "If you are trying to reach an ex-spouse for old time's sake, press 2-7-9-6-0."

But even if I got through, what would I tell him? That we're entirely different species is something we both figured out a long time ago.

Thin veils of fog slink up from the sea and twist through the marshes, get snagged in the stunted trees. The sky above is awash with the milky light of a shrinking moon that looks almost transparent, all by itself up there.

I've never felt as lonely here as I did when I was married. Not even in the dead of winter, with all the houses around mine empty. After a while our house seemed lonelier with both of us in it than when I was alone. I remember how I used to hope he'd learn that kind of loneliness, know someday how it feels when your skin can't keep you warm and your bones go hollow inside. But I was still fairly young then. If I hadn't still been, I could never have believed he wouldn't know, or that knowing he knew could make me happy.

The mosquitoes are bad this time of year, especially when we've had rain. The two boards I need to replace in the porch floor groan as I step on them. My clothes have gotten damp. I catch cold easily.

Still, I stand here for the longest time, shivering, my hand just touching the door.

Lokey Man

*T*hings, by which Kincaid meant his life, had come to a cold and cussed impasse.

Of all possible endings, standstill was the one Kincaid had never remotely imagined. He had envisioned death and divorce in all their anguished and ironic diversities. He had (Oh, the cheek of it, he can see that now!) conjured happily-ever-afters in settings that ranged from Sarasota to the South of France. His mind, embracing Gretel, her hair grown a becoming silver, boogalooed across ballrooms on cruise ships, waltzed stately at weddings where his children married the children of his dearest friends.

Kincaid, like any man, had his bosky side. Over the years, in his grimmer projections, he'd owned up to the growing feasibility of nuclear obliteration. Chapter 11 had figured in more than one dream. And once, on a rather inebriated evening at the Large Pond Country Club, Kincaid had watched the Bindleys' daughter BethAnn, newly married and voluptuous in the ivory satin on which no cost had been spared (her very nipples encrusted, for God's sake, in genuine seed pearls!) . . . yes, Kincaid's aging eyes had doted upon this spirited spanking-new wife of Keith Kyle Purdy as she danced the cha-cha in peau de soie pumps, her cleavage misted in a salty dew, and allowed himself for an instant to fancy a future as one fourth of a foursome that would volupt in adjoining split-levels right under the neighbors' noses on into an eternity blissful and spent.

But mostly there wasn't much margin between Kincaid's improvisatory fantasies and what he saw as his fate. His myth, his destiny, his own true fairy tale was gladsomely rooted in domestic soil, sown in the fertile if unremarkable spot where his actual life began when he met Gretel Faye Murchison in a class on management techniques at the community college here in this very suburb of Indianapolis and saw in her, his Gretel, the lusty appetites, common sense, and organizational flair on which an exemplary family could be founded.

Gretel was a) saving herself for marriage, b) a go-getter in the management-trainee program at Sears, and c) the unspoiled eldest of six children. She was responsible, cheerful, and strong. She was also fairly bosomy for such a petite girl. Kincaid knew a dream-about-to-come-true when he saw one. He'd grabbed hold tight and never let go.

Gretel's apartment, three homish and easeful rooms above a beauty shop in Brownsburg, not far from the Speedway, had made mush of Kincaid before his second Hush Puppy was over the threshold. The very clove-spiced air proclaimed Gretel a woman who could do about anything with next-to-nothing. Kincaid studied every flounce and knickknack with a yearning that stupefied him. He wanted to give her the world, then spend the rest of his life watching her make it corrigible and cozy.

Gretel, at first, seemed less than enchanted with Kincaid's proposal that they merge and mate. She was fond of him, she said, fond indeed. But—

Fond was, under the circumstances, a term Kincaid found not only disappointing, but downright desolating. His soul quite reeled from the single syllable of it, in fact. The *But*—, however, snatched him back a step from the slough of despond. Kincaid always perked up under the snoot of a challenge.

He looked thoughtfully at Gretel. "But what?" His voice was gentle.

"But—I don't know," Gretel said.

"I am your friend," Kincaid said. "You can tell me."

"The thing is," Gretel said, "I'm not sure I love you."

Something was making a shambles of Kincaid's insides, but he stood up straight and strong, as his grandfather, a railroad engineer, had taught him.

"There," Kincaid said softly. His eyes were as placid as Cecil Harden Lake. "Was that so hard?"

"I *want* to love you," Gretel said. Tears brewed along her lower lids, then sloshed from the corners of her candid hazel eyes. She covered her face. Her buffed fingernails looked like moonstones.

Kincaid's own hands were a ruination of rough work, scraped raw by asphalt shingles, punctured by roofing nails, stigmatical with pitch and paint. His right thumbnail, about to fall off any minute, was midnight blue.

Kincaid stared down for a moment at fingers long and shapely. These might, given a different life, have been beautiful hands, hands worth elaborate care, manicure and massage. But Kincaid's mitts had always been too useful for their own good. He shut his eyes, as in prayer, picturing a thin strip of gold . . . his fingers, clutching at air, sensed a dream about to slip right through them. He could almost hear his grandfather's cracky old voice. "This life of yours," the old man said, "sorry a thing as it's apt to turn out . . . you got to remember it's *you* up there in that locomotive, boy. You're the lokey man."

Kincaid's eyes snapped open like windowshades let go. Gretel stood across the room, in front of ruffled white curtains she'd made herself with a borrowed sewing machine. The curtains billowed out at the bottom like a wedding gown.

Kincaid crossed the room, his footwork resolute. Deploying his snaggy hands into realms of delicacy heretofore unattained, he uncovered Gretel's face.

"It's all right," he said. "Don't cry."

"I didn't want to hurt you, I just—"

"It's all right," Kincaid repeated. He kept hold of Gretel's hands. "Come here now, all right?" He tugged her toward the bedroom door.

Gretel pulled back, balking mightily. Her heart-shaped face was hectic and qualmish.

"I am not going to touch you," Kincaid said. "I swear to God I'm not."

After an unsettled moment, Gretel followed him from the sitting room.

Kincaid had, for several months now, but glimpsed her bedroom's allure from the other side of its narrow doorway. The room was, he saw fully now, a place made for dreams. The walls were grayish white, like fog, and the wide planks of the floor, whitewashed, were bare but for a small oval hooked rug beside the single bed, which was covered with a quilt of faded blues and lilacs. The pillowslips were chastely edged with strips of lace.

Kincaid saw a picture of an angel on the wall at the head of the bed. He pictured Gretel kneeling on the little rug, her knees ringed with pansies, her forehead at rest on the edge of the quilt, as she said bedtime prayers. He wondered if she ever prayed for him. His heart lost its mettle for a moment and he felt craven, cursed, spit out by heaven like a bitter seed.

"My intentions are one hundred percent pure," he whispered. "I want you to know that." Then he began to unbutton his frayed plaid shirt.

The bed was between them. Gretel looked too shocked to move or speak.

Kincaid unfastened his belt. "I won't lay a hand on you," he said, "though I do mightily long to." His worn blue trousers dropped to his ankles. He stepped from his shoes, from his pants. Then, standing on one foot at a time, he peeled off his socks.

His body was as beautified by labor as his hands were maimed. His chest was broad, his stomach narrow and flat and hard. His arms and legs were a sinewy wonderment of bulge and curve. The full-length mirror on the closet door behind him reflected a sun-burnished back, a set of shoulders any god might have made do with.

"I can bear a lot of brunt." Kincaid turned slowly, to show her. Then, keeping his back to her, he closed his eyes as if to witness with them this mad momentous deed he'd undertaken would undo him. He raised his hands to his waist and pulled down his undershorts. After stepping out of them, he opened his eyes but kept them lowered.

Slowly, Kincaid turned around. The intake of Gretel's breath, short and sharp, sounded like someone had squeezed her. Kincaid raised his head and looked into her eyes.

"There's not much of anything in particular wrong with me," he said. "Is there."

Her head might have moved slightly, he couldn't be certain. She seemed to be shaking all over.

"My heart and soul would likewise be naked if they could," Kincaid said. "I am not proud in that way." Gretel nodded then, he was sure she did. But she did not say a word.

Kincaid waited. After a moment that seemed too long by half, he bent to retrieve his undershorts, which were a disheartening shade of gray. "I expect I could put my clothes back on now," he said.

"Wait."

Gretel came around the bed with slow, firm steps, took the undershorts from his hands, and dropped them on the floor. Then she placed her hands on Kincaid's shoulders and turned him around to face the mirror again.

"Close your eyes," she said.

Kincaid stared at her.

"Please," she said, letting go of his shoulders.

He did. Then he waited for the touch of her fingers, her mouth, somewhere upon him. But that did not come and he was suddenly very cold.

"You can open them now," Gretel whispered.

She stood beside him in the mirror. Her naked body was the most of glory Kincaid would ever spy in all the long passage of his time on earth. Even his imagination would, he knew, never be the equal of Gretel Faye Murchison's radiant flesh.

He began to turn toward her, his hands rising.

"No," she said, holding his eyes with hers in the mirror's reflection. Then Gretel's gaze began to range up and down the length of the glass, where they stood side by side.

"We will have beautiful children," Kincaid whispered.

It was a Saturday in June. The late-day sun slanted through the window, making a kind of golden aura behind them. Kincaid wondered if Gretel saw it, too.

She just kept staring into the glass. After a moment, she touched her own breasts with a kind of wonder, as if she had never seen them before. Her nipples, large and rose-colored, stood up to the impingement of her fingers.

"Perfect children." Kincaid's voice was hushed and sweet, his rude hands a miracle of patience at his sides.

"Yes." Gretel's voice sounded solemn, almost sad. "Yes, I believe we will."

So had Kincaid's life as a man begun.

And now, rebelling from his imagination's constraints (and its perfidy, perhaps—Kincaid could not get over his lewd thoughts about the young newlyweds some years ago), his life as a man had sneakily ended. With all he had conjured and wagered on the future, how could visionary Kincaid have failed to foresee, to remedy, to prevail?

Kincaid's middle years had catapulted him into a riskish epoch, when it took real versatility to stave off all that might befall a man's tribe. Long gone the days when survival was a simple hunting-and-gathering proposition.

Kincaid had welcomed the gauntlets the eighties threw down, for he was in his prime, and his greatest talent, aside from his commodious imagination, was flexibility. Punches were made to roll with. In the quarter century of his husbandly existence, he had moved lithely with the transmogrifying times. His home was equipped with electronic eyes on watch against intrusion. His largish lawns watered themselves. His business was computerized, his offspring rigged for a competitive job market, his wife set up in a boutique ("In the Pink," it was called) in the Hoosier Village Mall, a worthy outlet for Gretel's well-known creative urges. So where had he gone wrong? Somewhere along the line, it seemed to Kincaid, he had succumbed to a massive failure of imagination.

On the face of it, Kincaid's existence as he approached his fiftieth birthday was a masterpiece of potential burst into full bloom. He began and ended each day with inventories of gratitude. Gretel had kept her shape, and the shop was turning a profit. Not that they needed it, really. Kincaid Roofing and Siding had hit the big numbers back during the energy crunch and had kept pace with an expanding market ever since. Greater Indianapolis had given way to a serious case of middle-aged spread, its population pooching out all over the place. That management course was sure coming in handy. Kincaid was a delegator now, a strategist, his hands never rubbing up against anything rougher than an OSHA report. He had seventeen guys working for him, plus two secretaries, a full-time mechanic for the trucks, and an accountant.

The life Kincaid had tailor-made for them—Gretel, the kids, and himself—was not, being human in size and shape, perfect. There were dark pockets, of course, lined with the lint of sorrow. The pattern he'd decided on would have accommodated five children, maybe six. Yet when all was said and done, there were only three. There had been a couple of miscarriages after the first child, a son, was born, another before Kirsten came along. . . .

And after that, swift and flattening as a tornado, the surgery that had put a necessary end to Gretel's childbearing.

She had, for some months afterward, been blue and touchy and a little vague. The house had started to look a bit frayed, and Kincaid often caught his wife studying him when she thought he wasn't watching. There was a perplexed look on her face, as if she couldn't quite fathom why he'd keep hanging around.

Still, the children they had, Kirsten not quite two yet, didn't leave much room in the house for ungainly griefs. And three, Kincaid told his wife, "was nothing to sniff at." At which mild remark his wife had copiously wept, while according him neither word nor glance. Indeed, Kincaid had marked during Gretel's convalescence a disconcerting tendency to avoid eye contact. Hormones rearranging themselves could set off some screwball symptomatology, he knew. A man who claimed to be more than a greenhorn in the republic of the female corpus was the worst sort of fool.

Gretel appeared, given time, to bounce back, though her eyes never quite lost their skittishness. Kincaid did not dwell on the loss, applying himself instead to gratitude. The more than quarter century, more than half their lives spent rearing kids, was a dream, the kind where you can't tell much difference between joy and chaos . . . and you don't much care to, either.

So what exactly (a sympathetic listener might inquire, should Kincaid ever begin to unburden himself, which he never would) is the current problem? What has transformed Kincaid into a man with his hands perpetually in his pockets, lint gathering under his chewed nails?

Kincaid, could he confront even for a millisecond the full range of his grief and bewilderment and pure dismay, might lay his head facedown on the nearest available surface and weep like a man whom death and divorce and exile and bankruptcy and global disaster and retribution for sexual excess had befallen in synchronous treachery.

But should the unbreakable Kincaid ever break in this fashion, it is doubtful even then that he should find in his innards the access code to the shame and sorrow festering in that black hole where his heart had so long lodged. What words would he use? What language and measure? How would he arrange the features of his unsaved face?

"Just *say* it, man," the listener (growing a tad impatient) might say. "Out with it, c'mon."

The tectonic plates of Kincaid's entire universe would rumba into upheave and utter wrack. His landscape would be leveled, each brick and branch of the safe-familiar tumbled into the abysmal yawn. No. Kincaid simply could not say it, not even to best friend, physician, family counselor, man of God. (Kincaid's brother-in-law Kenny is in some wise all these—but no. Gretel's big brother? It is out of the question.)

How could Kincaid, his soul a running sore, confess to anyone that he and Gretel have been sleeping in separate bedrooms since . . . well, let's just say for enough nights to add up to more than a couple of years.

He had been too sad, barred that first night from the marital bed, to recognize demise in the loop and slant of what was handwritten among the cornflowers on the guestroom wallpaper. For that very morning, Kirsten, the Kincaids' third, last, and most perfect child, had flown the nest . . .or the *coop*, as Kincaid had regrettably misspoken over lunch, thereby causing Gretel to shed tears afresh over her tortellini salad at the Greenery Café in downtown Indianapolis, to which they had repaired after watching Kirsten's plane take off for California at 11:14 A.M., darting into a cloudless blue that should have been consoling.

The TWA terminal, noisy and crowded, had reeked of nameless meats boiled to a fare-thee-well.

"Come on, sweetie," Kincaid said, aiming for a romantic jauntiness his bruised heart could not but take amiss. "Let's blow this joint. How about I treat my best girl to a nice lunch downtown?"

Gretel, wearing a severe gray suit befitting the departure of foreign dignitaries, wept upon the rock of Kincaid's shoulder. They both knew who his best girl was and had been for the past eighteen years and five months. His jauntiness struck them both as pathetic and smarmy.

"I couldn't eat." Gretel sounded like she was drowning.

"Me neither," Kincaid allowed. "But we've got to do something." They'd both taken the day off from work. Kirsten was their only daughter.

Lunch had been a misery, of course. The sprouts from Kincaid's low-cholesterol plate (called "The Slim Pickens Special" on the simpering menu) had scraped along his throat like barbed wire. Gretel's pasta salad ("Tortellini Fellini"), besogged by her grief, sat between them like a prop.

Kincaid, desperate for something to cling to, plucked a curly and wizened red leaf from the edge of his wife's plate. "What's this supposed to be?"

"Radicchio," Gretel sobbed.

"But what is it *for*?"

"Appearances." His wife's eyes accused Kincaid of low deeds and gaping deficiencies. "As in an arrangement," she snapped. "A *formality*."

The moment was, though he didn't see it then (Kincaid pillaging billfold for his Discover Card, momentary refuge for his red-rimmed eyes, his useless hands), the butt end of something. *Basta. Finis. Finale.* The end of the heretofore smooth road he would in nostalgic hindsight recognize as his life.

Gretel had regained some composure and appetite by sup-pertime. Their grilled chicken breasts and Caesar salad suffered little from the two phone calls that interrupted the meal. Doug called collect from Pennsylvania, where he was in his first year of medical school. Alton Jr., who was with an up-and-comer software firm in Palo Alto, had a company car with a phone in it now and was liable to be calling from just about anywhere.

"How you holding up, Dad?"

"Fine," said Kincaid. "Take a licking and keep on ticking, right?" He felt his throat closing up, signed off fast, and handed the phone to his wife.

Gretel talked to both boys with a breeziness that left Kin-caid aghast with admiration for her recuperative powers. Her lamentations at the airport, the heartbroken folly of their over-priced lunch, became the stuff of comic anecdote. Her laughter sounded wholesome and brave. When Gretel sat back down across from Kincaid at the butcher-block table, though, her mouth was as straight as Route 31 to South Bend and her eyes looked right through him.

Kincaid felt accused somehow. She thinks she's all alone now, he thought. *So where does that leave me?* was a question he could not bear to entertain.

"Things are sure going to be different around here," Kin-caid said, hoping to draw her out. He reached beyond his plate and hers to give her cold fingers some tender handling, but her reply stopped him short.

"Believe it, son," she said.

Son? Kincaid had not been thus addressed since his folks

passed on, and they had both died before he was twenty, leaving Kincaid, their only child, to the care and crabby companionship of an old man in mourning for the disintegration of America's railroads. His grandfather called Kincaid "boy," like a dog.

But "son"—what did it mean, on this of all days, to be thus addressed by one's bride, by the mother of one's perfect children, in that anything-but-maternal tone? Gretel sounded like a cardsharp, a sideshow shill, somebody's idea of an old coot . . . she sounded, did Gretel Kincaid the love of his life, like something suddenly less than a friend.

Kincaid was stumped, as well as heartsore and a little snockered, as he watched his wife stash their pitifully few supper implements in the coppertone KitchenAid dishwasher.

Then, without further word or glance for a Kincaid grown slightly queasy, she marched up the stairs and requisitioned the master bedroom for what would turn out to be this and all nights to come.

That's the thing about an impasse, Kincaid would come to learn: it has *Forever* written all over it.

Things came to a head eventually, of course. More's the pity that Forever lasted four years, seven months, and three days, which is to say one thousand six hundred and seventy-six nights minus those couple of hundred when the kids or overnight guests were on the premises and there were appearances to be thought of. But lying tense as an arm wrestler's tricep on the cold northerly perimeter of a king-size Serta DeLuxe Innercoil while his wife scrunched herself into a tiny south-central plot—why on earth, even if the sum total of Kincaid's lonesome dolor could be quantified, should those nights be subtracted from what his suffering amounted to? It was, the spirit-macerating agglomeration of those hundreds and hundreds of solitary nights, hideous in its prematurity, its lack of pity and reason.

Some mornings, drowned out by the sound of rushing water, Kincaid would stand in the shower stall and, looking into the porthole of his shaving mirror, would cry like a little squirt.

It had come to that.

Doug, against all advice and despite such pressure as Kincaid deemed sporting, got married in his last year of medical school. The heart-to-heart to which Kincaid subjected his second son made not a dent in the nuptial schedule.

"Your life is going to be tougher than an armadillo," Kincaid said, "and not a whole lot prettier, either."

"I guess I know that, Dad."

"I'll keep on paying your tuition, but I can't do much more. The bacon's yours to bring home."

The kid nodded like he'd already figured out that part. "We'll make out," he said.

Doug was, in some respects, Kincaid's least perfect child. He was slight, myopic, stubborn, and brainy. He seemed to have inherited his father's taste for adversity. Kincaid adored him.

"If the girl is pregnant," Kincaid lowered his voice, "there are other options besides matrimony, you know."

"I guess I know that, too." Doug was laughing and Kincaid had to join him—his son had already decided to specialize in OB-GYN.

Kincaid had trouble stopping, once he started laughing. It

felt like something had cracked inside him and whatever kept him on an even keel was leaking out.

"It's going to be okay, Dad." Doug handed him a paper cocktail napkin with a paunchy-looking golfer in a sand trap on it. Kincaid wiped his eyes with the sleeve of his sportcoat and stuffed the napkin over his mouth, trying to stifle hysteria.

"The thing is," Kincaid said, struggling for control, "marriage is . . ."

"No bed of roses?" The kid was trying to help him out.

"That, too." Kincaid sobered and sighed. "More like a confoundment, I was going to say. A man can get pretty balled up."

Doug was examining his father through little wire-framed specs, looking very much, Kincaid realized, like a doctor. Suddenly Kincaid wanted to lay his head down on the table right there in the country club lounge and pour his puny and muddled heart out. To his *son.* Good God. Kincaid rammed a palmful of beer nuts into his mouth.

"Dad, is something wrong with . . . you know?" The kid's face was hosting a war between worry and embarrassment.

"Wrong?" Kincaid said, his cheeks pouched out with nuts. "Nah." He slugged back some Old Milwaukee to rinse out his mouth. "So, when do we get to meet your girl, Dougie?"

"That's one thing I thought maybe I should mention. Max isn't exactly a girl, Dad."

"Max?" Caught mid-swig, Kincaid began to choke. Doug slapped him on the back. Some doctor. I am in a cartoon, Kincaid thought. The hapless father. They ought to put me on a cocktail napkin.

"Maxine, Dad," Doug said. "She's a little older."

Than what, Kincaid wondered, the Statue of Liberty?

"And she's got a little kid."

"Little," Kincaid said. "How little?"

"About yea-high." Doug's smile seemed to glitter in the dim bar. "His name's Reg. He's seven."

Doug must have been getting into his first tux for the prom around the time this woman was going into labor. Big year for both of them.

"Max and Reg," Kincaid said. "Wow. Sounds like a ball team."

"And there aren't going to be any more kids, Dad. Max can't."

"She can't?"

Doug shook his head. "I've thought about that, though, and I've decided it's okay."

A whoosh of air went out of Kincaid, as if he'd taken a punch to the solar plexus.

Doug leaned forward. "Maybe I can't prove it right now," he said, "but I know what I'm doing, Dad." The boy's eyes, behind the thumbprinted lenses of his glasses, were glossy with faith. "It's Max I want," he said. "You know?"

Kincaid had to fumble deep down in his querulous heart for a full minute before he could find what the moment called for. On a TV up in a corner behind the bar the Bulls were creaming the Knicks. Everybody was saying Chicago would never recover from losing Jordan. Still, maybe the kid did right. It was probably better to quit at your peak.

Kincaid reached across the table and snatched his son's pale smooth hand from midair. Then he leaned over and planted a beery kiss in the golden fleece on the back of it.

"You're the lokey man," he said.

———

The first time his daughter-in-law opened her mouth in his presence, Kincaid fell in love with her.

"So this is America." Keen brown eyes whittled their way across the house's redwood facade, around the half-moon driveway, along the three-car garage, and snagged on the gazebo. "Yikes," she said.

Max was a nurse, a tall, broad-shouldered package of sass with an edgy and oddly handsome profile, something like a young Joan Baez, Kincaid thought. Max was from Chicago. She talked out of one side of her mouth, like somebody who'd done time.

They had been married for months by the time Doug brought Max to Indiana to meet the folks. Their so-called wedding at city hall in Philadelphia had been on short notice, a weekend both groom and bride were scheduled off from the hospital. "Next time that happens oughta be right in time for the golden anniversary gala," Max said.

Kincaid and Gretel hadn't even heard about the nuptials until after they were over. It was disappointing, but understandable. Gretel sent Max a locket that had belonged to her grandmother, a dainty bit of filigree she'd have grounds to reconsider once she got a good look at the bride. Kincaid sent Doug a cashier's check for ten thousand dollars, with a note: "Even an armadillo's got a tender spot when it comes to love. Be happy, son. Be brave."

Doug and Max sent a framed picture of the two of them standing in front of the Liberty Bell. Max, who was wearing a red dress and sunglasses with rhinestone frames, looked like she was three or four inches taller than Doug, who had a long-stemmed rose clamped between his teeth. The shades made it hard to guess the bride's age. The rose didn't make Doug look any older.

"Hoo-boy," Kincaid said.

Gretel didn't say anything. But in April, when the kids finally came to visit, Gretel fell in love with her daughter-in-law, too. Max, in the flesh, was irresistible.

"We were sorry your little boy—"

"Reg," Doug said. "He's with his dad this weekend."

"I wish he could have come with you."

"You've been spared," Max muttered from the corner of her mouth. "I just hope my ex is getting everything he deserves. All in one weekend."

A loud laugh busted out of Kincaid. He sneaked a look at Gretel to see how she was taking it.

"Seven-year-olds can be—"

"A real pain in the patoot," Max said.

Gretel's face blossomed in a flamboyant smile, a candescence so long denied Kincaid that he nearly winced at its brightness.

"I remember." Gretel put her arm around her new daughter-in-law's waist and led her up the driveway toward the kitchen door. "And I'd give anything to have my hands full like that again," Kincaid heard her say.

Doug's face looked thin and bushed and utterly love-frazzled. He was waiting, Kincaid saw, for a paternal verdict.

"I say we give her the title," Kincaid said. "Shut this pageant down."

"Yeah." Doug sighed. "Max would be pretty hard to beat."

"If you inherited a smidgeon of your old man's good sense, I don't guess you'll try," Kincaid said, cracking one side of his mouth. "What a dame." He sounded, he thought, like George Raft.

———

Spring had come early to Indiana that year, and stayed, hunkering down and taking over like an overindulgent visiting mother-in-law. The back fence was smothered with azaleas so gaudy that you had to squint to admire them. Jonquils had jumped the sternly edged flower beds to effuse on the lawn. The nights, sometimes so warm that the birds forgot to stop singing, kept Kincaid in a tizzy of yearning.

It was Saturday afternoon, the grass didn't need a trim, and Kincaid felt a sense of well-being sunk so deep in him that it wasn't much different from an ache. Dougie and Max didn't have to fly back to Philadelphia until Monday, so the weekend still seemed uncramped, magnanimous. Tonight the house would be full of their friends, coming over to meet Dougie's bride. A shame Alton Jr. and Kirsten couldn't be there, of course. But they'd be back, they'd always be back. Kincaid looked up at a bachelor-button sky and thought maybe life wasn't such a bad trade-off, really.

Gretel was in the kitchen. It had been ages since she'd baked anything, Kincaid realized. He smelled peaches and cinnamon and butter in the air around the back door, competing with the perfume of the lilacs that bowed and scraped along the side of the garage. They could have used a snipping, but somehow Kincaid's hands lacked their habitual itch. Leave well enough alone, he thought.

Doug and Max, hauling a blanket, a cooler, and a portable cassette player with double headphones, had wandered off to lie in the sun somewhere. Max, wearing a pair of Kincaid's old paisley boxers and a tank top one of the boys had left behind, had smeared Wesson oil on her pasty white legs before they left. "Philadelphia resort wear," she said to Kincaid. "Criminey, I'm a mess."

"You look good enough to eat, honey," Kincaid said.

"Sorry to wilt your willy, bub," Max said. "The doc here says you gotta cut down on fat." She slapped the cushy span of her hips. If ever a woman looked equipped for making babies . . . Kincaid, catching the thought red-handed, shoved it aside and jammed his hands in his pockets.

"She's also a little on the salty side." Doug kissed Max's chin and Kincaid had to look away from the bare adoration in his son's eyes.

He stood in the driveway now, alone, and remembered that look. The kid was gaga over his wife and Kincaid didn't blame him. Wasn't a man supposed to be? Through the kitchen screens Kincaid heard a winsome clatter of pots and pans, a gush of water. On the radio Tony Bennett was singing "I've Got the World on a String" and Gretel was humming along. Kincaid, feeling like a beggar looking for a handout at his own back door, let a breeze give him the bum's rush out to the open land beyond the pampered yard.

The fields were a scalding green and screaming with bugs. Kincaid, somewhat stiff in the knees, set himself a strenuous pace. Insects he couldn't see swarmed his nostrils, jumped up inside his pants cuffs, and weaseled their way into his socks. He felt crawly all over.

He was moving so fast, trampling the weeds so recklessly, that he flushed out a pheasant. "Blam," Kincaid said. "Right between the eyes."

The bird gave him a decidedly jaded look before blustering away through a high screen of feather grass and into a clump of chokeberry.

The midafternoon sun was hellacious and Kincaid was working up to a headache. He aimed for a little dip in the field where a copse of stunted alders crowded around a feeble creek the kids had loved to stir up with their sneakers for those few halcyon years before they discovered video arcades and skating rinks.

Kincaid had never been sure whether the creek was on his property or not. He'd always meant to check out the land survey to figure the exact boundaries. But then the kids were all of a sudden too savvy and hormonal to be dragging him out here and it just didn't matter anymore. Now, though, Kincaid wished he had some way of knowing if it was his own ground he was standing on.

He'd almost made it into the shade when, up to his knees in bindweed, Kincaid came to a frozen halt. The breath felt wrung out of him so hard that he had to bend over a little bit. At the edge of the grove, in a pool of baffling sunlight, lay his son and daughter-in-law, stark naked and flat on their backs.

They were surely asleep, Kincaid thought, or they would have heard him, plunging through the brush like a stag, slamming a lid on birdsong. Their nonchalance irked him. Even with those little plugs and wires in their ears, they should have been alert to his approach, protecting themselves and sparing him.

Kincaid, his ankles snarled in vines, stood rooted to the spot. The sun beat down on his exposed head. Sweat dropped from his brow and stung his eyes.

Their mismatched bodies were white as unsavory jungle blooms, spongy from workdays too rigorous to allow healthy exercise. Yet Doug and Max together possessed a peculiar beauty, a sheer comeliness neither, separately, could approach. Kincaid, feeling indecent and fearful, feasted his eyes on the sight of them, their limbs in a splay of exhaustion and perfect trust. Kincaid recalled a summer about five years ago. Kirsten was in high school, hardly ever home. Gretel kept bringing up the idea of a picnic out here, just the two of them. But the notion of this place without the kids made Kincaid imagine a wasteland and he'd just kept putting Gretel off.

Kincaid's skin felt scratchy and constricting, like a winter suit that no longer fit. The wind shifted. He could hear the sluggish music of the creek he'd imagined must have dried up and vanished because he'd so long neglected to keep an eye on it.

They weren't even touching, Doug and Max, just lying there side by side, asleep on a vaguely familiar old quilt of faded blue and lilac squares.

Kincaid, his head bowed, turned away and walked slowly back to the house, crossing rough land he may or may not have owned. The sun was like a mallet at the back of his head.

Streamers of yellow light from the slatted nightlight in the hallway fell across the master bedroom door. Cordoned off like a murder scene, Kincaid thought. Sealed until further notice.

Max and Doug had taken off that morning after breakfast. The stillness they left behind felt suffocating. Kincaid had watched their rental car pull away with a heart that felt, quite literally, like it was sinking. Their absence rose up and choked him the second he came through the door, home from work.

Now his bare feet sank, mute, into the deep pile of the Oriental runner as he approached the light-striped door and raised a meek fist. Then he found he couldn't do it. Could not even raise a knock on his own door. His hand uncurled and fell to his side, and he just stood there, looking down at the seam of light at the bottom of the door. He wondered if she could hear him breathe.

"Gretel?" he whispered. "Honey?"

Of course she couldn't hear him. He was hardly giving it a try. Kincaid turned from the door and started pacing, making not a dent in the house's implacable silence.

Max and Doug would be working now, at the hospital, jet-lagged and wired on long-stewed coffee, perhaps meeting like strangers with eyes on the make in some elevator or underground passageway. Something lewd might escape from the corner of Max's mouth. Dougie might sneak a love tap to his wife's white nylon flank. But they'd keep on the move. They had to. At dawn, as Kincaid stumbled to the curb for his morning paper, the newlyweds would finally be getting to bed. Reg, Doug said proudly, dressed himself, made his own breakfast and even his own sack lunch, on such mornings. The schedule constantly changed. Kincaid imagined the boy heading into the day alone, without fuss, so his mother and the kid she married could grab their few hours of rest. What kind of life . . .

"I don't envy them," Kincaid murmured. Then he clenched his jaw. The lie felt like something tough and gritty caught between his teeth.

Like a sleepwalker, Kincaid wound up in the bathroom without quite knowing how he got there. At night Gretel kept a fat candle burning in a little milk-glass dish on the back of the commode. As if there were always small children or guests in the house, Kincaid thought. The candle's waxy vanilla fumes made his eyes run.

He did not understand how he could feel so tired and still be unable to sleep. Gretel didn't sleep much either, he knew. Sometimes the TV was still on at three, four in the morning, and Kincaid would hear a woman weeping: Lana Turner, Bette Davis, Loretta Young. Joan Crawford was the one who really got to him, though. When a woman that tough broke, it was something to cry about. Kincaid hoped Max never cried. Or, if she did, that he'd never have to see it.

Kincaid tore off two squares of toilet paper and blotted his eyes. Then, the heels of his hands heavy on the rim of the sink, he leaned over and looked into the mirror above the vanity.

The flame's dim and unsteady light, catching him from below and off to one side, brought out the worst in his face, distorting his features into a tapestry of shadows and unwholesome creases. I even look like a stranger, he thought. He wanted to turn around, slip off his bathrobe, study the whole of himself in the full-length mirror on the back of the door. But he was afraid what he might see. He weighed exactly what he'd weighed when he got married—his weight had never varied more than a pound or two. But his body hardly looked familiar anymore.

Overcome by weariness, Kincaid shut his eyes for a moment. The picture that came to him, displacing his own sad-sack face, was indelible: his son and daughter-in-law, just the two of them, bathed in sunlight. The keen beauty of their slack and ill-proportioned bodies cut into his mind's eye like a shaft of light, sudden and far too bright. When Kincaid opened his eyes, he couldn't see a thing.

He groped for the light switch, but he couldn't find it, could not even remember where it was supposed to be. He twisted around and his arms were, for one panicky moment, hopelessly entangled in the shower curtain, clammy and slick. He banged his shin on the edge of the tub as he flailed his way out into the hall, stumbling on the fringe of the runner, catching himself on a bookcase before he fell. The feckless husband, he thought. A cartoon.

Kincaid crimped his eyelids tightly together, colluding with the dark. He needed neither eyes nor light to find his way to the bedroom.

"Gretel?" he said. Then he twisted the fluted brass knob and the door swept open wide for him. It had probably never, Kincaid realized, been locked. He had always wondered, but he'd never touched it.

Gretel had fallen asleep with the television on. She looked lost, Kincaid saw, in the wide white bed, a mountain range of snowy lace-edged pillows surrounding her. It shocked him to discover that even without him there, Gretel confined herself to a stingy portion of the mattress's southerly edge.

"Honey?" Kincaid said.

Her eyes clicked fully open, wide and glassy.

"Are you awake?" Kincaid said.

Gretel sat up, clutching the covers to the frilly front of her nightgown. "What's wrong?" she said.

Her beauty, his own lack of immunity to it, sideswiped Kincaid's heart. He sucked in his breath and held it.

"Alton, are you all right?"

"No," Kincaid said. "I don't believe I am."

Gretel started to get up, the blanket slipping from her bosom. Her nightgown was satin, the color of French vanilla ice cream. "Are you sick?"

Kincaid shook his head. "Don't get up," he said. "You don't need to."

Gretel stayed poised on the edge of the bed, one foot dangling to the floor. Her painted toenails were scarlet droplets on the bone-white rug.

Kincaid turned and switched off the television, choking off the sound of a great many people laughing cooperatively.

"I need to talk to you," he said. "This may or may not be an emergency."

When he turned around Gretel was staring at him. Her eyes, very green in the lamplight, were twin signals of blinking alarm. "It's the middle of the night," she said.

"It's eleven-forty," Kincaid said gently.

"I was asleep."

"I know," he said. "I'm sorry."

She sighed.

"I need to ask you something," Kincaid said.

"Couldn't it wait?" She was sufficiently awake and reassured to be cranky now, which Kincaid found strangely comforting.

"I don't think so." He swallowed hard. "I would like to know if you love me," Kincaid said. "Or if you ever did."

"Love you." She was stalling for time. Humoring him. Making no promises. Kincaid didn't blame her. She thought she was having a conversation with a lunatic in her nightgown in the middle of the night. "I married you," Gretel said cautiously. "Didn't I?"

"You did." Kincaid nodded. "You married me and made me . . . whatever it is that I am."

She started to say something, then stopped herself, her lips remaining slightly parted.

"You didn't answer my question," Kincaid said.

She just kept staring at him.

"I am your friend," he said quietly. "You can tell me."

"Of course I loved you." Gretel sighed.

"Then?" Kincaid said. "When you married me?"

She nodded.

"And now?"

Her pursed mouth gave way just a little. "Always," she said, the word like a small defeat.

"There," Kincaid said. "Was that so hard?"

"Why are you doing this?" Her eyes had a trapped look. "I don't understand."

Kincaid sat down heavily at the foot of the bed. He could not look at her now. "Gretel," he said in a low, hoarse voice, "the brunt may be coming up to where it's more than I can handle."

"You're tired," she said. "You work too hard."

Kincaid shook his head. "What I am," he said, "is lost." He looked up, scanning the room, eyes everywhere but on his wife. "This would appear to be my life," Kincaid said. "But I seem to have got myself misplaced."

"Can you tell me," Gretel said, "what you're talking about?"

"In all likelihood," Kincaid said, "no." He turned then, taking in his wife's face. Gretel looked pale, puzzled, even sympathetic. But what was she thinking? That he could not venture a guess terrified him.

Next door a car started up, then the engine was cut off again, as if somebody had forgotten where it was they meant to go. Kincaid got up, walked a few feet from the bed, then paused there. After a moment, he unknotted the sash of his maroon velour robe. He let the robe drop to the floor, where it spread around his feet like a harrowing stain.

When he turned around the lamp shot a bolt of light into his eyes and Gretel was a mere outline against the huge white bed. "Do you see me?" Kincaid whispered. "Am I still here?"

During the incalculable moment of his waiting, it dawned on Kincaid that the birds were singing again, or still, oblivious to the dark, the late hour. At the windows the white curtains puffed out, then flattened, then puffed out again, as if the house were breathing.

Then Gretel was moving toward him, into the shadows,

where it was not quite so hard to see. As she moved closer, Kincaid's orphaned imagination made mirrors of her eyes and he saw himself there and he was very small.

Gretel leaned down and picked up his robe, wrapping it around him, holding it tightly closed under his chin. "I'm here, too," she said.

Kincaid hardly noticed that she led him to the bed, pulled the covers over him, turned out the light. He only knew that as they lay there in the dark they huddled close together, like children lost or left behind. The birds kept singing as if they'd forgotten how to stop.

Finally, at the very same moment, Kincaid and Gretel fell asleep. It was steep, their fall, and swift. They slept as children will, pure tuckered out by long and labyrinthine days of trying to fathom a world they keep losing track of in dreams.

Adult

Education

*S*eems like we do everything backward, Gabriel and me. Which wouldn't be surprising if we were the kids we been acting like. But Gabriel, he's nearly fifty, and I am forty-four. You might think by now a body'd have better sense.

On the night we met, which was on a New Haven city bus that petered out at rush hour in a part of town makes you want to hold your breath till it's behind you, like a cemetery, we wound up in bed. Just to get acquainted. Things worked out so good there, couldn't see much reason not to keep on like we started.

"I mean to get to know you real good." Gabriel declared it in a testifying way. Nobody having said as much to me before, not even the two men who married me, I wanted to shout Hallelujah! and Amen. Seems like Gabriel's making some kind of believer out of me.

Still, it's hard to excuse myself for doing something so crazy, going off with a man I didn't know from Adam and landing between his sheets like that. I'm not trying to excuse myself when I say it might have been because I was just so cold.

And because he was so kind when the world looked anything but.

A lot of people got off that bus the minute the motor died. The black smoke spouting up out of it was not a hopeful sign. But me, I was far from home and in no place a woman would care to find herself alone after dark, which would be soon. My car battery had died that morning. I couldn't see but the one choice: sticking it out.

I was squeezed in beside the window in a two-seater toward the back. The man beside me had his bony knees stuck halfway out into the aisle in a way I could tell meant not to crowd me. With the trousers of his post office uniform pressed so slick, he looked more like somebody on his way to work than from. But his delivery bag lay on the floor between us flat empty, and if the man that dropped it there stood up he'd be, you could tell, a little stooped. His crispy close-cut hair was dabbed with white around his ears and high forehead, like somebody'd got after him with a powder puff. Wiry as it was, it looked like it would be the softest thing to touch, that hair.

He caught me peeking sidewise. "Our lucky day." When he smiled his brown face creased into long wrinkles along his cheeks and short ones around his eyes. His eyes, small and dark and shiny, somehow made plain what a deep-down nice person lived behind them.

"That way so far." I smiled back. "You figure sundown should change things?"

He looked like he was thinking it over. "Been a tough one?"

"Just my car picked this morning to give up on living." I shrugged. "We all gotta go sometime."

The bus heater wasn't working, of course. His laugh warmed the air between us. "That's a thing I admire," he said, "a philosophical outlook."

"Yeah, well, life's a good teacher," I said. "Strict."

He nodded. "Still," he said, "evenings ought to be more kindly than mornings, don't you think?"

Lotta things oughta be a way they ain't was what I thought to say. But his face had a peaceful look I didn't want to chase away with hard words. It was just a broke-down bus, after all, not the end of the world.

"We're liable to set here awhile," I said. "You may as well lean back."

He studied on me for a few seconds. His fudge-color eyes had a look like I said something to startle. After a minute, though, he eased into the ratty seat and swiveled his knees in, close beside mine but not touching.

"Person in your line of work must be right run-down," I said, "by the end of a day."

"Run-down and wrought up." He sighed.

We didn't have a good lot to talk about, him and me, but we made do the way strangers will when they get stranded like that. He told me about things that happened to him, out carrying the mail. It sounded like a combination of fighting in a war and working in a mental home. He showed me where a dog had torn up his wrist weeks before. The skin there was pink as my own, but mending nicely. He also told me about an old lady years back who'd come out naked as a jaybird to take the mail from his hand before he could drop it through the slot in her door, morning after morning.

"Not that the poor soul got a thing but bills and circulars," he said.

He knew it was a sad story he was telling and I liked how he didn't try to make it sound funny.

"It was me first noticed when she passed," he said. "One morning she didn't come out. All the lights burning away inside like it was nightfall. I took one look at that window and I called 911. I just knew," he said.

"It's like that with bad things," I said. "You'll feel them coming."

He gave me a sweet off-kilter smile. "Sometimes with good things, too," he said.

Right across the aisle from us, up overhead, was this sign: ADULT EDUCATION. A little notepad was attached, where you could tear off a slip to sign up for evening classes.

He was bound to notice, after a while, how my eyes would wander after that sign whenever our talk stalled out.

"I got that in the back of my mind," he said.

"Going back to school?"

"Likely to have time on my hands once I retire."

"What would you take?"

It was an idle question, but answered so quick I knew he'd spent a good bit of time with it. "History," he said. "A man oughtn't to leave this world without some understanding what makes it tick."

"Be nice, wouldn't it?" I said. "Things starting to look like they might make some sense."

He nodded. "What about you?"

"Not me," I said. "School near about killed me the first time."

"But you're different now," he said. "Ain't you." Wasn't no way I could take it for a question.

The sign's red letters seemed to glow above us as the bus got dimmer.

"One of them classes on how to read faster might not hurt," I told him after a spell. "I got some catching up to do."

"Don't we all." His smile fell short, seemed like, of what it was aiming for.

After the most part of an hour, when the bus still hadn't so much as coughed or spit and the stand-in bus never came, he stood up. A tall lanky man, he was a bit stooped like I expected.

"You giving up?" I said.

"Hollering uncle," he said. "Uh-huh."

"Good luck," I said. "Nice talking with you."

He just stood there, looking down at me. The day's last light had dwindled near to nothing and I couldn't make out the features on his dark face. Then, bending to retrieve his mail pouch, he dipped into a stream of streetlamp light trickling through the window. I caught sight of the gentleness in his eyes and smiled again.

"Come on," he said. "I'll see you get home."

"That's okay," I said.

He sank back down in the seat beside me. I slanted my face toward the window. Traffic was in a snarl all around us. I could feel him studying me.

"I'll get there," I said. "I always do."

"You don't rightly know me, do you?" He sounded surprised.

When I turned to look he was holding out his hand. "Gabriel Thurston Bolling," he said. "Jr."

"Pleased." The way I took his hand must have cried out I didn't want to.

"You got to trust somebody," he said. "Besides, your lips are blue."

"Been told it's my best color," I said. "Blue."

His kindly face crinkled with that smile again. "My brother-in-law borried my car, but I reckon he'll be back by now." *Borried*, he said, just like my people back home. "I'll get us a lift to my place, then drive you."

No rapist's apt to be walking around in a postman's uniform was what I told myself, never mind with all that sweetness in a smile. When I followed Gabriel off the bus I couldn't feel my feet, which made walking kind of tricky. He held to my arm as I climbed down the steps.

Him finding us a cab in two minutes flat dropped a miracle into a day everything had up to now seemed bent on going wrong in. He wouldn't let me even pay my share. "Let me be an angel of mercy," he said. "For once." He sounded right serious about it.

The man driving the cab was white and old and looking at us kind of nasty, like he was certain a black man and a white woman together couldn't amount to no good. It made me mad enough to let Gabriel pay because it seemed like he needed to have some pride about it, only I hoped he wouldn't give the old man a tip, which he did.

"You got a mighty kindness about you, sir." I said it plenty loud enough for the driver to hear.

The taxi peeled away from the curb in a way made clear getting slush all over us was no accident. I didn't mind so much about me, but when I saw Gabriel's blue-gray uniform all wet and spotty—well, I must've been plain worn out, I guess. How else could something like that start me crying?

Gabriel said a word I ain't been hearing in the longest time, not since I was a child. *Pshaw*. Then he said it a couple or three more times in a velvety voice like singing a lullaby.

"Pure meanness," I said. My teeth were chattering.

"Don't amount to—" Gabriel took hold of my arm and

steered me into a house I couldn't, between darkness and tears, hardly see.

"Need to get you warmed up," he said. "That's what."

We were in a little vestibule. I remember it smelled like toast.

I remember that he took my boots off for me and left me in a big old armchair with my stocking feet on a heat grate in the floor.

I remember my wet coat hung on a brass hook beside the door and an afghan snugged up around my shoulders. The afghan was all different colors and a cup of something hot was between my hands.

"What is this?" I asked him.

"Just sugar and water, mostly." He smiled. "And a little something to take the chill off."

I can't for the life of me remember how we got up the stairs. But I know the going wasn't against my will and that for the longest time I did not stop crying.

Gabriel's bed lies wide and smooth under a soft Indian cotton bedspread the color of strong tea. He has a whole lot of pillows. The pillows mostly have jungle animals' faces and are fringed or tasseled on the ends.

I don't even own a bedspread. I sleep on a foldout foam rubber contraption that tries to look and act like a chair in the daytime. Its stubbly plaid covering leaves a rash on my skin.

Imagine how different things would have turned out if it was my place we went to that first night.

I haven't let Gabriel see where I live yet. I got to do some fixing up first.

I had me some decent furniture once. Well, twice, to tell

the truth. The exes have it now. First time around I told Buddy to keep everything. He was so sad about me leaving like I had to. And the way he grew up, his mama run off with his baby sister, and his daddy yanking him from one trailer park to another until he knew every dead-end road in northern Kentucky, Buddy was real partial to permanent things. I even let him keep my mama's collection of pink Depression glass, though I told him I might ask for it back one day.

"Gloriacious," he said (that's the name Buddy made up for me; I'm really only Glory), "you come back anytime. You can have everything back." His eyes took a deep dive into mine. "All of it," he said. "Anytime."

"You never know," I said. Which I guess was a little white lie.

Buddy's round face went all pink and puckered. I took off maybe a little quicker than a woman ought to have after six years, but I meant it as a kindness. The cleaner the break, likelier the healing. I never looked back. Buddy must've known I wouldn't.

The second batch of furniture was harder to part with. Curtis Randolph sold used cars outside of Wheeling and did real well for a drunk. He saw to it that I got things even my dreams never bargained for: a red velvet humpback loveseat that looked like a Valentine candy box, an honest-to-God Tiffany lamp. Our maple dining room suite come with not just a sideboard, but a hutch. Mama's Depression glass would have gone so nice on those shelves, when I think about it. And that glass was all she had to leave me when she passed on. But Curtis would've only smashed it all up one Saturday night. I might still be picking pink glass slivers out of my sorry hide now, if I hadn't thought to be good to Buddy on my way out the door.

Like it was, I was lucky to get loose of Curtis with a couple changes of clothes. I made off with one satchel and two shopping bags. That time I did look back, I can tell you. I hardly knew where I was headed except for out, and far, and quick. My eyes stayed in the rearview mirror of that turquoise Mustang that was thank God in my name, until Pittsburgh. Even now, ten years later and four states between us, I'll catch myself glancing over my shoulder every now and again. Curtis wasn't one to give up easy on anything he felt entitled to.

So I maybe haven't got much to show for myself . . . never figured to stay in this little apartment so long, I guess. One good look at this place would be apt to put a steady soul like Gabriel's in mind of words like *fly by night . . . will o'the wisp.* Next thing he'd get to wondering if a woman with so little wouldn't be bound to want, to *need,* too much. Going to his place, anyhow, means I can leave whenever I want.

I had never been so naked, I remember thinking that first time. Gabriel's skin is a deep, dark brown so smooth you'd think it was polished. I got to feeling almost lonesome, lying there beside him in a skin seems pale enough to see through. My hide is no home to me, no protection or resting place. I wanted to crawl inside Gabriel's skin, just stay there safe and hid.

But his hands wouldn't let me be, no. Gabriel's hands took me places I'd never thought to go, places beyond naming or intending. Sounds unheard-of filled the dark, one minute growls, pure song the next, wild noise my own throat could not deny having everything to do with. I was the stranger to be scared of, not Gabriel.

When he asked me why was I crying I said I didn't know.

I had never been so naked.

The words that passed between Gabriel and me those first couple of weeks you could write on an envelope and still have room for an address and a postage stamp. He told me about growing up in Pennsylvania not a hundred miles from where I was reared myself, and about his daddy dying young with the black dust in his lungs. He told me about coming to New Haven after he got out of the Army because an uncle there said he could get him a post office job. Gabriel told me about his wife, but no more than I needed to know.

Evelyn Grand Bolling, Ph.D.—I saw her name all official on an envelope left lying on the kitchen counter—is younger than Gabriel or me. And greedier, I'd guess, than a person's got call to be. She got what she wanted off him—education and a meal ticket and a government pension to look forward to—then lit out for California and a job where she can tell a bunch of people what to do, which sounds like what she is best at. This Evelyn got everything she wanted and she doesn't want Gabriel.

"So how come y'all aren't divorced?" I said. "Not that it's any of my beeswax."

"She don't believe in divorce. You make your bed you got to lie in it, Evelyn says."

"She don't appear to be doing much of that."

"I been on the back burner a good while, Glory." Gabriel said it like he thought that's just where he deserved to wind up.

It's not like he's a married man, I tell myself. Not really.

"Are you waiting for her?" I ask him. "I mean, do you expect she'll be back?"

"I been waiting for something." Someday I must tell Gabriel that so small and tender a smile is not to be risked in a world like this one we got. "Maybe it's you," he says.

"Hush." It's not a sound you can give sharp edges to. "Gabriel, don't," I say.

His smile just goes on taking chances.

I always leave by eleven o'clock. I never promise I'll be back. But Gabriel knows. He'll put on his house shoes and, no matter how cold it is, he'll walk me to my car. "Be seeing you." He'll say it like a promise. When he punches down the lock button and closes the car door, it feels like he's tucking me in.

Gabriel's house is narrow across the front, just room for one small window beside the front door. He keeps the curtains drawn night and day. The house is wood and painted blue. At night the street light makes the paint look purple and you can't see how it is peeling. Sometimes I drive by during the day, when I know Gabriel's off on his mail route, just to look at his house, to keep a clear picture of it and to know its true color. At night it always looks different again. I want to remember everything.

Gabriel's two hands reach out like one thing and pull me into his vestibule, where it is always warm. He kneels down and pulls off my boots. The round rag rug on the linoleum floor is bumpy and warm through my thin cotton socks. Gabriel's hands are under my coat, inside my sweater. He closes the door by pushing me against it. I lean there, my clothes falling away, dropping to the floor, light and soundless as curls of peeling paint.

I am naked at the front door of Gabriel's house and he is naked, too. The television is on in the next room, the only light. I stand out white and chilly as the moon, while Gabriel melts into the warm dark. I smell bacon and toast, lemon dish soap, and floor wax. Gabriel's house is cleaner, warmer, than any place I ever lived.

My fingers are digging into his back, narrow and hard and smooth. My own back, pressed up against the wooden panels of the door, arches. Gabriel is leaning down, his open mouth feeding on the skin and muscle between my arm and breast. I wonder what I taste like there, bitter or salty or sweet. Gabriel smells like grass.

"Upstairs?" he says, one word. I picture a hand, neither his nor mine, writing it. The envelope is still mostly blank. There is room yet for a list of what we might run out of, a long foreign address, wings stamped in blurry blue, a simple map to a place some ways away, where I've never been before.

"Glory?" he says. "Honey?"

I want plenty of space left for things I might need to say later. I shake my head. Then I kneel down, there in the dark vestibule, my knees creased by the ridges in the rag rug that I need to remember is brown and gold like October.

I wonder if Gabriel leaves the TV on to give God something to watch when we're best left on our own.

I was, as a youngster, forever falling in love—not just with boys, I mean, but with old folks, little children, bus drivers and librarians and clerks in the five-and-dime. Anybody who'd bother to show me kindness, was what it came down to, I expect. Recklessly I'd attach myself at the flimsiest excuse, hanging around where, stumbled over, I might stand the least chance of being invited in.

"Glory," my mama would ask me, "you been making a nuisance of yourself?" Then she'd remind me of these little sayings she was partial to: *Absence makes the heart grow fonder. Good fences make good neighbors.* And: *Familiarity breeds contempt.*

I tried for the longest time to disbelieve the truth she meant to acquaint me with. But life makes no bones about teaching the hard way what your mama would try to soften, of course.

Gabriel says, "Why you want to make yourself so scarce around here, Glory? Don't you know I been missing you?"

"Busy," I tell him. "Things I got to get done." And if I happen to be looking into his eyes right then, I'll maybe say, "I missed you, too," or some such. The part about not wanting to be a nuisance I keep to myself.

The third week, on the nights I don't show up at his house, Gabriel starts calling me up. We've never talked on the phone before and the first time he calls I get all rough-tongued and shy, like a teenager.

He asks how was my day.

"Fine," I say. Which it must have been, since I can't recall a thing about it. I went to work, I guess, because if I didn't that would be something to remember.

I clean houses in the pretty little towns along the shore, Guilford and Madison mostly. I hardly know the people I work for, because they're off at work all day. There are two young couples without children, and four singles. I keep them straight in my mind by what their belongings ask of me: Mondays the oriental rugs and parquet floors, Fridays the eggshell wall-to-wall shag needs fluffing up with a bamboo rake after it's hoovered. Wednesday, though, is the worst: huge white-tiled his-and-hers kitchen with double everything and the copper-bottom pots that always need scouring. I can't for the life of me figure what two people could be doing with so much food. Not to mention three bathrooms.

"That's it, fine?" Gabriel laughs into the phone and I feel warm breath on my ear. I go weak in the knees.

"What's up?" I say.

"Just checking on you," he says.

"You don't need to." I sound a little huffy. He must figure being so loose with him, I wouldn't draw the line elsewhere.

"Hey," he says. "I said *checking*, not checking up." Which leaves me nothing to say at all.

"I was just missing you, Glory."

"Oh," I say.

"And also I wanted to ask you something."

I wait.

"Can I take you out to dinner?" Gabriel says. "I was thinking Saturday night."

"Why would you want to do that?"

"Why wouldn't I?" He laughs again.

All I want to do is touch him. "You mean like a date?" I say.

"Like I should have done in the first place." Gabriel's not laughing anymore. "I want to treat you right," he says.

"You treat me fine," I say, thinking how we've never had to keep being ourselves with anybody else watching and that might be hard and I don't want a thing about us to change.

"I know this real nice Italian place."

"We got to decide this now?"

"Give me time to get a good hard shine on my shoes."

"Gabriel Bolling," I say to him, "what are you up to?"

"Just making some plans," he says. "There's a few things need doing, Glory."

"Well, if it's me they'll be done to, you'd best let me in on it."

His laugh is rough and warm as pure wool. "I want to court you, is all."

"You think we're kids?"

"I know we're not. That's just it. I got serious intentions."

Well, that about knocks me over.

"Want my friends to meet you, Glory. I got a mind to take you places, show you off, see you eat right."

"I eat just fine," I say. "And I'm hardly a thing to show off."

He goes quiet for a moment, sad like he gets whenever I try to make light of myself.

"Gabriel?" I say. "Aren't we past such as that?"

"I got things to make up for," he says after a while.

"You got nothing to make up for," I tell him. "Besides, what's the point of trying to go back?"

I can almost hear him thinking. "Go back far enough," he says, "I might find you all over again."

My throat's shut tight, like a door swelled up with dampness.

"You reckon folks like us could get that lucky twice?" Gabriel asks me.

"If luck's what this is," I tell him, "maybe we oughtn't push it."

"Hadn't thought of taking a lady out to dinner like that, pushing my luck." He tries to make a chuckling sound, but it snags on hurt somewhere at the back of his throat. If I was sitting beside him, my fingertips would find their way to what words can't mend or comfort.

"I hate the telephone," I say. "You know it?"

"Come over," Gabriel tells me.

"It's cold," I tell him. "It's late."

"I'll come there."

Reckon he hears my No in the silence I can't quite say it into.

"All right," Gabriel says softly. "It's all right."

"Just seems we maybe shouldn't rush things, is all."

"Already done that, I'd say."

And now we got to pay for it, is what I hear myself thinking. I know it don't make the least sense. "Gabriel?"

"I'm right here," he tells me.

"I know." I try to picture his face, as if *right here* really was where I could find him, touch him. But the face I see, mean as a mug shot, is that taxi driver's. How would I ever be able to eat, somebody looking at me and Gabriel that way? "Could we just wait on that dinner a little while?"

"We can do whatever you want," Gabriel tells me. "You just got to let me know what you're ready for."

And what about what I ain't ready for?

My bones recall the warmth of him. My chapped fingers already know the flow of his blood, so close below the skin that clothes him. Right at my fingertips . . . would living there teach me, in time, to ask what I need to? A body moves backwards long enough, could it turn out to be forward she's been moving all along, only just with her back turned on what's ahead?

I'm still trying to figure it out the next evening when, around six, Gabriel calls again.

"I'm making grilled cheese sandwiches," he says. "You want one?"

When I say sure, he asks do I want tomato on it.

The first time we went to bed together it was like we both knew everything we needed to know about each other. Eating with Gabriel, though, is liable to take some getting used to.

The grilled cheese sandwiches are huge and messy—great hunks of buttery black bread with two kinds of cheese, yellow and white, slices of tomato, chopped black olives, hot peppers, and avocado.

"I got carried away," Gabriel says. He is wearing a clean white shirt, nice gray slacks with a pleated front. He's got a dish towel looped through his belt.

"I guess you did." The table is covered with a pressed yellow cloth. Real napkins, green cotton with fringed edges. A big skillet of fried potatoes sits in the middle, on a quilted pot holder shaped like a turtle. A whole bunch of little glass bowls congregate in the middle of the table—ketchup, mustard, okra pickles, deviled eggs. Two tall glasses with ice in them. Two cans of Dr Pepper.

Gabriel stands there for a moment and looks over the table, frowning. His eyes are sharp and full of worry, like a school crossing guard. "Almost ready," he says. He puts two red candles in glass holders on either side of the skillet, lights them, then turns out the overhead light. He helps me with my chair.

While I'm trying to think of something to say, Gabriel jumps up from the table. In a second he's back, sprinkling paprika on the four deviled eggs.

"There," he says.

When Gabriel sits down across from me, his face is damp and the candlelight shines on it. I want to reach across the table and unbutton his shirt. He looks like a husband, I think. For a second I need to close my eyes.

"Glory?"

My eyes pop open. "Just saying grace," I say.

He smiles at me. "Amen." Then his hands get busy, piling food on a huge blue plate which he hands me when no room is left on it.

"What are you trying to do to me?" I ask him.

Gabriel just smiles and smiles, like we both know the answer to that and nothing else needs saying.

I could never eat half what he's given me, but I'd best try. He's not about to let me touch him again, I'm sure of it, until I've cleaned my plate.

When he asks am I ready, I say I reckon I am.

How is it that, coming together so gently, we wind up breathless and bruised? For all I can't be certain of, I know I have never run into a thing as tender as Gabriel's loving, as careful as his hands. Still, the loving seems to carry us away to some place where what is running us has stronger concerns than looking after limbs, skins. Never for a moment has his touch ever hurt me. Mornings in the shower, though, I'll find these petals of pale blue and lilac opening up on my skin. How on earth do they get there? They almost seem like miracles, marks of holiness, like those saints that would start bleeding for no good reason but maybe God's.

I do not bleed anymore. I stopped early, like my mama did, which seems to me just as well. I was never cut out to be having babies, not anyhow when looking after myself turned out to be such a job. It took every bit of strength I had just to put that low sorry corner of West Virginia I started from behind me. I been being careful all my life. Now, in one way at least, I don't need to anymore, which strikes me as a blessed thing.

These thoughts that come riding through my head now, raising little swirls of dust, stuff about blessedness and God and holy wounds, aren't like me. It isn't that I don't believe, but I can't say as I've had more than a passing acquaintance with the

Lord. I've mostly just tried to be decent and to trust that would suit Him. Now, though, when I'm behaving a far cry from decent, when I can scarcely think of a thing worth wanting but somebody else's husband, it seems like God's all over me. "Hey," I feel like asking Him, "where You been keeping Yourself?"

Sometimes it makes me want to laugh, this idea that the Lord's taking a sudden interest in my life. I don't mean no disrespect. It's just, how else could all this happen? How could backwards turn out to be the right way to go about things, unless it's God giving the directions?

I lay in that big bed now, the jungle animals gone all tame and Gabriel wrapping every bit of himself around me, and I can't help believing God's come into it somewhere. How else are you going to explain the two of us who both got cars riding the bus one single night and finding each other in New Haven, this place such a far cry from where either of us belong?

Or the light in Gabriel's eyes that, when the light goes off, seems enough to see by?

Or me, all of a sudden singing?

Outside the March night is cold and windy and wet. Below, on the street, somebody curses. A car caterwauls around a corner and a metal trash can crashes to the pavement. The wind slaps the window with a sheet of freezing rain and the glass rattles in its loose frame.

When Gabriel sleeps he gets hotter and hotter. I wonder what is burning him up inside and if the heat is something his dreams have learned to cater to.

It must be long past midnight. I know I should make myself scarce. I just can't remember why. I keep thinking of Evelyn, Gabriel's wife, who even in California must get cold at night.

Between my legs I am wet and warm, a little tender. For a

moment, what with the dark, I can almost believe I am bleeding again.

Gabriel's head is lying on my belly, the weight and heat of it like something I just gave birth to, a creation come of the extra blood and flesh and bone I didn't know I carried in me. And now the cord that runs between us might be cut, but what ties us one to the other will always be there, strong and permanent and severe.

"Glory?" Gabriel whispers.

"I'm still here," I say.

"Don't go," he says, "all right?" He is talking in his sleep.

He would wake up if I asked him to. He would leave the warm mussed bed and, without putting on a light, would gather up our clothes, sort them out. He would button my blouse up to the chin and smooth down my hair. He would not want me to leave but would help me to go, if I told him that's what I wanted.

"Go?" I say. For a moment I can't imagine where. It has slipped my mind that I might live anywhere else.

Some kids with a boom box are raising Cain across the way, over where the project preoccupies the street with ugly red bricks and barred windows and heartache. They are high on something, those kids, always high and bound for trouble. I am praying for them in the back of my mind, wanting them to live through everything long enough to get to the place where I am now. Those kids deserve to know, I tell the Lord, what I am learning.

"Gabriel?" I whisper.

He hitches himself upwards. "What is it, love?" He sounds a little scared.

"Tomorrow you'll come eat at my place," I whisper. "All right?"

His head settles on my breast. His breathing evens out. Gabriel's mouth is always on me somewhere, his breath hot as July.

"I'll ask you again in the morning," I tell him. "In case you forgot."

I chance a tiny, defenseless smile on the drowsing animals. My throat is full of praise. Blue wildflowers spring up on my skin. I can feel them blooming in the dark.

Song-and-
Dance Man

eth, you're growing wistful."

Seth Branfeldt looked up from the quartered *Virginian-Pilot* wedged in beside his breakfast plate. His baby-blues were dreamy.

"You *are*." LaDonna, Branfeldt's former leading lady in the Toledo Footlighters and his wife of twenty years, emoted an award-winning sigh. "Darling, don't tell me you're not."

At forty-six, Seth Branfeldt wore the face of a Little League All-Star. The freckles on his snubby nose had neglected to fade. His hair was red and thick and plucky. But too much time in the sun and a tardy parting with Pall Malls had left his boyishness looking pickled, hermetic. Frisking his plump repertoire, Branfeldt hit upon a hankering curve of lip, the one his Billy Bigelow broke hearts with. *Carousel*. Held over two weeks, he remembered.

"Shit," Medea, his daughter, said. "He's gonna sing."

Branfeldt gazed at his child with what he hoped passed for pathos.

"Pass on it, Dad, okay?"

The girl, an acerbic seventeen, had real presence. Branfeldt winked at his wife, then sucked in some air. It all started in the diaphragm.

Soon, Branfeldt sang, she would leave him. His voice grew so plaintive, he felt like he could *see* it: his baby girl gone off in the mist of day, never to *know* . . .

He got choked up.

LaDonna fluttered her eyelashes like Carol Channing.

"Always some routine." Medea, her Levi's so snug she moved like a mermaid, snaked a curvaceous hip out from behind the breakfast nook table. "You guys," her exit line, was tossed off in a huff.

Branfeldt applauded.

LaDonna snatched the paper and clouted him on the ear.

Upstairs a door slammed.

"We bombed," Branfeldt said.

"Not the first time, sweetie."

"Or the last."

Branfeldt looked around the breakfast nook, recently redecorated. Snagged velvet shades looped with gold cord hung at the windows. The walls were plastered with playbills, posters, rave reviews. Over his wife's right shoulder Branfeldt, a callow Marryin' Sam at twenty-five, was leering at his then-betrothed. LaDonna's cleavage was framed by an off-the-shoulder polka dot blouse. "The kid's got talent," he said.

"Why do I encourage you?" LaDonna said.

Branfeldt grinned. "Somebody's got to."

But LaDonna was back to the original script. "You're living in the past again, Seth."

"I am living, dear heart, in paradise." Branfeldt flipped his paper to the real estate page. "I'm a stranger, is all," he said.

When he looked up again his wife was gazing out the window. Gold curls lapped at her cheeks. LaDonna was still a showstopper. But her ingenue days were over. Branfeldt wondered what she was staring at. She looked a little scared.

The spoked wheels of his new gold LeMans spun across the causeway. The moat around my castle, he thought. Tidewater property had gone over the moon the past few years. The waterfront was kaput. Branfeldt wasn't, thank God, in the market. He scanned prices and terms just to test his capacity for astonishment.

The sun was like a spotlight, the sky a stagy blue. Branfeldt squinted. On a clear day you really *could* see forever, if you looked. There were probably a million guys on their way to work right this minute whose dreams included a week at Virginia Beach with the wife and kids in August or July. And *fishermen*—Christ, I'm taking up room in somebody's heaven, Branfeldt thought.

An ovation of gulls burst out in the cloudless sky . . . every morning another encore. His life was starting to remind him of *The Fantasticks,* a run that went on and on without making a whole lot of sense. This plum was too *ripe* . . . what was that supposed to mean?

The gulls were screaming. "You're on! You're on!" Nervy birds.

"So I'm going already." Branfeldt played the line with the amused world-weariness he'd have given Tevye in *Fiddler.* Only he'd lost the part to an older guy. *You just haven't got the gravity, Seth,* Ken Burrus, the director, said. Branfeldt's shrug now was a triumph of resignation.

Many a man, he knew, succumbed to nostalgia around his age. Moving up on fifty, if you had any vision, any *grasp,* you began to take stock. You'd feel these little gusts, maybe hear a click, and you'd recognize the sound: doors to possibility, windows of opportunity, slamming in your face.

Wistful? Some guys got downright frantic. You saw it all the time—the lipstick-red Miata, the hair weave and eye tuck, the twenty-three-year-old wife skipping off to aerobics class in a leotard and springy little shoes.

Branfeldt's boss, Morley Tyson, had run through that whole scene about a year ago, jogging to Sting tapes on a Walkman, long lunches with the pretty paralegal who hadn't lasted past the first act.

Morley was back with his wife now, but his kids still barely spoke to him and whatever surgery he'd inflicted on his savvy sad-sack face had left him with two permanent shiners.

Morley was too tolerant of screwups and lapses these days. Branfeldt missed the old chief, missed the snap-crackle-and-bite that had given them both their edge.

It wasn't like Branfeldt screwed up that often—P.R. director for a rinky-dink industrial park wasn't exactly a challenging role and he had his cues down pat. Still, he'd grown a little slack lately—mistimed press releases, missed meetings. He'd even misquoted Morley a time or two to reporters. Five years ago that would have got his flabby butt fired in a New York minute. Now all of a sudden Morley seemed programmed to forgive anybody just about anything. His new humility fit him, Branfeldt thought, like a bad off-the-rack suit.

Things at the park were going great, 100 percent occupancy and an expansion in the works. But Morley was playing it like a guy who was all washed up. His long upper lip was always a little sweaty. His handshake felt like a flounder.

The road to the Tinker's Island Industrial Park splayed across the marshlands like a withered limb, shapeless and emaciated. The job of persuading the Feds, the Commonwealth, and half a dozen fire-breathing citizen groups that a 350-acre enclave of light industry wouldn't snuff the wetlands had, praise the Lord, fallen to Branfeldt's predecessor. The Tinker's Island complex—"TIP," as the locals called it with that chumminess Branfeldt still mistrusted in Southerners—had opened in the mid-seventies. By the time Branfeldt became its mouthpiece in '82, things had simmered down. The job came with some terrific benefits, his ticket out of Toledo being one of them. He'd made his entrance with the brisk optimism of a soap star doing regional theater—he'd shown he had stuff nobody would have guessed.

His moxie got a quick diluting, though, his first day on the job. Branfeldt showed up early, clutching a five-page memo he'd hammered out over the weekend, changes he planned to implement his first three months on the job. "Ready to get this show on the road." He put the old glitter in his eyes as he held the memo across the polished plane of Morley Tyson's teak desk.

Tyson, a little razor blade of a guy with dark barbed eyes and a gunmetal silk suit, ignored the memo. Reaching inside a desk drawer, he pulled out a book: Roger Tory Peterson's *Field Guide to Eastern Birds*, a spanking-new edition.

Branfeldt blinked.

Tyson didn't. "First tool of the trade," he said.

Branfeldt worked up a roguish grin—*Guys and Dolls*, Toledo '75—and waited for the punch line. Something about loons, he figured. But Morley Tyson's expression was hard and humorless as a condor's.

"Cram," he said. "You don't just cover my ass here, you upholster it."

A dimmer switch reset Branfeldt's eyes. He folded up the memo and stuffed it into the pocket of his new blue blazer.

"Pay close attention to your accidentals," Tyson said.

Accidentals? Something about insurance maybe. This Tyson could sure make hash out of an upbeat agenda.

Now, for more than a decade, Branfeldt had been ferrying prospective tenants and investors through the gates of the industrial park and down its skinny salt-grayed road. Seemed like some official swamp warden or other came nosing around each week, doing a head count on herons and cattle egrets, ibises and frigate birds. Branfeldt kept Roger Tory Peterson in the glove compartment, the Accidental Shorebird section dog-eared. He'd showcased terns and petrels, pumped himself up over godwits and curlews. He'd even once talked the chief into springing for a pair of imported trumpeter swans, a semi-shady deal. But the fly-by-night couple hadn't hung around long enough to give much mileage. Branfeldt had found their eerie cries depressing anyhow. Almost as bad as the loons, who always sounded like they'd lost something they couldn't live without.

Branfeldt still savored the tricky turn, how the visitors first took it in. You came to what looked like the end of the road. Then the silvered asphalt hooked like a claw. It was the last place you'd expect to find an office. Watching from the corner of his eyes, Branfeldt could see the weathered cypress siding, the low-slung screened porch and fieldstone chimney and shake roof doing his job . . . if the birds hadn't already done it, the office would close the deal.

"Nothing fancy," Branfeldt liked to say. "Didn't seem like we should go poking a finger in Mother Nature's eye, is all."

Even the professional tree-huggers would go mushy then, forgetting to ask how many birds there used to be and how many pines cut down and where do you suppose the sewage all went to?

Morley's Town Car (the Miata having split with the girl-friend) wasn't in its usual spot, a surprise since Branfeldt was running late. The chief had been putting in fourteen-hour days since the last of his wild oats got off-loaded. Branfeldt bounded up the steps and closed the screen door softly behind him. Had he forgotten a breakfast meeting somewhere?

Felicia, the office manager, was not at her desk. The old schoolhouse clock above it showed nearly nine and Felicia's sky blue Taurus was backed in against a cluster of scrub pines out back like it always was by 7:30, but otherwise there was no sign of her. Or anybody else.

It felt kind of creepy being alone in the office. Howard, the accountant, was out on loan this week, Branfeldt remembered. Duckblind, Inc., the newest tenant (or *member*, as Morley insisted on saying, like the industrial park was some exclusive club) had run into some auditing snag. The novelty outfit was already shaky—a couple dozen Filipino girls who didn't look old enough to work (green cards, who knew?) stenciling turquoise and olive mallards on cheap plastic window blinds hustled in from Taiwan. Better to help them over the hump, Morley said, than lose the rent.

"Felicia?"

The Mr. Coffee was stone cold. She must have gone off with Morley somewhere. Maybe there *was* a meeting . . . Branfeldt ran through a list of "members" in his mind: MagiMix Soups'n'Dips, Land-O-Goshen Learning Aids, Critterlitter, Rite 2-U Coupons . . . nothing came to him. Hadn't been a hitch or a flap in months, except for the Duckblind thing, small-fry.

The phone console on Felicia's desk began to whine, the

private line. Pam, the so-called receptionist, ought to be in any second. But the noise was driving him batty.

"Tee-Eye-Pee Management."

"Who *is* this?" The voice, a woman's, sounded strangled.

"S. Branfeldt, P.R. Can I help you?"

"Oh, Seth—"

"Felicia?"

"You're *there*." She was crying. "Thank God."

Branfeldt hunched his shoulders and ducked his head. "I'm here," he said. "Where are you?"

"I think you better come get me."

"Sure."

Branfeldt waited. Felicia, a sixtyish widow with an iron maiden figure and a hairdo like S.O.S. pads, had been with Morley Tyson all the way back to Pittsburgh and the death throes of an obsolete container business his grandfather had dumped in his lap.

"Felicia?" Branfeldt waited another minute. "Maybe you could tell me where you are?"

"Chesapeake General."

"You're hurt?"

"Don't be silly," she said.

She'd come in earlier than usual. It wasn't until she left her desk at 7:45 to start the coffee that she noticed Morley Tyson's sleek silver car aslant at the foot of the road.

"They don't think he's going to make it, Seth."

"An accident?" Branfeldt said. "But how—?"

"Stroke." Her voice was suddenly all business. "Massive coronary occlusion," she said. "Isn't that a stroke?"

Didn't *coronary* sound more like a heart attack? "You sit tight," Branfeldt said. "I'm on my way."

But the woman could not stop talking. She'd found Morley

Tyson slumped over the steering wheel, a pool of vomit over-flowing his limp cupped hands and staining the calfskin uphol-stery. She'd had to shoulder him aside to squeeze into the driver's seat and—

"All right," Branfeldt said. "Okay." He thought about how people died in plays: mostly offstage, or in clean white beds, loved ones hovering to catch last words, to learn from them and be transformed. Then the spot would shrink. Or the lights would dim, change color. The dead person's face would be peaceful, pure white. Some weeping in the darkness, perhaps, but only for a moment. The houselights would come right up, if you could just . . .

"Hold on," he said. "You stay put."

"They won't let me see him," Felicia said.

Branfeldt's breath let go in a thin, quiet stream. "I'm al-ready on my way," he said.

Morley somehow squeaked by. "Stroke and heart attack both." His wife, Martha Rose, sounded almost appeased.

"Morley's a tough old bird," Branfeldt said. "Be his old own self in no time." He'd almost said "like a new man," had just caught himself. Martha Rose had had a crawful of *that*.

By the time Morley got out of ICU and into a private room, the Board of Directors had met and named Branfeldt Acting CEO. A few days later, over a quick nine holes at Bow Creek, the Chairman, Adm. Quinsey Tuckerford (Ret.), told Bran-feldt, "The *Acting* is only temporary, remember."

"Sure thing." Branfeldt blew a giveaway putt. His grin felt loose. He'd given up the stage years ago. Did Tuckerford think he was a dreamer or something? They must've run a back-ground check, nosed around in Toledo . . .

Sickening under a blast furnace sun, Branfeldt recalled his last performance, a musical version of *Some Like It Hot,* and him, in the Tony Curtis part, wearing a merry widow and a petticoat. At the end of the big number he'd flipped up his flounced hem to show a red garter belt over his jockey shorts. His picture had even been picked up by the Cleveland *Plain Dealer.*

"Guess I'm kind of surprised you'd bring that up now," Branfeldt said cautiously.

The old admiral's complexion, in full sunlight, looked like a crustacean's. He pressed his lips in a bivalve smile. "You're a man of tact, son," he said. "Show real stick-to-itiveness." He whacked Branfeldt's backside with the shank of his putter. "Would have made a fine officer," he said.

"Acting's just——"

"Just for now," the admiral agreed. "Give that poor cuss Tyson time to adjust, tally up his limitations, then the job's yours. Free and clear. No more *Acting.*"

Branfeldt blinked once, then weaseled a plaid handkerchief out of his back pocket and mopped his face.

"No more *Acting,*" he said. "No, sir."

One gander at his daughter in a pink cotton sundress, a small swell of new bosom edging up over a scoop of ruffle, and Branfeldt's heart fluidified.

It was four on a Sunday afternoon, hot as blue blazes, and he'd just shot eighteen holes with some of his Kiwanis buddies. Still sun-stunned and a tad beery, he lay in a hammock threaded through the patchy shade of sibling runt pear trees. Steam rose from his body. A shower had only poached him.

LaDonna, slim as her daughter in a linen shift the brash

yellow of marigolds, stood beside Meddie in the encroaching sun. Together they looked like a dream.

"Been gallivanting, you girls?" Branfeldt said. "Don't know as I relish the pair of you all dolled up and gone off without a chaperone."

"We went to visit Uncle Morley."

The light behind them was so bright Branfeldt couldn't read his daughter's face, but he was just upwind of her rebuke.

Five weeks after landing in the hospital, Morley Tyson had been transferred to a rehab center in Portsmouth. He was now in his second week there. Branfeldt, who'd been sending plants and elaborate floral arrangements at least twice a week since Day One, had yet to drop in.

"Well, the sight of y'all must've been a considerable cheering up," he said.

"Daddy," Medea said, "he can't *talk*."

Branfeldt just couldn't picture it, Morley mum. "He will, though, right? I mean, after a while?"

His daughter made a dismissive sound. "Sometimes I don't get you, Dad."

Branfeldt closed his eyes against the glare. When he opened them again, LaDonna had stepped into the shade, placing herself between Branfeldt and their child.

"He's doing lots better, Martha Rose says."

"Martha Rose was there?"

"Felicia, too."

"That's nice," said Branfeldt.

"But Dad, he's all by *himself*."

Branfeldt winced. "I hear you, honey," he said.

There was a rustle of crisp cotton, the slap of a sandal sole, the rattle of a screen door. The girl was gone.

"I don't understand it myself," Branfeldt said. "What's keeping me."

LaDonna just nodded, her face all kindness. After a moment Branfeldt held out his arms and she dropped into the hammock beside him. Her hair, sticking to his damp face, was like the flowery suffocation of a funeral home. The hammock lurched and swayed. Branfeldt, moist and rank, felt like a slab of raw meat beside his wife.

"I'm just lousy in that kind of scene," he said.

"You'll get there, honey," LaDonna said. "When you're up to it."

It was the height of summer by the time Branfeldt got himself in hand and went to see Morley. The heat had been ferocious, no letup since April. The papers were filled with drownings and crimes of passion. A small plane had gone down in flames, the lives of a whole Ohio family, the youngest only two, sizzling out in the lukewarm waters of Stumpy Lake.

The sky looked like the sheets of glass afloat on the sea of molten tin in the Toledo plant where his father had worked for thirty years, Branfeldt thought. He'd worked for the same company himself, after graduating from Bucknell. But Branfeldt, an intern in public relations, had set foot in the glass plant only to lead through groups of schoolchildren the first and third Fridays of each month. His old man had never seen the inside of the corporate offices.

Branfeldt had been a big hit with the youngsters. Not understanding the production process very well himself, he was able to make it sound like magic, how a liquid could be so thick and tough you'd swear it was a solid. *Clarity, flexibility, tensile strength*—he'd spun words above the youngsters' heads like juggler's pins.

The kids were always most astounded by the heat, though. *Twenty-nine hundred degrees Fahrenheit*, Branfeldt would boast . . . *more than twenty-five times hotter than the hottest day any of us will ever live through*. Then he'd play at wiping his brow, cool as a cucumber, and do a little hotfoot dance as if the plant floor were on fire. He made sure the tour never lolly-gagged anywhere the old man might catch his act.

Back at the gate, before getting the kids on their yellow buses, Branfeldt would hand around little blobs of molten glass that had been dropped into cold water. The lumps were called Prince Rupert's Drops, Branfeldt explained, and they couldn't be smashed, not by the strongest man in the world with a hammer the size of a kettle drum.

Even Haystacks Calhoun couldn't do it, he'd say. *But if you can find the tail of the drop and pinch it with a pliers, the whole thing will crumble like a sugar cube*. He'd worked up a nice little pantomime of crumbling that made even the teachers laugh.

The rehab hospital's windows shone in the late afternoon sun like fire-polished crown glass. An elevator that felt like a walk-in freezer hauled Branfeldt up to the top floor, where a skinny girl in a white nylon jumpsuit directed him to Morley's private room.

Branfeldt found the right door, then stalled in the corridor, leaning against the wall. His breathing felt funny. He hadn't been in a hospital in eight years.

It had eaten up most of a day, flying from Norfolk, by way of Washington and Pittsburgh, to Toledo. He'd have done better to drive, could have made an earlier start. His father had departed only twenty minutes before Branfeldt arrived. His sister, Evie, had used that word: *departed*.

It was day's end then, too. Branfeldt remembered a washed-out pink sky above the Maumee River, a sinking sun with all the fire gone out of it. In his father's room curtains were drawn against the sunset, across the window, around the bed. Evie led the way, pulling back a flap of limp green cloth. Branfeldt felt like he was entering a tent. Then his sister was gone and he, afloat in a faint watery light, was alone with his father for the first time in years.

The skin around the old man's mouth and eyes was so cracked and dried it looked like his face had shattered. He seemed to be shrinking as he cooled.

The wake, the funeral . . . the chores and errands of death . . . Branfeldt had moved through the next few days like a trouper, doing his best in a role that was beyond him. He knew he was mugging. He couldn't get a handle on what he was supposed to feel.

The day he was to fly back to Norfolk, Branfeldt met with a lawyer and signed over his half of everything, such as it was, to his sister. Evie and the two kids were already living in the old man's house, since her second husband had flown the coop the year before.

Evie, the younger by two years, looked ten years older than her brother. It hurt Branfeldt to look at her.

"It's me you call now, if you need anything. You got it?" The line fell flat on its face.

"Seth, I wasn't supposed to wind up with everything. Why are you doing this?"

"Why?" The question amazed him until he realized he didn't know the answer, either.

"It's so you won't ever have to come back here," Evie said. "Isn't it?"

Branfeldt stared. She'd always reminded him of their mother, a plain gentle woman who'd died years ago. Now he saw the old man's suspicious eyes set like rivets in his sister's placid face.

It was late November. The sky was grizzled and thick. They were standing on Monroe Street in front of the lawyer's office, just a few blocks down from the art museum, where there was glass that was three thousand years old, Branfeldt recalled. Glass from Egypt, Mesopotamia, and Greece . . . vessels older than God as Branfeldt knew Him.

A paralyzing wind struck their faces. Branfeldt raised his arms, as if he could shelter his sister from the worst of it. "I owe—"

"You don't have anything to make up for, Seth." Evie leaned against him for a moment. Branfeldt held her, but she felt breakable. His grip went lax.

"He loved you," Evie said.

"He was never there."

"Where?"

"Where I wanted him to see me," Branfeldt said. "If just once he would've come . . ."

His sister drew back and looked up at him. Her hair, the sepia of old photographs, was thin. Her scalp showed through where the wind parted it. "You scared him, Seth." She tried to smile. "People ought not to stand out, he said."

"It wasn't—"

"I know." Her worn leather glove touched his face. Her eyes were, had always been, like their mother's. "It's not your fault," she said.

"Maybe it was all that glass," Branfeldt said. "He always had to try to see *through* everything."

"He loved you, Seth."

"It was only Toledo," Branfeldt said. "You think I didn't know that? It's just, I was never that good at anything else."

The wind drove something into his eye. He rubbed at it mercilessly. He missed his wife and daughter, stuck back in Virginia with some virus, both of them. But he was glad they hadn't come. Toledo was a sorry place, and the old man had missed one last chance to piss on what Branfeldt had to be proud of.

After a minute he took his sister's thin arm and stepped off the curb. "You figure we got time to stop for a bratwurst?" he said. "Might be a while before I get another chance." He was shivering.

The hospital corridor was beginning to smell like a school cafeteria. Branfeldt heard the rattle of heavy crockery. Feeling queasy, he pushed at the numbered door and stuck his head around it, engaging grin ready to go.

Morley Tyson, a stained napkin under his chin, was asleep. His mouth gapped open a little, its two sides somehow mismatched. His left hand, limp beside him on the white bedding, looked like something the life had gone out of.

Branfeldt hovered in the door frame. For a minute he didn't even try to breathe. The room was like a jungle. Greenery sprouted everywhere, crawled across the nightstand and windowsill and dresser, inched along the floor. A bird of paradise perched on the rolling bedtray that seemed to cut Morley's body in half.

The only sign of animal life was the irregular rise and fall of Morley's bony chest, a slight movement of the cloth that covered him. And a faint smell, something like decay so far gone that it could almost be overlooked.

After a moment, breathing again, Branfeldt looked away from Morley and started counting plants. There were twenty-three, plus a couple vases of flowers. Each plant had a little card sticking up out of the dirt on a plastic thing that looked like a tuning fork. Branfeldt didn't want to see his name, scrawled over and over by unfamiliar hands.

His eyes homed in again on Morley, not himself in any way Branfeldt could see. *Fatigue fracture*, he thought. The flaw can be there for years, invisible. But what's in the very air around it is making inroads all the time, weakening, undermining, until one day the whole thing just falls to pieces.

Branfeldt jammed his hands into the pants pockets of his Palm Beach suit. He ought to look cheerful, in charge, just in case Morley was watching from behind those transparent-looking eyelids in their bruised sockets.

And maybe he was. Because no sooner had Branfeldt put the finishing touches to his pose than Morley's eyes snapped open, bright and beady as a spider monkey's.

"Anybody home?" Branfeldt said.

Morley's tough old features wandered some, then settled into a lopsided grimace.

"Hey, boss man."

"Huh."

"Didn't I tell Felicia you'd be mouthing off again in no time?" Branfeldt grinned. "Ole Fleesh," he said. "Wish you'd get back to work. I mean, how long you think I can handle her?"

"Huh," Morley said.

Branfeldt stepped closer to the bed. "Don't tell me that's all you got to say for yourself," he said.

"Huh," Morley said. "Huh-huh."

The sound, a far cry from human, took the starch right out

of Branfeldt. He sidled up to the foot of the bed and gripped its iron rail. "Aw, shit, chief," he said.

Morley nodded, sort of.

"Damn it all to hell," said Branfeldt. "Give me a monologue and I bomb every time."

He hadn't understood that Morley was smiling until he stopped. The old man's eyes narrowed and the stringy flesh around his mouth collapsed. He raised his right hand and, with surprising authority, waved Branfeldt toward the door: *Take a hike, asshole.*

"I hear you," Branfeldt said. "I know what you're saying."

He'd left the door halfway open. He looked at the gap with longing. "Jesus, Morley," he said. "It's kept me on the run, trying to play you. I'm nothing but a song-and-dance man, you know?"

He waited for Morley to concur: *Huh.* But there was no sound from the head on the pillow, no forgiveness in the small hard eyes. No encouragement, either. Branfeldt felt like all those plants had sucked the last gasp of air from the small room.

"You probably want some shut-eye, right?"

Morley stared at him another moment, then closed his eyes.

" 'Atta boy." Branfeldt began backing toward the door. "Things are swell out there in birdland, chief. Not a worry in the world."

Morley's face was still and glazed.

"You remember that old barnacle goose?" Branfeldt grinned. "Not Fleesh, nah. That big ole bird with the white mask . . . looks like the Phantom of the Opera?" Groping behind him, he found the door handle, gripped it. "Old bastard showed up again last week," he said. "Can you beat it?"

Out in the corridor a man let loose a noisy laugh. Then it sounded like somebody clapped a hand over his mouth. "Sorry," a voice said in a loud whisper.

"Yeah, they all make a comeback," Branfeldt said, "you give 'em a little time."

The sun was taking a nosedive into the Elizabeth River when he pulled away from the hospital. The days seemed to come up short so suddenly in August. One day you'd notice it and realize you should have been paying closer attention to how long the light used to last.

The sky was wan by the time Branfeldt got home. When he hit the button on the little black box clipped to his visor, he was surprised LaDonna's sherry-colored Saab wasn't tucked into its berth in the garage.

The kitchen, spotless, smelled of lemony dishwasher soap. No sign of supper. "Anybody home? Meddie?" Branfeldt, keeping his back to the breakfast nook, filled a short glass with crushed ice and headed into the living room to pour himself a drink.

The long room, entirely white and mostly glass on the western side, was brighter than any room had a right to be at dusk. LaDonna, in recent years, had trained her theatrical gifts on the house. The results, though he wouldn't have said so, were sometimes a bit much. Still, Branfeldt had to admit the stark sunken living room was a knockout.

Looking down, negotiating the three steps, their edges tricky with thick shag, he didn't notice the mess until he was halfway to the dry sink in the corner.

"Sweet God!" he whispered.

A crystal lamp beside the white silk sofa was overturned. A pair of cream-matted prints of wildflowers in thin gold frames had gone tipsy. A spun-glass figurine, swept from the mantle, had crash-landed on the pale marble hearth, not far from a felled basket of marsh grass. At first Branfeldt had trouble remembering the glass figure had been an angel. He wondered if Meddie, who had loved it as a child, would even miss it now.

He wheeled around then, amazed to find the long glass wall scatheless. The sky above the hedges of the yard had hardened to alabaster. The three splotches of blood were strewn on the glass like red blossoms on a bone-white table.

A blank space yawned. He was being swallowed up by his own life. Branfeldt tore through the house, trying to cry out the names of his wife and child but unable to make a sound.

A trail of his daughter's clothing, bereft of her shape, led him from a tossed bed through a door to a porcelain tub, several strands of bright hair scrawling a desperate cursive around its drain. Scarlet-blotted tissues littered a marble counter. His wife's absence screamed in a spattered mirror. Their scent was everywhere. Still Branfeldt did not find them.

What he did find, eventually, was a battered wren with a broken neck, fallen behind the sofa back.

Holding the bird in both hands, Branfeldt studied its commonplace markings for a long lost time. Its back and wings were the warm reddish color of sandy soil. Its tail feathers were notched with black and the breast was pale. A long slash of white ran above each eye, giving it an astonished look. It wasn't a species he'd had any need to pay attention to. Such birds were around everywhere, all the time, by the millions. What a puny critter, Branfeldt thought, to have done so much damage.

By the time LaDonna and Meddie got home, loaded down with fragrant white cartons from the Szechuan carryout at the mall, Branfeldt had buried the bird out back, below a hem of wisteria. He had wiped the blood from the glass and was setting things back to rights as best he could. Carelessly, he'd tried to scoop up shards of the shattered angel with his bare hands. Slivers of glass were embedded in his palms and fingertips.

Branfeldt walked out into the deepening twilight to meet his wife and daughter, his arms raised as if to stop them.

"Honey—" His clumsily bandaged hands dropped to his sides. "I'm afraid things are kind of a mess," he said.

LaDonna just looked at him.

"Dad," Meddie said. "What did you do?"

The pale beauty of their faces, rendered nearly identical by alarm and shadow, staggered him. Branfeldt thought about the long wall of light, the glass he'd been promised could never shatter. His lips felt like something not his own. He held out his arms again, ushering his wife and child inside the flimsy enclave of his protection.

"It could have been worse," he said.

It was not quite dawn when Branfeldt returned to the hospital. On the upper floors the windows looked dull, tarnished. Only half a dozen cars, all of them expensive, sat in the doctors' lot. The LeMans seemed to belong there. But just to be on the safe side, Branfeldt chose a space away from the lights.

Fumbling into his clothes in the dark, he had tried to dress the way he thought a doctor would, his suit a summer-weight worsted of charcoal gray, a starched blue shirt, a navy rep tie. The tie was loose, its knot askew. LaDonna had removed the glass slivers from his hands and the bandages were gone, but his fingers felt balky and sore. Branfeldt hustled to the staff entrance, hoping the tie lent him a real doctor's harried look.

A security guard slumped behind a battered desk just inside the door. The old man, working a crossword puzzle, looked half asleep. Branfeldt spotted a dull gold name tag on the beige uniform shirt, then slanted his face away, looking preoccupied.

"Morning, Max."

"Hey, doc." The old man tapped his dentures with the eraser end of a stubby pencil and didn't look up.

The rest was a piece of cake. Branfeldt skirted the nurses' station, where a beautiful Indian girl in a white maternity smock leaned toward a computer screen, her belly balanced on her knees. As he passed the staff lounge he smelled fresh coffee and heard a sleepy murmur of women's voices. "One more hour," someone said through a yawn. Then Branfeldt was home free.

A silver-blue nightlight glowed on a panel above the bed. Below it, in shadow, Morley's half-open eyes seemed to stare at him without recognition. His head had rolled from the pillow to crook in an odd way. Branfeldt thought of the bird.

"Morley?" He bent over the bed. "Buddy?"

The old man let loose a gust of rancid breath. The right side of the ruined mouth wrenched into something like a smile.

"Jesus." Branfeldt gripped the bed railing. "You scared the shit out of me."

The frail chest jerked up and down a few times and Morley's eyes teared up. *This is where laughs wind up*, Branfeldt thought. He smiled sadly. "Quite the card, chief."

A tear leaked from the corner of Morley's left eye. Branfeldt blotted it with a blue French cuff. Morley reached up with his good right arm and pinched Branfeldt's lapel, rubbing the suit's fine fabric between his thumb and two fingers. His right eyebrow arched, warping the rest of his face.

"Seemed best to clean up my act a little," Branfeldt said. "If I had any shot at filling in for you."

"Huh." The old man's face seemed to harden.

"Yeah," Branfeldt said. "The reviews have been sort of mixed."

He crossed to the window and drew back the curtain. The

sky, about two shades lighter than his suit, was rouged now at the tops of the trees. "Going to be a beauty," he said. "Still hot, though."

He turned around. Morley closed his eyes like a man flat out of patience.

"You don't give a shit, right?" said Branfeldt sadly. "I keep forgetting."

Morley's mouth twitched.

"Do things get easier?" Branfeldt asked. "When you stop giving a shit?"

The air in the room seemed to be solidifying, the window growing more transparent as the light came up. When glass cooled too rapidly, the whole process came to a halt, Branfeldt recalled, freezing everything in its last fluid moment. Then no more random changes were possible, the shape was there to stay.

"I can't act my way out of a paper bag," he whispered. "Never could."

Morley's head slipped down further, canted now at a tortured angle.

"I could sing, though." Branfeldt's eyes grew dreamy. "Jesus, could I sing."

The old man made a sound deep in his throat, something like a growl.

"Oh," Branfeldt said. Leaning down, he scooped up Morley's skull in one smarting palm and set it back on the pillow. "Okay?"

The scrawny old rib cage started moving up and down again, an elastic solid.

Branfeldt switched off the nightlight. Dawn's eerie blue glow filled the room. Fists of leaves the blackish green of a cyclone sky seemed to tighten around them. The air smelled of damp earth. Branfeldt lowered the bed railing. At the foot of the bed, the old man's feet made a mound under the blanket. Sighing, Branfeldt settled himself beside it.

Morley's eyes opened again, cunning and griped. Like they can see right through me, Branfeldt thought. He allotted the moment a small smile. "Any requests?" he said.

"Huh." Morley slanted his face toward the window.

"Last chance, chief." Branfeldt cleared his throat.

The voice had frayed some, he knew, with time and smoke. But its sweetness had not been lost. He knew that, too. I've always been a singer, Branfeldt thought. Never claimed to be more.

Morley was drifting back toward sleep. Suddenly Branfeldt couldn't remember a single tune. He studied the old out-of-whack face. He felt like it was trying to coach him, pull from him something he knew he had but couldn't quite reach on his own.

The stillness ticked. Branfeldt lifted his eyes to the window. The sun had bellied up over an ocean the lay of the land was doing its best to hide. A dark band of birds festooned the breeze, then vanished.

Beside him Morley's breaths grew syncopated, edgy. Branfeldt inhaled and exhaled slowly. He imagined the sounds he could have made, singing his heart out. He pictured his whole repertoire flying out through the glass, dissolving in a flood of rose-gold light.

Finally, Branfeldt opened his mouth. He sucked the available air from deep in his diaphragm, then pushed it out. He heard a wind, puny and yonder. Frightened, he reached out and laid a scored hand on the bony mound of Morley's feet.

The ticking stopped.

He heard the wind again. It sounded a little closer this time.

Only me, Branfeldt thought, in the offing.

What
I Remember Now

We'd spot each other from halfway down the street in town, was how it started, me going into the store for a tin of baking powder, him ducking into the P.O. to pick up a package or stamps. I'd wave: big flurry. Two beats, then, like he was agreeing with something he'd thought over, he'd nod.

Before long, I guess I never really went anywhere without looking for his bright blue pickup. We'd pass on the road and I'd wave and he'd lift two fingers from the steering wheel, which is pretty much how people up here say hello, not going out on any limbs. But always we'd both be smiling, him mostly in the eyes, me with my gums showing. No matter how long I live in Vermont, it will always be obvious I'm from Illinois, I'm afraid.

It wasn't like I came here looking for something. Solitude suits me. I knew that much when I was young. Some people do best on their own. Which is mostly how I've been for thirty-six years now, on my own. Still, with him I got to be kind of like a kid with an imaginary friend, having him to talk to in my mind. He kept me company from a distance.

I remember the first word he said to me: *Hey*. It was back around late October and things were pretty well shut down along the reservoir road, except for the Kit'n'Caboodle, which Ham Bouchard liked to keep open as long as he could for the hunters. I'd stopped in because it was a sunny day and the roads were still clear and I wondered if anything was going on. Ham being someone who'd always know, and tell. But mostly I went for Gladys Bouchard's maple cream pie, which if I didn't get some soon, I wouldn't taste again until June. The Caboodle staying open would definitely file down the points some on winter's teeth.

I was perched on a swivel stool, Dexters swinging and a mouth full of butter and sugar and cream. Ham was telling me how Fowler Oldensberg had stepped in it big-time the night before. The item on the town meeting agenda was public decency at the little man-made beach on the south end of the reservoir. It's one of those issues that gets a public airing once a year, whether it needs it or not. Every September these college kids will motorcade up from Bennington and Middlebury, sometimes even from Dartmouth, to play Frisbee and drink beer. And every once in a while, given enough sun and beer, they'll go skinny-dipping. Big deal.

"So Fowler gets all hot under the collar," Ham is telling me. "I think it unclogs his arteries or sinuses or pores or something. Anyhow, he keeps referring to *gazongas*, like it's a term he picked up in some medical book. Meanwhile his poor wife's sinking down through the seat of her chair and the women from that commune herb farm place over on the Covered Bridge Road are getting tighter lips and redder faces by the second."

Ham shakes his head. " 'Anti-Gazonga-Exposure' . . . a town ordinance. You should have been there, Junie."

Gladys shoved her round face into the serving window from the kitchen. "Lucky to miss it, I'd say. Pure waste of a working person's time."

"This pie's from heaven," I told her.

"The pie's from *Vermont*," Gladys said. "You still don't know the difference?"

"Don't weasel out of winter like you two, either," I said.

"Talk to me after forty-odd winters," said Gladys. "Maybe you'll get some sympathy."

"Might even get an invitation to come down and see us." Ham levered his chunky forearms on the counter in front of me. "Available man or two down there in Vero Beach," he said.

"Ham, leave her alone." Gladys was using the flat, automatic voice she'd use to say *Order's up*.

It was well past the local idea of lunchtime. The rush at the Caboodle is 11:30 or so. Nobody in the place at 1:15 but me and the slick-haired UPS man, reading yesterday's *Leader* in the corner booth and having a bowl of bean soup before heading on to St. Johnsbury.

Ham moved closer, leaning in on his elbows and giving me the kindly uncle look. "Should I?" he asked.

"Leave me alone?" I smiled. "Might be worth a try. Something different."

"Just seems like a waste, is all," Ham said. "You carry keeping to yourself too far, Junie."

"What if I like it that way?"

"Sweet-looking lady like you." He shook his head. "Put on a couple pounds, yank that curly mop off your face so a body could see you . . ."

I looked at my watch. "I ought to go."

Gladys's head reappeared in the window. "*He*'s the one ought to go," she said. "How about we lobby Fowler for an anti-buttinsky ordinance?"

"You wanna turn this place into a ghost town?" Ham said. I laughed.

"Finish your pie," Ham said. "I'll meddle with you some other time."

"When are you closing?" I asked.

"For the season?"

"Not soon enough," Gladys said from the kitchen.

"Weekend after next," said Ham. "Saturday lunch."

"Might be summer next time I see you."

"Don't hibernate," Ham said. "You need to get out, join in."

"Ham," I said, "I'm not in the market."

"What I want to know is, how come?"

"None of your beeswax." Gladys was back.

"Oh, but it *is*," I told her.

"She's gonna get cute now," Ham said. "You watch."

"Want to make sure when you finally dump him that I'm free to make my move," I said, tossing my hair back over my shoulder.

Ham nodded. "Figured it was bound to be some cockamamie thing like that," he said.

After my pie was gone, I stayed at the counter, watching Ham scrape down the grill and top off the ketchup bottles while I waded through a second cup of coffee. I heard somebody pull up out front. A minute later the door opened and a draft hit me between the shoulder blades. Ham nodded at someone. "Right back," he said. Then he ducked into the kitchen with a tray full of dirty glasses.

I turned my head just a fraction. Swatches of blue plaid flannel and faded denim floated in the corner of my right eye.

"Hey." He sat down at the counter six stools away.

"Hey." Just my eyes leaned into the smile, perfect Yankee. But then I had to go and ruin it: "How you doing?"

I never knew before that a person could nod using just one side of their head.

After that, for a good six months, we always said *hey*. And if I slipped—*How you doing?*—I'd get that half nod. That was all.

It seemed like he was watching me a little closer now, though—not in a creepy way, but nice, like you'd watch ducks winging low along the shore, a usual sight you'd still enjoy noticing, no matter how many times you saw it.

In December I got a surprise royalty check and took it right to the big mall in Burlington. I went into one of those walk-in places and got a few ragged inches trimmed off my hair. The girl who did it made a pitch for putting in some streaks to camouflage the gray starting to show at the front. "Highlighting," she called it. "We could keep it real subtle."

"Maybe next time," I said.

My head felt a little easier to hold up, with some of that excess hair gone. I treated myself to lunch in a real restaurant, rather than fighting the Saturday food court crush. I didn't leave the french fries on my plate like I usually do. Then I went into a full-price department store and bought myself a red down jacket.

I needed a heavier jacket if I was going to stay here, which after three years it appeared that I was. I'd been looking on the drab side lately—like Ham was trying to tell me, I guess. A little color couldn't hurt. But red? I probably wasn't looking too hard at my own motives. It seems kind of obvious now that I was making sure I'd be easy to spot.

Winters being what they are up here, you can go for days at a time without leaving your house. The guys on the town plows do a terrific job, but even so, the kids can have so many snow days to make up they barely make it out of school by the Fourth of July. It was going to be one of those winters.

Artists make good shut-ins. Being freelance has its drawbacks, of course. A lot of people can't take the uncertainty. I don't mind flying by the seat of my pants, though, not when the rent is cheap and I can call my time my own.

My work, after I moved up here, got cleaner somehow, like I can look at a thing now and filter out the parts that don't matter. My illustrations—greeting cards and calendars are my bread and butter, but I get magazine work, too, a book jacket now and then—seem like they're catching on since I simplified things. I've even got a couple of semi-steady gigs, one with a classy little private press in Iowa City, another with a midsize Boston publisher. Winter's a good time for my work. Loneliness has never been a big problem with me.

Recently I'd started fooling around with an idea for a children's book. The main character, a raccoon, was a pie bandit trying to reform. He started a support group for other animals with sticky fingers. My illustrations weren't bad, but the text came hard. I couldn't make up my mind whether the moral had to do with stealing, gluttony, or good intentions. For kids, more than one moral gets too confusing.

Anyway, even with a lot of snowed-in days, I'd see him maybe once a week, at the post office or the general store or just out on the road. One weekend when the Congregational church was having a bake sale, I saw him getting into his truck with what looked like a coconut cake. I don't think he spotted me, though, which made me wonder how many times he saw me when I didn't know it. Distant sightings, a weekly *hey* . . . not a lot to get by on. But knowing he was around, or might be, made me happy in a funny way.

I knew his name by then, of course. You know everybody's name and general history (some version of it) in a place this small, even people you don't know well enough to say *hey* to. The way people talk amazes me. I don't think there's real spite in it, not like small towns are usually made out to be (mostly by people who never lived in one). It's just that there isn't all that much to talk about, so we talk about what's here: the weather, food, and—in this case—about eight hundred other people. If you had kids, of course, you'd talk about them. And if you had a really good friend, you might talk about God.

Barter Cunningham (that's his name, Barter—isn't that something?) looked like a man who, if you ever really got to know him, might talk about God. Or at least listen when you did.

April's where you can hit rock bottom. Just when things are reportedly easing up in the rest of the world, here comes another snootful of snow, another licking of ice, and what's started melting freezes solid again. You stop believing in summer the way you stopped believing in Santa Claus, a loss of faith that strips the gloss off life. Ice brings down the power lines and you lose your sense of humor and you need a hair dryer to thaw out the pipes before you can take a shower and you swear to God you're going to move to a saner place the second the plows dig you out.

This April caught me in a worse frame of mind than usual

because of my father dying in March. After that, everything felt a little out of balance, like the world was tilted or something.

The morning I was supposed to fly to San Diego for the funeral, I got up at five A.M. If you plan to be gone for more than a day, you can't just lock up and leave. You'll need, for one thing, to drain the pipes. My bag was standing by the door, full of dark clothes bound to be too heavy. During the night another two feet of snow had been dumped on top of the two or three feet we already had and I couldn't get the front door open. When I couldn't open the back door, either, it dawned on me that I wasn't going anyplace, not even to my own father's funeral.

We weren't close. I doubt my father was close to anybody, really, and it scares me sometimes that maybe I take after him. When I was a kid he was a drinker. By the time I finished high school he and my mom, who's dead now, were divorced and Dad had straightened himself out. He moved to California, got some training, and found work as a court reporter. The job suited him, he said.

I asked didn't he get depressed, hearing about crimes and accidents all the time.

It wasn't like that, he said. Ninety-eight percent of what he took down was boring, cut-and-dried.

"If it's boring, how can you like it?" I said.

"You concentrate on one letter or number at a time," he told me. "What they add up to's none of your business."

"But you must get emotionally involved sometimes."

"That's exactly what'll drive you nuts," my father said. "Getting emotionally involved."

It wasn't like we were estranged. I saw him every few years, usually at my brother's, after Davis got into insurance and moved to La Jolla. But our attempts at family get-togethers always left me feeling sort of hollow.

As a drunk, my father was vague, sentimental, unreliable, and silly. When I was a child he embarrassed me. Sober, he became a Jack Webb type, terse and cryptic, prone to see things in either/or terms. He wore brown suits, complained of poor digestion, and showed a flair for meanness that mostly wasn't aimed at me, but made him hard to warm up to.

If I wasn't crazy about either version of him, I was still awed by the way my father transformed himself. It takes guts to beat the bottle. Maybe the fact that I'd never said I was proud of him was what made getting to his funeral feel so urgent.

There was just no way. I called my brother. "Act of God," Davis said. "You're covered."

"I wanted to be there," I said.

"Why?" He sounded genuinely curious.

"Damned if I know," I said.

My brother sighed. "He really was one shitty father, wasn't he?" If you didn't put too much stock in words, my brother sounded kind. Davis has my mother's bent for forgiveness. It can get him into trouble. His first wife took him to the cleaners. The one he's married to now looks sullen in every picture I've ever seen of her.

"You ought to come visit, Junie. I miss you."

"If there's ever a thaw," I said.

It was five days before I could leave my house, two of them without power. The afternoon my father was being cremated, I worked by the light of two oil lamps, finishing a second version of the children's book about the pie-stealing raccoon. The first draft had focused on paying for your mistakes. The second was more about good intentions. Both probably ended a little less happily than books for young children are supposed to.

———

Then I hit kind of a dry spell. April went from bad to the usual worse. One Saturday, after a shut-in week wasted trying to paint New England wildflowers I could no longer imagine, I decided to give myself a day off. The roads, for the first time in weeks, were clear. I fixed myself up a little, put on a fringed scarf with my red jacket, and drove to Montpelier.

Seeing Montpelier for the first time, people can't get over a state capital being so small. The whole downtown's just a few blocks, a sweet and sort of mixed-up little hamlet where farmers and artists and politicos seem to get a hoot out of rubbing elbows. The bumper stickers alone could be a tourist attraction. Greenpeace and the NRA can cozy up on the same bumper. For me, though, the big draw is a terrific bookstore.

That's where I was—in the bookstore—when I ran into him. In Montpelier. I couldn't believe it.

I was squatting down to look through the children's books like I could get inspiration without paying for it. Raccoons weren't exactly an untapped resource in children's literature, I was finding out. Good intentions didn't look like such an original idea, either.

Sweating in my heavy jacket, I was starting to think about wandering up State Street to find some lunch when I spotted him in a back corner of the shop. He was flat-out reading, not even pretending to browse. The fat hardback in his hands had a glossy red cover with a close-up of JFK in black and white. Barter Cunningham was crying.

I ducked my head quickly and stayed hunkered down. My knees were stiff. When I tried to shift my weight a little, I lost my balance. A big picture book slipped from my lap and slapped the floor.

"Hey."

I ducked to retrieve the book, pretending not to hear.

"Hey, I said."

"Oh—" I glanced up. "I didn't see you," I said.

He laughed, a low, warm, scratchy sound. He seemed oblivious to the tears running down his face. All I wanted to do was get the hell away before he realized he was crying. People hold it against you, seeing them when they wish nobody did.

"Don't worry," he said. "It's just that I can't afford it."

"What?"

"The book," he said. "It's thirty-four ninety-five." He closed the cover gently, leaving his palm lie against JFK's cheek. Because he so clearly wanted me to, I laughed, but it wasn't much of a laugh.

I stood up slowly. "What are you doing way over here?"

He glanced around as if he'd forgotten where he was. "I seem to be weeping unabashedly in a bookshop." He smiled. "A small hobby of mine. I like it because it's not competitive."

I nodded. I must have looked dazed.

"And you?" he said.

Did I neglect to say that Barter Cunningham is beautiful? Perhaps I skipped over this fact because it makes my small fixation seem tawdry, too easily understood. His hair, nearly the exact shade and sheen of copper, fell over the back of his collar then in a short, thick braid. His beard, slightly darker, more auburn, had streaks of pure white in it. His eyes are not the expected shades of blue or green you find in most redheads, but a brown so deep it would come cheap to call them black. Barter Cunningham is beautiful.

At that moment, his lashes wet and his face winter-pale, his eyes seemed even darker. A hard season appeared to have thinned him down, and I wanted to lay my hand on his slightly gaunt cheek just as his own was resting on the dead president's.

He'd asked me something, but I could not recall what it was, so I told him what I had told no one. "My father died," I said.

He nodded, as if this could have been an appropriate reply to what he'd asked. Expected even. "I'm sorry."

"It's not like we were close," I said.

"Still," he said.

"Yes," I said.

The exchange seemed to complete something for me.

"It's amazing," Barter said, tucking the JFK book back into its shelf. "Here I am carrying around this present for you, then you go and show up like this."

His jacket was brown leather, ancient and cracked, a maze of pockets he began fumbling through.

"A present?" I assumed he was joking.

"Right," he said. "Here." He held out a small roll of paper with a red rubber band around it. "It's only a bumper sticker."

I unrolled it. *Invite someone dangerous to tea*, it said. The saying was framed with little green cups and saucers.

"I don't know anyone dangerous, I don't think," I said.

"You know me."

"Not really."

"And to think you have such an honest face." He shook his head sadly.

"But I don't," I said. "Know you."

"I better introduce myself then. I'm Barter Cunningham. I live in—"

"I know," I said, laughing.

"There, you see?"

He wiped his eyes with a red mitten he'd pulled out of a pocket. I concentrated on rolling up the bumper sticker. The rubber band snapped. I pinched the small tube of rolled-up paper between my forefinger and thumb. "I was wondering," I said. "Would you consent to have tea with me?"

"High tea?" Barter Cunningham said. "Or low?"

I thought for a moment. "Low might be best," I said. "Under the circumstances."

"Bereavement?" he said.

I nodded. "And April."

"A tragic history," Barter said.

"And an uncertain future," I agreed.

"A depressed economy," he added in an undertone.

"I know just the place," I said with uncharacteristic firmness.

He took my arm. "Don't tell me—"

I nodded. "I'm afraid so."

"Vermont," we said in perfect unison. And we were hardly more than strangers.

Each week or so, as the wind began to lose its edge, the snow its staying power, he would come to my back door. Always late at night, it always caught me off guard. The ways he touched me seemed to turn me into someone else, someone famished and audacious.

He would not let me turn on a light when he left. A blade of cold sliced through the darkness of my kitchen as he slipped out the door. I'd lift a corner of a curtain to spy on his shape as it shadowed the snow, then vanished. I knew I'd not see him again, ever, and so each time he left I would cry. Often it would be morning before I could get warm.

When we passed in town or out on the road, nothing was

different, my reckless smile, the subtle rise of his two fingers from the wheel, the startling blue disappearance of his truck in my rearview mirror.

That afternoon in Montpelier, drinking tea and eating glazed whole-wheat doughnuts (a delightfully *low* low tea, we concurred), Barter demanded I tell him everything I knew about him.

His eyes made me helplessly forthright. I recited his name, a competent description of his farmhouse and its location, the year, make, and model of his truck, the numbers of his post office box and license plate.

"You like coconut cake," I said. "And Doritos and Milky Ways. You drink Red Dog ale, but moderately, and you recycle the bottles. You are a night owl."

"You've observed all this?"

"In passing," I said.

He smiled. "But what have you heard?"

"Heard?"

"Give," he said.

I nodded. "You grew up in that house where you live, now, alone. Your parents are dead, but you have a sister somewhere . . ."

"So far so good."

"Are you close to her?"

"Later," he said. "Go on."

"You lived in New York," I said. "The city, for quite a few years . . . something on Wall Street?"

"Let's not get bogged down."

I took a deep breath. "You were married," I said. "To someone you met while you were away at college. But when you came back here a few years ago, you no longer had a wife."

The doughnut shop was steamy. My face had started to

perspire. Barter reached across the table and blotted my upper lip with a paper napkin.

"Error," he said. "I have a wife. She happens to be elsewhere, so it's an understandable mistake."

"Your wife is—"

"No longer a consideration." He smiled a crimped little smile. "At her own insistence."

I tried to nod with just one side of my head.

"Don't lose your momentum," Barter said softly.

I drew in my breath, then let it slowly out. "Your favorite color is blue," I said, "and the source of your income is a matter of much speculation."

"To myself, among others." He laughed.

"Questions now?"

"Patience," Barter said.

An elderly waitress with a great many rings on her bent and speckled fingers refilled our tea mugs with hot water. "It'd be another quarter for fresh bags," she said. "Each."

"Please, ma'am," Barter said. Then he looked at me. "I'm buying."

"With ill-gotten gains?"

He held one finger to his lips. "Not now," he said.

"This isn't fair," I said.

"Oh, but it is," he said. "It's already your turn now. You see?"

Then, for an uncomfortable moment, he studied me. The lines around his eyes were meticulous. I wished that I could indulge, unobserved, in a long and close look at him. I would have done a pencil drawing of his face, exactingly detailed, to try to parse its beauty. But what a pity, I thought, to lose the glorious palette of his beard, his hair, the faint blood-shadows beneath his fair skin.

"You are more alone," Barter began, "than folks here deem . . . proper. For a woman, that is."

"You are reporting, I take it? Not editorializing?"

"Absolutely." His face grew solemn. "There are those who would be glad to lavish some pity on you," he said. "But your smile thwarts that ambition at every turn."

I nodded. "Good."

"You are some kind of artist, but no ostentation of canvas or clay or stone has been displayed in these parts. Your medium, whatever it may be, evidently comes and goes in small, neat packages. Their labels suggest you learned Palmer Method in your youth, hence are most likely Catholic. You do a boom business at the post office."

"Not bad," I said. "Are you finished?"

"Hardly." Barter took a substantial bite out of his second doughnut, chewed slowly, swallowed. "You look dazzling in red. Your '93 Nissan is going to need a new muffler soon. Your taste in reading is somewhat childish. You have a weakness for pie, particularly maple cream and boysenberry. You bear up bravely under ambivalent grief. You are a keen observer, with a better-than-average memory. You are—"

"Please." I held up my hand. "Enough."

"I'm almost done," Barter said.

"All right."

"You have a soft spot for men who weep."

"For anyone who weeps," I said.

"I stand corrected," Barter Cunningham said.

As it happened, we never got around to the questions. No time, Barter pointed out, if we intended to make the three o'clock matinee—a double bill, two of the old *Thin Man* movies. A shame and a pity and pure disgrace, Barter claimed, that I'd never seen such classics. "You will lose your heart to William Powell," he said. "I am getting jealous in advance."

I sat beside him in the dark, thinking of all the questions I'd eventually ask him.

It was dark when we came out, the cold an affront after the overheated theater. The sky, clear and lavish with stars, reminded me of a navy blue dotted Swiss party dress I had when I was a little girl. I can picture it hanging in my closet, its full skirt and sleeves stiff with starch, though I have no recollection of wearing it.

We shared a black olive pizza and Barter talked about Myrna Loy, her sense of style. He knew whole blocks of dialogue from both movies by heart. I laughed too much and never got to ask him a thing. We split the check because I insisted. But after it was paid, he bought two large teas to go. "It's going to take forever to get back," Barter said. He took the ends of my long fringed scarf, looping one around my neck, the other around his own. "Forever and ever," he said. Then he touched his cup of tea to my cheek, a kiss that, lasting a second longer, might have been scalding.

"Hey," I said.

In my car I sipped the tea sparingly, warming my hands on the Styrofoam cup and trying to make it last. Barter's headlights, in my rearview mirror, doted on me all the long way home.

But a few nights later, making love to me on the ratty couch I'd meant to reupholster back when winter still seemed endless, he kept his eyes closed. His lashes, long but pale, all but disappeared against his skin. Sometimes there's an unfinished look to his face. I like to draw him that way.

There are so many things, even now, I've never asked him.

_____

May was the usual tease, mud and false hope and one last snow-blast. But finally the snow and ice were gone for good. Then June slipped into place, making up for everything. The trees filled out. The hills greened and grew bosomy. Fiddleheads unfurled overnight along the streams, and wildflowers, so improbable just weeks before, grew commonplace.

I was trying my hand at some erotic drawings. In the town library I'd found an old book of sailors' knots and studied the most intricate of them. Brazen strokes of India ink splayed across page after page in an oddly willful way. The couples, intertwined like rope, kept their faces hidden.

Sometimes, working on these drawings, I'd suddenly find myself before the pier glass in the bedroom, stripped, touching myself. Then I'd be back at the drafting table, shivering, my bare breasts pressing into the paper as I leaned into the light.

I suspect I have never done better work. These drawings reveal a woman I do not know. Her exposure leaves me feeling, by comparison, impoverished. The drawings are concealed at the bottom of a file cabinet drawer now. I rarely look at them, but I sometimes imagine myself showing them to Barter. I'll destroy them someday soon, I think.

By Flag Day (no minor holiday in this town, thanks to Fowler Oldensberg and his VFW cronies) the Caboodle was still boarded up. I kept on the lookout for Gladys and Ham whenever I was in town. Finally, toward the end of the month, a for-sale sign from Poindexter Realty went up in front of the café.

Gladys had had a stroke in February, I found out. She was in a nursing home in Fort Pierce. Ham had put their Vero

Beach house on the market and moved into a little apartment, close enough to visit Gladys three times a day. He'd never rest easy about her eating right, he'd told Martha Poindexter, unless he fed her himself.

I thought I might call the real estate office, get an address, maybe send flowers or something. But I kept having second thoughts. Ham and Gladys were fun to talk to, and it wouldn't seem like summer without those pies, but we were hardly what you'd call friends.

It wasn't long after I heard about Gladys, I think, that Barter mentioned he might be away for a while. That's something I remember, the way he said *might*, like he couldn't be quite sure. Even though we didn't see each other all that much, certainly not what you'd call regularly, I imagined how each day would have something missing, him not around to run into, catch sight of.

" 'A while'?" I said.

I could see right away he didn't like being asked. "A week or two." He didn't look at me. I knew better, of course, than to ask where he was going.

"I've been thinking about a trip, too," I said. "Maybe later in the summer."

"Katmandu is lovely this time of year." Barter's smile translated easily: *Sorry I'm a little touchy.*

"Been there," I said, "done that." I gave his braid a tug: *All forgiven. Don't mention it.*

Wherever he went, Barter came back without his beard or the braid. I passed right by him, he told me later, going into the hardware store. And that night, when he appeared at my back door, even after I recognized his voice, I felt a little scared.

"Hey," he said.

I held the screen door open for him. It was like letting

a stranger inside, knowing better. "What happened to you?" I said.

He kissed me on both cheeks, like a Parisian. "Shorn in Jericho," he said.

"You went to Israel?"

"Long Island." He laughed. He looked exhausted, suddenly older. "Didn't seem right, having my kid mortified at his high school graduation. I looked like some old hippy, he said."

"I like old hippies," I said. "You have a son?"

Barter nodded. I just stood there staring at him, this man, this *father*, who bore only the slightest resemblance to someone I knew.

"Well," I said after a minute. "Did you have a good time?"

"As barbershops go." His smile, a faded, threadbare thing thrown over his face, did nothing for him. "What about you?"

"I'm all right," I said. "I missed you."

He looked startled. Or embarrassed, maybe.

"Was that out of line?" I asked.

"More like out of the blue." He was looking past me, into the dim and ordinary room at my back. I wondered if he thought somebody else might be there.

"Barter," I said, "what is it?"

He shook himself a little, like he was trying to wake up. Then he reached for me with both hands. He pulled me against him, locking my head in under his chin so I couldn't look up at him. "I missed you, too," he said.

I hadn't realized until that moment that Barter never used my name. The way he said *you*, I might have been anybody.

My arms knotted around him. My hands reached for the back of his neck, where the braid used to rest, the skin there so soft, so exposed now. I raised one foot, twining my leg around his, like a vine on a trellis.

"June," I said. "Junie."

He held me tighter.

I wrenched my head back, pulling it free. "June." Keeping my eyes closed, I mouthed my name over and over, my tongue painting it over the smooth skin of his chin and cheeks.

My nose nudged across his upper lip, the shocking nakedness of it, but there was no getting used to the new taste and smell of him and when he sighed his breath poured wordless into my mouth and down my throat and I felt like I was choking.

"We're all right," he whispered. "Aren't we?" His faded blue shirt was damp across the back. Inside it, he shivered. "Isn't this all right?"

He made love to me differently that night, tending to my body with a kind of gratitude, like a man who knows he has lost his charm. His trying so hard to please was what made me so sad, I think. And after we were finished, we both cried and didn't ask each other why.

For a long time we didn't talk at all, but just lay there, twisted around each other like strands of something frayed but still loosely holding together so long as no pressure's brought to bear, no weight. I thought about the India ink drawings I'd made in the spring. I was glad I'd never shown them to him. What would Barter have made of such diligent passion?

A beeswax candle the color of pale honey was burning down in a chipped saucer on the bedside table. I kept an eye on the flame as I lay there, cramped and numb, latticed with a man I didn't recognize and barely breathing. The room began to smell stale. I pictured Ham's big fist tamed around a soup spoon, coaxing Gladys into a few more drops of something she couldn't keep from leaking out of the corner of her mouth.

With each deepening breath, I could feel heat and hardness draining from Barter, could feel my arms begin to imagine letting him go.

But then, just when I was sure he was asleep, he started talking.

Barter told me about the dairy cows lowing in the barn behind his house when he was a boy, how he hated the smells, the sounds of ceaseless mourning, the filthy mindless work alongside his silent father in the dark before sunrise. He told me how his father, an old socialist with dream-encrusted eyes and a tongue stilled by disillusion, had named his three children for the verbs of his lost beliefs. A sister, Share, lived in an ashram in Connecticut now. She had renounced the world in order to meditate. An older brother, Teach, had committed suicide at seventeen. Their mother had willed her own disappearance in November of 1963, as if shock and grief on a mass scale could cover her insignificant tracks and drown out the cries of those left behind.

"She died in Taos last year," Barter said. "That's when I found out where she went."

The candle burned down to nothing, the blackened wick collapsing into a puddle of wax and leaving only a wisp of smoke to trail above the bed.

"I never told my sister," Barter whispered. "Would you?"

I didn't take it for a question, really. It was just something he said.

We could not see the sky. The room was still pitch-dark. But daylight must have been starting to leak around the eastern horizon by then, because the birds began to sing.

Barter told me about the wife he would not divorce, did not know how to stop loving, even now that she loved someone else, a woman, and was happier with her than she had ever been with him.

I couldn't think of a question to ask, not a single one.

I dozed a little, maybe, but it wasn't like I stopped listening. Barter Cunningham talked the sun up over the scalloped green border at the end of the world up into a true blue sky. And even if I did fall asleep finally, I never stopped listening to the sound of his voice.

I remember that when I woke up I had a headache.

I remember wondering if his calling out to me was something I heard, or something I dreamed.

I remember how he never said the names of his mother or his wife. But he told me his son's name, John—just that, John Cunningham, a name no one would ridicule or question, a name that expected nothing. The boy, seventeen, was the spitting image of his mother was the last thing I heard Barter say.

Things I might have asked him come back to me sometimes, things like where his money comes from and how often he cries in bookstores and whether he believes in God.

Mostly, though, what I remember now is what it felt like to pass him out on the road yesterday, to see his naked face gleaming like something slightly dangerous behind the dirty windshield of that bright blue truck. I remember watching the scant lift of two fingers from the steering wheel, a smile that never escaped past his eyes. I remember wondering which of us let go first, and then thinking, like I do whenever I spot him, that we could almost be strangers. There are quite a few people around here that, although their secrets have been whispered to me, I really don't know at all.

In France
They Turn to Stone
When They Die

The old woman drowsed beneath an overhang of Orphan Annie hair. The blast of orange swirls and curlicues was blinding in the sun. Monsoon wondered how the old lady could sleep with all that brightness in her face.

His backside was going numb against the pavement. Blinking, he scooched up sideways for an up-close look at her. Wasn't looking none too good. The old woman had the sort of face reminded you there was a skull behind it. Her skin was bluish white, taffy speckled. Her mouth looked like some kid had crayoned it in to fill the gap between the sharp points of her nose and chin.

"Baby," Monsoon crooned. "Ooh-ooh, baby."

The old woman opened her eyes and stared at him without expression. Her eyes were the straightforward blue of the larkspur spikes along his granny's fence back in Macon. His granny hadn't got no eyelashes, neither, at the end, no brows to speak of. Old ladies lasted long enough, they always got around to having a naked look.

"Fuck off." This one's voice, though, she

sounded like a little girl, even when she got to cussing him out. "Fuck off," she said. "I mean it."

Monsoon smiled like he'd accomplished something. "Hey," he said.

"What do you want?" Her chin pointed at him like a finger.

"Want to eat you," Monsoon said. "Want to eat you up, babe." He grinned. A few of his teeth were missing. Those left were very white and looked like they'd been filed down to render him harmless.

"Uppity nigger," the old woman said.

"White bitch."

They smiled at each other like parties to an agreement. The street around them was empty of people, crowded with debris. Something as pure as sunlight seemed a sin. The old woman, still smiling, shut her eyes. After a minute Monsoon did, too. "Lap you up like cream till you scream," he said.

"Load me up on the spuds," Monica said. "Forget about that green stuff."

The girl behind the steam table smiled. There was mist on her glasses. Monica wondered how she could see.

"Where are you going to get your vitamins?" the girl asked.

"You don't want to know," said Monica.

The girl, a student from some college, was always there on Thursdays, always asking questions. She wore loose khaki shorts, even now, in November. At twelve-thirty, when the line was shut down on the dot, she'd come out from behind the counter and wander from table to table, butting in, making people talk who didn't want to, interrupting those who did. Her name was Karen. Her legs reminded Monica of butterscotch pudding, thick and lumpy and yellowish. Every time Monica saw Karen's legs, she wanted to kick her in the shins.

A spoonful of instant mashed potatoes landed beside a slice of Spam that had a ring of pineapple and a cherry nailed to it with a toothpick.

"You can do better than that," Monica said.

Karen's smile dimmed. She dropped another dab of potatoes on the gray plastic plate. "All right?"

"Don't go overboard."

Monica pushed past a little kid in a Roger Rabbit T-shirt who had big eyes for the day-old doughnuts. All the ones with frosting were gone. At the end of the line she snatched up three slices of dry white bread, slipping them into a pocket. Thursday nights, supper was in a church basement halfway across town. She might not feel like making the trip.

She was late because of falling asleep in the library, in a little room where they kept the magazines and a couple of almost-comfortable chairs. You weren't allowed to sleep in there. She probably should thank the biddy with the fuzzy blue hair for throwing her out. Otherwise she would have missed out on lunch today.

Monica stood by the end of the counter and looked around the room. The white cinder-block walls were painted with clouds and rainbows and flowers that looked like they had faces. The low ceiling and the pipes that ran across it were blue, as if they could fake the sky. As far as Monica could see, there was no room for her anywhere.

The tray was getting heavy and the straps of her backpack cut into her shoulders. A lot of people were finished, just sitting there taking up room. Bastards. Monica thought about sitting down right where she was and eating on the floor. Probably wouldn't get as far as swallowing the first bite, though. Make anything they call trouble, you weren't allowed back in for two weeks. Monica'd been put off limits more than once. They meant business. "The bastards," she said.

Her legs were swelled up but good today. She could feel the pain pushing up through the rest of her, like something was getting ready to bust. Monica squeezed her eyes shut. *Gusher*, she thought. The word came back to her from a movie she saw once. It was in Texas and had Montgomery Clift in it. Monica pictured blood bursting up out of her head, black and thick, covering everything. Nobody who got anywhere near her would ever be able to wash it off.

Monica's arms had started trembling, when the tray's weight was suddenly lifted from them. Her eyes flashed open. She saw the food moving out of her reach. It looked better than it had when the girl was dishing it up.

"Come on, babe," Monsoon said. "Got you a sit-down."

"You," Monica said.

He kept walking.

Monica followed, trying to keep up with him. The throbbing in her ankles felt like sucking mud. "Who the hell do you think you are?"

"You got all day," Monsoon said over his shoulder, "maybe I tell you."

Monica spotted two empty chairs at a long plywood table near the back of the room. A tray with a half-eaten meal sat at one place. The other was empty.

"Think I'm about to eat with you," Monica said, "you got another think coming."

"Meaner you talk, the hotter I get, mama." Monsoon set down her tray and pulled out her chair. "Gon' wine and dine you."

Monica came to a halt, looking up at him. He was more

than a foot taller than she was, snaky through the hips, wide as a garage door at the shoulders. She thought he was maybe forty, but it was impossible to tell with people who weren't white. He was too damn old, anyhow, to act like he did.

"I'll eat," Monica said. "But I ain't talking."

He grinned, his small white teeth flashing behind a beard like a cloud of black smoke. "Suits me," he said.

Monica struggled free of her red backpack and eased it to the floor. Her coat, a flare of shredding purple satin with nibbles of yellowed white fur at the collar and cuffs, fell heavily on top of it, the contents of its pockets clanking. She began peeling elbow-length black gloves from her bent fingers.

"Woo," Monsoon said, "take it *off*!"

Ignoring him, she plunked herself down on the metal chair. Her feet didn't touch the floor. Pale flesh puffed out over the tops of her blue bowling shoes like bread dough somebody forgot to punch down.

"You better not look at me, either," she said. "I'm armed."

He didn't know what got him started watching her, why lately it was starting to seem like a habit. She just tickled him sometimes. But mostly the old lady was like a bad accident, Monsoon thought. You didn't want to look but couldn't seem to stop yourself.

They'd both been on the street for a few years now, Monsoon since the old VA hospital shut down, Monica since the rooming house on Diversey burned up. Not that this was the first time for either of them on the street. Just the longest. And maybe the last, the way things were looking. Monsoon made out all right. Seemed like maybe the old lady was wearing down, though.

"What do you want from me?" she'd ask him sometimes when she caught him staring at her. "What the hell are you after?"

"Want to sniff your drawers," Monsoon would tell her. "Find out is white meat sweet as they say."

The more impervious the old woman seemed, the harder Monsoon tried to get under her skin. She brought out his poetic streak. "Want to lick your knickers," he said. "Take a spin through your skin . . . won't never let me out once you get me in."

Monica just gave him a jaded look. "You're no James Whitcomb Riley, bub," she'd say.

Monsoon didn't understand more than a tenth what she talked about. Hello and goodbye, please and thank you, didn't exist in her language. Sometimes when Monsoon laid hold of a bottle, he'd share it with her. The old lady favored apricot brandy and gin, but she'd drink anything, long as she wasn't expected to show gratitude for it.

One spring night—must have been back in May, it wasn't really warm yet—they'd gnawed on sweet-and-sour baby spareribs bones in the alley behind Café Polynesia, meanwhile polishing off a whole fifth of peppermint schnapps Monsoon had risked his neck to come by. Old dude who kept the package store over by the Greyhound had a gun down under the counter. Wasn't nobody didn't know it since the Preston boy got blown away for a pint of Ron Rico and a couple Slim Jims.

"Stuff tastes like Colgate," Monica said.

"Ain't nobody making you imbibe, old woman."

" 'Imbibe'?" The old lady had a laugh like a maggoty old myna bird he'd seen in a whorehouse in Bangkok, sound to make a man's cock keel over limp as collards.

"Means *drink*." Monsoon was haughty.

"I know what it means," Monica said. "What I don't know is where you get off sounding so uppish." She tossed back another mouthful before passing the bottle back to him. "Pegged you for a phony the first time I saw you."

"Nothin' phony 'bout me," said Monsoon. "Not like, say, that hair you wearin'."

The old woman grinned. "How about your *name*?" She sniffed. "Monsoon. Gimme a break."

"They give it to me in the army," he said. "Means a storm."

"Somebody say I needed an interpreter?" She snatched the bottle and took a long swallow. "Ferocious like a storm, huh? That's what I'm supposed to think?"

"Hot and wet and—" He licked his lips and smiled dirty. "Liable to start up out of nowhere and go on for weeks."

The old lady shrugged. "I seen some real storms," she said.

Monsoon looked her over. "I can see that," he said.

At dawn, behind a Dumpster smelling of tropical fruits and rotting fish, they'd thrown up together. Monsoon hardly remembered that part, though, except he'd lost his taste for peppermint schnapps since then. What came back to him afterward, locked onto his mind, was how the old lady, once she got oiled, had jabbered on through the chilliest part of the night, telling him in a dreamy voice about some old church outside of Paris where the corpses of kings and queens were just lying right there where you could see them.

Monsoon had run into a few corpses himself. The Mekong Delta was full of them. But in a church, left to lie for more than a hundred years and nobody even burying them?

Their fingers were as long and tapered as silver dinner knives, Monica said. And their faces looked snooty, like they were turning up their noses at heaven.

"Must stink in there," Monsoon said. "All them dead carcasses."

Monica shook her head.

"Must." Monsoon was definite. "And flies . . ."

"In France they turn to stone when they die." The old woman laughed. If it was a joke, Monsoon didn't get it.

"And maggots," he said. "Shit."

Monica just kept laughing.

Her daddy been some Frenchie stonecutter, she said, who made marble angels and swans and lambs to decorate gardens and graves. They lived up north, in Vermont. When Monica was sixteen, her mama died in a mill fire. Her daddy took in mind to sell their house and use the money to take his one and only child to see the dead kings and queens in the church where he got baptized when he was just a week old, and they went on a big boat.

"I was sick the whole way," Monica said. "My father just stood out on the deck and stared at the sea, never said a word. The waves got as big as those high-rises over there." She nodded toward State Street. "He looked like a statue," she said. "I saw it coming."

"What?"

"Just never you mind," she said.

Monsoon was skeptical. "You really been to Paris, France?"

Monica nodded. Her eyes were an ocean away.

San Denny, she called the place, or something like that. "I tell you, death don't make a dent," she said.

"I know what you mean," Monsoon said after a while. He wanted to tell the old lady about the times he'd walked away from it himself. But she'd gone fast asleep in the crook of his arm by then.

When he was sure she was out, Monsoon touched her hair. It reminded him of something you'd scour out pots with. With the lipstick gone, her mouth was just a little round opening. Her lips made a soft popping sound that sent a sour minty smell up around his face.

Before long, Monsoon, his back propped against the restaurant's concrete back stoop, dozed off, too. He dreamed about the church he'd never seen and could hardly believe in. The dead kings and queens and even Jesus on His cross were all turned to stone. When he woke up, Monica was gone. His bottle was bone-dry, and the sky in the east, yellowish and full of long stringy clouds, looked like egg drop soup.

Been on top of things, Monsoon thought, woulda seen trouble coming and headed it off. Like it was, though, too busy working at getting a rise out of the old woman. So it was easy for Darnelle to come sneaking up behind, the loony shine in her eyes like usual, only brighter. Picking pink gristle out his teeth and talking trash left them both, him and the old lady, wide-open.

"Gon' bury my nose in your panty hose" was what he was saying, a new one he'd been saving up for her. "Stroke your leg till you beg."

Monica, her mouth crammed full of white stuff, was paying him no mind.

"Mama in for a treat 'cause I'm a—"

Darnelle swooped down like a flighty blackbird, all flap and claw and cackle. Next he knew, the old lady was laid out flat on the floor, food and spit running down her chin and her legs splayed out pale and puffy and advertising her serious need of some underwear.

Seemed, though, like Monica didn't know what was left to showing, her dress bunched up at her waist that way. Her hands had no thought but to cover her head. Meanwhile, crazy Darnelle Featherstone's dancing out the door toting Monica's wig like Salome with John the Baptist's head on a plate, a sight so unreal that it maybe explained why didn't nobody even try and stop her. She wasn't right in the head, Darnelle. Wasn't nobody didn't know it. Monsoon knew it better than most.

Monica wasn't getting up.

"You all right, mama?" Monsoon said.

What come from her mouth hadn't a thing to do with words. The soft, weak sounds were worse than screaming. They made heads turn away. Folks gave up eating. Even Monsoon, for a second, had to shut his eyes.

When he got himself together enough to open them again, Monica was still on the floor, all nakedness below and ruin above, her head like an egg in the nest of her small freckled hands.

Monsoon knelt down beside her, yanked down her skirt. "Let's fix you up," he said. With his bare fingers he wiped the food and spit from her face. Then he rubbed his hands on his pants.

"Come on." He stood up slowly, then reached down to pull her up.

The terrible soft sounds kept leaking from her mouth, her hands kept hold of her skull. A few wisps of hair, white and flimsy as spiderwebs, were pasted to her scalp.

Leaning down, Monsoon grasped Monica under the arms and lifted her to her feet. There was hardly any weight to her. She went silent, pressing her lips together. Eyes like nobody's home.

"We'll see to her, thank you." The steely-eyed sister in

charge was all of a sudden in his face, that nosy Karen behind her. Making hushing sounds, they bracketed the old lady and led her away. She looked like a tiny child between them. They vanished into the corridor behind a fire door that said STAFF ONLY.

When Monica didn't return after more than half an hour, Monsoon got up to go. The dining hall was empty, the tables cleared and scrubbed down. Clanking pans and rushing water made a racket in the kitchen. The hot room smelled of Lysol and overcooked food.

Before he went out to the street, Monsoon picked up the old woman's things and placed them on the table. The backpack was heavy. Seemed like even the thready coat packed more heft than she did.

He didn't see her at the soup kitchen, or anywhere, for four days. Not that he was actually looking for her, but the old lady wasn't anywhere.

After it snowed on Sunday night, though, Monsoon couldn't stop thinking about that crazy purple coat of hers. Like something Billie Holiday might have been wearing to slink out from a limo and in through the Cotton Club's stage door. Only that would have been fifty years ago, when the coat was almost new. And not in winter, either. Empty out them big pockets, that rag wouldn't add up to a pound on a cheating butcherman's scale.

He knew everywhere to look. Wasn't a warm spot or dark corner in the city Monsoon hadn't ducked into himself a time or two. But he didn't know a soul to ask. It dawned on him now what a loner the old lady was. He'd never seen her hanging out with nobody. Fact was, he might be about the only one she ever talked with. If you could call that talking.

Thing was, she'd need to eat. And get in out of the nights, now it was down to freezing. There was only so many places. She wasn't showing up at none of them.

Monday nights, the Salvation Army dished out chili at the shelter in the old armory. The chili, lukewarm and gluey, without a bit of spice or meat in it, was something he'd look forward to about as much as withdrawal. Rather go hungry Monday evening than pass Tuesday morning in the bus station lavatory with the trots. Monsoon figured he'd swing by the armory, though, in case the old lady wandered in. She had a cast-iron stomach. Maybe he could choke down a cup of their stewed coffee while he checked things out.

Monica wasn't there. But Darnelle Featherstone, crazy bitch, was. Monsoon saw her traipsing through the line, had on red and white knee socks like one of Santy's elves with them stiletto-heel pumps she been wearing till they got ground down to bitty stumps. The old lady's hair was hanging from Darnelle's belt loop like a scalp on some damn Injun warrior.

Monsoon dawdled back by the coatrack, making himself scarce until Darnelle got her some chili and sat down on a wooden bench along the wall. He let her get a big mouthful half chewed before he got the jump on her. The wig came off the belt with a ripping sound.

"Ought to kill you," he said.

He expected her to let loose with a yell. Darnelle was famous for that. Every couple months she'd clear a place out— the soup kitchen or bus terminal, a schoolyard, even a church, she didn't care—with her haint hollering that made your heart stop and your eardrums hope to hell you were dying.

But she must have been losing steam, Darnelle. Or on something. She just looked up at Monsoon with those how-now-brown-cow eyes and kept right on eating.

Monsoon bent down, bringing his face right next to hers. "See you fuck with that lady . . . see you fuck with *anybody* again like you done," he said, "I will seriously mess with you."

Darnelle laughed, her teeth all stuck with them mashed brown beans. "Been hopin' you do somethin' to me, baby. It's a while now, ain't it?"

Monsoon, looking at her, felt sick. He had done, once. Darnelle never let him forget it. High as the moon and crazier than she was, back then. She said he was her baby's daddy, even though the little girl got born two, three years after that one sorry night.

Monsoon crushed Monica's wig and shoved his fist into his pocket. Darnelle's smile was sweet, loose like her mind.

"How you getting on?" Monsoon said after a moment. "How's Jamiel?"

"She missing her poppy." Darnelle licked her teeth, then smiled again. She looked almost like the fine young thing she used to be, running the streets with Monsoon's baby sister when he had one.

"She—what—four now, Jamiel?"

Darnelle blinked. "Six," she said. "Ought to come round and see her."

"She with you now?" The little girl had been, so far as he knew, in foster homes since she was a year old.

Darnelle's placid brown eyes went hazy. She mumbled something, her mouth full again.

"Say what?"

She was staring across the room at a long span of empty bench. The chili wasn't selling too good. There weren't twenty people in the huge, cold room.

"Say, I got pitchers," Darnelle said. "Come by and see her, all right?"

Monsoon sighed. "Maybe I do that," he said.

Darnelle hunched over her bowl, her eyes half closed. Her jaw muscles were twitching up and down. Monsoon couldn't tell if she was chewing or praying or shivering.

"You take care now, Darnelle," he said. "Hear?"

She started humming "Here Comes the Sun."

Monsoon shoved his hands deep into his pockets as he headed out into the cold. The old lady's wig felt cool and shapeless and stiff, like something left dead at the side of a lonely road.

Nothing he tried to find her turned up a clue. The old lady didn't leave tracks. When he finally got mad and gave up looking, Monsoon nearly tripped over her.

At first he thought she was dead. The old lady was laid out on a marble slab at the foot of a side altar in the little Catholic church on Market Street. Her backpack was shoved under her head like a lumpy pillow, her coat spread over her. A painted statue of Mary and the Baby Jesus was backed into a carved-out hollow above the little altar, a bank of stubby candles in red shot glasses burning below. Their light made Monica's small, sharp profile look like marble, pink as dawn and veined with blue.

A church would have been the last place he'd think of to look for her. He wouldn't have gone in himself if the night wasn't so damn cold and the church the first place he saw that he could get inside. St. Martin de Porres was the only church in the whole city that kept open all night now.

When the council had passed a law that all churches had to be locked after dark except with services going on, Father Mack, the pastor, raised holy hell. The homeless had to have someplace to go, he said. The city got all heated up over it. Hazard, they said. Public nuisance, they said. When Father Mack and St. Martin's got a judge to see things right, the council retaliated by yanking all the benches out of Buchanan Park.

Nobody took much advantage of the church, for all of that. It was dark and damp and barely heated. From spring to fall, though, the park benches had been sort of like a club. Folks felt safe there, clustered under the big amber lights. Sometimes a band got going. Now everybody was on their own.

Two old bums in one raggedy sleeping bag were filling the church vestibule with snores and the smell of cheap bourbon. Monsoon nearly stepped on them on his way in. Not that they'd likely notice. The candles drew him up front to the side altar. From a distance their pale red light looked warm.

The toes of his boots stopped only a few feet short of the old woman. Monsoon froze for a moment. Her chest didn't seem to be moving.

He dropped to his knees and lowered his cheek near her mouth. Her lips were just slightly parted. He felt the fever from her skin before her breath touched his face. "Oh, shit," he said.

Her eyes, purplish black in the candlelight, gave away no surprise or alarm. She just looked at him. "You again," she said.

Her hands were clasped on her chest, outside the covering of her coat. She lifted them slowly and touched her head, her palms over her ears, her fingers like claws. When she felt the black knit cap, she pulled it down more snugly, then her hands dropped away. "What the fuck do you want?"

Monsoon tried to come up with reason or rhyme, but he'd lost the taste for sass. Heat radiated from her scrawny body, washing up over his knees and thighs like a warm tide, rising up to his belly, his chest, as he knelt over her.

"Where you been, mama?"

"Around." Monica struggled to sit up.

"Been lonesome for you."

She turned and looked at the statue of Mary and the Child. "What a crock," she said.

"Brought you something."

Her eyes brightened a little. "To drink?"

"Better." Monsoon reached into his pocket and pulled out the wig. The curls had gone tangled and flat. He tried to fluff it up a little before passing it to her.

She dropped the wig on the altar without a glance. "You got anything to eat?"

"You want prime rib or turkey?" Monsoon grinned. "Woulda brought ribs but they kinda messy."

"You're a real hoot," Monica said. "You know it?" She lay back down and pulled her coat up to her chin, folding her arms under it.

"Look like a damn mummy," Monsoon said.

She didn't answer him. Her legs, exposed to the knee, were bare, and one was badly ulcerated, an overblown rose festering just above her ankle.

"Under the weather, ain't you?" Monsoon slipped off his army jacket and covered her legs.

She kicked at the jacket and it flew off the marble step, landing in the darkness below them. "I'm all right."

"Oh, yeah," Monsoon. "You fine. I can see that."

She shut her eyes.

"Ought to take what you can get," Monsoon said gently. "If it's all somebody got to give you."

Her eyes flashed open. "You can go to hell," she said. Then her eyelids lowered again and she pressed her lips together until her mouth disappeared into itself.

"Remind me of a aspirin," he said. "Bitty old white thing, all hard and sour."

The old woman stayed locked in behind her eyes.

Monsoon, still kneeling, dropped his butt to the floor beside her. The marble was cold and slick as ice. "Okay," he said. "That's how you want to be."

After a time his own eyes grew heavy. He reached down below the step, found his jacket, and laid it over her legs again. Then he sidled closer to the heat of her and closed his eyes.

"And you can just stop looking at me, too," Monica said.

Monsoon laughed softly. "You carrying again?"

She was staring at the statue. Mary's head was bent in what might have been modesty or sorrow or shame. But the Child's eyes, penetrating, full of light, seemed to be taking in every-thing—the old lady, Monsoon, the sleeping bums and the empty pews, the small spill of light and the infinite darkness beyond it.

"I can see perfect in the dark," she said. "Always could."

Monsoon wrapped his arms around himself and rested his forehead on his knees. "Me, too," he said.

"We shoulda been spies."

"Right," Monsoon said. "But which side?"

The old woman's hands crept out from under the coat and stroked a snip of pale fur. Her breathing whistled like the wind.

"Overboard in a storm on the way home," she said.

He figured she was talking in her sleep, like you would with a fever. Monsoon had heard the courthouse clock strike three—seemed like hours ago, but it hadn't chimed four yet. Though he was far from sleep himself, he wasn't really awake, either. The old lady's breathing had got to sounding tough and tangled now, like weeds she couldn't get through.

"The captain tore up the letter. If it was an accident, I'd get some money, he said. The little bits of white paper flew up in the air and I never saw them touch the water."

Without raising his head, Monsoon reached out to touch her face. His fingers were too cold to tell if she was really getting hotter. Seemed like it, though. "Shh," he said. "Get back to sleep now."

"The angels' heads were always bent down," she said. "Their wings kept folded up tight."

"All right," Monsoon said. "Shh."

"For a long time I remembered that like something that only happened after she burned up. You know?"

"Uh-huh." Monsoon's palm smoothed her forehead. "You hush now."

"But when I got older than him, which was soon, I knew he was always sad." She sighed. "Always. Even the garden angels with the sun all over them made me cry. You couldn't see it, but the wings were always broken."

"It's okay," Monsoon whispered.

"Some people are an accident before they even get born." She tossed her head, and his hand slipped from her brow. "You think I'm dreaming," she said bitterly. "You're making a big mistake if you think I don't know the difference."

Monsoon lifted his head from his knees. The old lady's eyes were wide-open, intent on his face.

"No," Monsoon said. "You're not dreaming."

After a moment, she nodded.

"Probably ought to be getting some rest, though."

She laughed hoarsely. "Nod out now I miss the best part."

She coughed, her body going rigid. The will she exerted to stop was like another person between them. When her body finally went lax, Monsoon, alone with her, felt frightened.

Her eyes were watering. He wiped them with the cuff of his sweatshirt.

"Listen, you," Monica said. "I can handle it."

"Never said you couldn't."

She smiled. "For a long time I thought I knew what I was waiting for. Exactly."

He waited.

"The fucking angels would rear up their heads like wild horses," she said. "Christ."

"Ain't nothing like that." Monsoon said it as if he knew.

"It's like the kings and queens," she said. "All stone and stillness."

Her voice had gone weak. She was shivering.

"Got to warm you up."

"For what?" Her laugh was strangled by a cough.

"Never mind." Monsoon unknotted himself, stretching his arms and legs. Then, moving slowly, he inched down beside her.

"Don't," she whispered. "That's close enough."

"Okay." He slipped an arm under her neck, lifted her head from the backpack, and cradled it in the crook of his arm.

"You should have seen me." Her breath wreathed his face, bitter and steamy.

Monsoon drew her closer. "I reckon," he said.

"He put my face on every damn one of those angels." Her eyes brimmed and shimmered. "I saw myself everywhere."

With surprising strength and quickness, Monica grabbed the shoulders of her coat and flipped it up in the air. Her pockets were empty now, had to be. The purple satin sailed, spreading out wide, hanging above them for a moment. Then it floated down again and enfolded them both inside it.

"I want you to get out of here," Monica said.

"It's freezing." Monsoon tightened his hold on her. "Long ways yet to morning."

She wrenched her head around and glared at him. "Fuck morning," she said.

She didn't talk for a long while after that, but Monsoon knew she wasn't sleeping. Her breathing was too labored, her body too tight. The clock chimed four. She stayed close, letting him keep hold of her but slanting her face away. He wondered if she saw the statue. Monsoon kept trying not to look at it.

The old woman let the echo of the fifth chime fade away before she rolled away from him. "Get going," she said. "I mean it." Her voice was firm and clear.

"No way."

She moved farther away, widening the chilly space between them. Monsoon could have held on, but he let her go. She didn't have much stamina. He wanted to fight fair.

"Go?" he said. "Why should I?"

She turned her back to him. "Because I'm telling you to," she said.

Monsoon sat up and rubbed his eyes. Still nothing but blackness to the church. "It's almost daybreak," he said. "We get some breakfast in you and—"

"Get the fuck out of here." She rolled onto her back and stared up at him.

It seemed like he was caught in her eyes forever. Her cap had fallen off and lay beside her on the floor in a pool of reddish light. Her head was nothing but a skull.

"Just wait, all right?" he said. "Hold on."

"I been waiting all my life," she said.

Monsoon smiled. "Think you can do a number on me, old woman?"

"Do anything I want," she said. "I'm armed."

In the back of the church one of the old men moaned in his sleep, then began to snore again. Monsoon stared at Monica. Her eyes, fixed on the statue, looked like polished dark stones. He looked up. For the first time Monsoon noticed that the Child held something round and gold with a little cross on the top of it.

"Please," Monica said.

The globe, gleaming a dull orange in the candlelight, looked too large, too heavy for the infant's hand. Monsoon sucked in his breath. Finally, he nodded. "Your call," he said.

"Thank you," the old woman said.

When he nodded again, his head felt like an impossible burden for his neck, and his shoulders ached.

Monsoon stood up slowly, easing his way back into his cramped limbs, his numb feet.

"Don't forget your jacket."

"You keep it."

"What the hell would I want with something like that?"

"Right." He picked up the jacket and put it on.

"See you," Monica said.

Monsoon hesitated. "What if you change your mind?" he said.

Her laugh, like the cry of a frenzied bird, wheeled through stillness.

The dark, when Monsoon stepped off the altar, seemed bottomless. One hand raised, he turned around and reached back toward the light, as if its frail radiance could steady him.

The old woman's profile was stony and white. His arm dropped to his side. "Be seeing you," he said.

Keeping his eyes on her, Monsoon backed into the dark. The blackness seemed to stretch at least as far above as it did below.

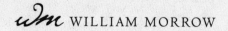 WILLIAM MORROW 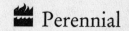 Perennial

New in Hardcover November 2001 from Susan Dodd:

THE SILENT WOMAN
A Novel
ISBN 0-688-17000-5 (hardcover)

A hypnotic and erotic tale of loss, obsession, and recreation featuring an unforgettable trio of characters: the artist, Oskar Kokoschka; his bedeviling muse, Alma Mahler; and Hulda—the servant girl caught in their dangerous web.

Also by Susan Dodd:

MAMAW
A Novel of an Outlaw Mother
ISBN 0-688-17001-3 (paperback)

The story of Zerelda James, the fearless mother of the country's most wanted, despised, yet idolized men: Frank and Jesse James. Based on historical fact, Susan Dodd has created a new legend in the name of Mamaw.

THE MOURNERS' BENCH
A Novel
ISBN 0-688-16973-2 (paperback)

"A novel that does a splendid job of showing two people engaged in a last-minute effort, fueled by both love and guilt, to understand the present and the past." —*The New York Times Book Review*

O CARELESS LOVE
Stories and a Novella
ISBN 0-688-17773-5 (paperback)

"A dazzling range of characters and settings, a compassionate understanding for connection, a zest for negotiating the contemporary sexual battlefield, a keen ear for snappy, tart dialogue and a felicitous use of language distinguish Dodd's [short story] collection...a standout." —*Publishers Weekly*

Available wherever books are sold, or call 1-800-331-3761 to order.